7/12

DISCARD

D1548531

Sandra Levy Ceren, Ph.D., a practicing clinical psychologist lives in Del Mar, California.

PRESCRIPTION FOR TERROR

When rape and murder strike young, single women on the sun-drenched San Diego coast, police are stumped. One of the victims was Dr. Cory Cohen's patient. The trauma triggers flashbacks of Cory's own terrifying rape. Her attacker went free, but she vows this one will not. Armed with psychological expertise, she is determined to uncover his identity. In her relentless pursuit, she risks the loss of an important friendship, and worse, places herself squarely into the killer's path.

SANDRA LEVY CEREN

PRESCRIPTION FOR TERROR

Complete and Unabridged

ULVERSCROFT
Leicester

First published in 1999 in the
United States of America

First Large Print Edition
published 2003

British Library CIP Data

Ceren, Sandra Levy
 Prescription for terror.—Large print ed.—
 Ulverscroft large print series: thriller
 1. Suspense fiction
 2. Large type books
 I. Title
 813.5'4 [F]

 ISBN 0–7089–4719–0

Published by
F. A. Thorpe (Publishing)
Anstey, Leicestershire
Set by Words & Graphics Ltd.
Anstey, Leicestershire
Printed and bound in Great Britain by
T. J. International Ltd., Padstow, Cornwall

This book is printed on acid-free paper

Acknowledgement

My deepest gratitude to the many people who have graciously helped me navigate the transition from psychologist to fiction author. Special thanks to Jean Carroll, founder of the South Coast Writers Group for her guidance and encouragement, Shirley Bellero for her screen-writer's eye, Judy Loeb for her thoughtful critique, Frederick Collins, former investigator of the Orange County Sheriff's Department for providing his insight and knowledge of law enforcement procedures gleaned from many decades of experience. To Ann Liddel, my editorial helper for her thoroughness, support and friendship, my husband Ely Levinsky for his technical assistance and my children Pamela Duncan and Daniel Ceren for their astute suggestions and reassurance.

Prologue

A quarter moon lit his path through the thick oleander shrubs of the condo complex. Confident that this evening would go as well as the others, he scanned the area, darted between the heavy foliage and stopped to tighten the hood of his black sweat suit. Though remote, the risk of getting caught sent an exciting current up his spine and made him feel alive. Soon, soon, he thought, reassured by the weight of the knife in his pocket.

He imagined the young woman emerge from the shower, wrap a terryrobe around her slender body and doll herself up for their date. Just like the others, she was in store for a surprise certain to terrify her and delight him. The anticipation of stifling her screams and turning her joyful expectation into a bloody horror aroused him.

The scent of vanilla wafted from a window, no doubt, from hers. She had invited him for coffee and probably baked in his honor. Set the table with flowers, switched on the stereo, too, as the others had done. What stupid bitches they all were!

A grin spread across his face as he

considered his clever scheme. Choosing vulnerable, unsuspecting targets, his impeccable methods produced for him a package of pleasure wrapped in secrecy. Better than the time he had worked the night shift as a psych aide in the hospital. No one had suspected his wee-hour marauding. Cat-like he had slipped into the beds of female patients. Recalling those adventures, he had an erection. No, not yet, he told himself.

When the hospital had to cut costs, they discharged him. He felt that peculiar admixture of pleasure from his covert activities and anger at the dismissal. Now, when he thought of that time, his muscles tensed and his head throbbed.

Sheltered behind the stout trunk of a date palm tree, he poked his head out and saw the young woman silhouetted against the window shade. He stepped closer for a better view. A dog barked and another echoed in response. He could not calculate the direction of the barking, but he knew she lived alone and had no dog to protect her.

Someone opened a window and flashed a light in his direction.

Quickly, he crouched behind a camellia bush. The flash went out and the window closed.

He waited a few minutes. All was still. He glanced at his Rolex and strolled toward the rendezvous.

1

It was a strange day. Devil winds often brought the unexpected and unnerved Cory. Sounds seemed louder and colors brighter. Jolted by the ringing phone, she grabbed the receiver.

'Hi. It's Grace Myles.' The woman on the line hesitated. 'Sorry to bother you, Dr. Cohen, but I can't keep tomorrow's appointment. Have you time today? I'm anxious to see you.'

Knowing Grace found it hard to ask a favor, Cory would skip lunch.

'Sure. Can you come at twelve?'

'Perfect. See you then.'

The hot sun streamed in through Cory's breakfast room window. She closed the shutters, nuked her oat bran cereal in the microwave and dug into a juicy, pink grapefruit picked from her garden. She hoped the fresh-brewed dark roasted coffee would shift her into gear, but still groggy after draining a giant mug, she splashed cold water on her face and thought a beach run would perk her up.

It was late autumn in southern California,

but hot enough for shorts and a sleeveless T-shirt. She pushed her long, black pony tail, her concession to femininity, through the hole in the back of her blue baseball cap and trudged to the shore.

Hot dry Santa Ana winds from the desert made her skin itch, and her eyes gritty. A large palm tree bent and swayed against a clear blue sky. Complaints of irritability and poor concentration, often the result of this remarkable weather condition, could bring an increase in new patients. She needed to be ready.

A line of brown smog from L.A. clung to the western horizon marring the bright blue sky, an artist's smudge of pastel on paper. A flock of small winter white sandpipers scurried at the water's edge. Long beaks poked at the shoreline searching for sand crabs. Energetic birds ran back and forth on their long thin legs chasing the waves. Cory envied their enthusiasm. Some people enjoyed the hot, dry weather and played in the surf, but Santa Ana's weren't her thing.

She slogged along thinking of Grace. The sensitive, intelligent young woman reminded her of her daughter Rachel who was a few years younger, but Grace was naïve and lacked self-confidence. Cory's two children did not suffer from those afflictions. The sole parent, she took credit for their good mental health. Now young adults, Rachel and Noah were traveling abroad with Cory's dad who adored them. A few years ago, he stepped in to fill the void their father had left behind.

Cory thought of the strange legacy she had bestowed upon her children. Her own mother had abandoned her when she was three years old. Thereafter, Cory's paternal grandmother took over. Was it coincidental that Cory married someone who would also abandon offspring? Could she have foreseen it? For the most part, Freud hadn't believed in coincidences. Cory had spent many years with a fine therapist looking within for an answer, but had sparse clues.

Grace, orphaned at three, emotionally neglected and fragile, brought out Cory's maternal feelings. At times she wished Grace were her child so she could cradle her in her arms, tell her she was lovable, and protect her. What an odd duo we'd make, she thought. Grace so fair and petite and I, tall, dark, Eurasian. The best she should do was foster her growth in ways that therapy allowed.

Encouraging Grace's talent was one of Cory's goals. At a recent museum lecture, Cory had collected an application for an art scholarship and planned to surprise Grace with it. She could hardly wait to see how it would brighten her young patient.

After fifteen minutes of jogging, Cory ran out of steam.

She strolled home and showered. The strong rush of water invigorated her. Toweling off, she wondered why Grace was eager to see her.

Cory dashed to the office and almost collided with the young woman as they entered the reception room where Ann, her Person Friday, busy straightening magazines, turned her curly blonde head, and waved a greeting.

Grace sat and crossed her ankles. Ribbons of sunshine from the open slats of the window blinds fell across her blue denim dress, paling the fair skin on her thin arms and legs. Her face and blonde hair appeared translucent, ghost-like. Avoiding the glare, she scrunched to the shady side of the chair. Cory adjusted the slats.

'Thanks for fixing the blinds so it doesn't hurt my eyes. Gestures like that are a big deal to me. After my parents died, no one, apart from you, has given me consideration, has paid me much attention. Not one damn bit!' She cleared her throat. 'I hope I haven't blown it asking for a session change, but I have to attend a work seminar tomorrow.'

'Of course not. I'm glad you've come a day earlier so I could give you this.' She handed Grace the application.

The look of delight on her patient's face made Cory wish she had a camera handy to capture it.

'You think I'm good enough for a scholarship?'

Cory remembered Grace's well-crafted drawings of lone dark creatures, a metaphor for her loneliness and depression. 'Definitely. I'm not an artist, Grace, but I appreciate art. I think you have talent.'

Shrugging her shoulders, Grace smiled a joyful, child-like smile. 'I'm glad you have faith in me. Nobody else did. Not my aunt or uncle. They called it a waste of time. They never cared for me or my work.' She sighed. 'My old boyfriend also thought my art wasn't saleable. He thought of everything in monetary terms. Billable hours and saleable art.'

Cory shook her head.

'But you ... you really do believe in my talent?'

'Yes. You've a lot to offer. Intelligence, compassion ... '

Unaccustomed to compliments, Grace's blue eyes welled with tears. She yanked a tissue from the box and blotted her face.

'You're likable. Talented. A beautiful young woman.'

Blushing, Grace bowed her head.

'You seemed anxious to see me today,' Cory said.

Like a tot with a new toy, Grace looked up and clapped her hands. 'I wanted to share good news. A client of the firm is interested in me. He's been phoning me a whole lot.'

'That's nice, Grace.' Cory smiled. 'Tell me about him?'

⋆   ⋆   ⋆

Grace pondered the question and realized she was so thrilled by the interest the man had shown her, she hadn't found out much about him. It hurt to think Dr. Cohen would judge her as foolish.

'Uh . . . I'm ashamed to say, I haven't asked him a whole lot.' She squirmed and waited for a response, but the therapist looked as she wanted her to continue. 'He sounds well educated. He said he's an executive in a big corporation. He's too shy to date and keeps to himself. Until he feels more comfortable, he prefers being phone friends with me.'

⋆   ⋆   ⋆

'How does that strike you?' Cory asked, curious about a shy executive.

'It suits me fine,' Grace said, cupping her chin in her hand. 'Hmm. I just realized, he seems to know more about me than I've told him.'

'Such as?'

'Last week I turned twenty-five. Because I didn't want a fuss made about it at the office, I didn't tell anyone, yet he called to wish me a happy birthday.'

'That's odd. Maybe he asked about you at the firm.'

'It's possible, but he'd have to know someone in Human Resources to get privileged data. He must be really taken with me to go to all that trouble. I'm not rushing into anything. For now, it's simply phone friendship.'

Cory understood that Grace was needy and when smitten, her intensity could be over-whelming to herself and others. As though reading her mind, Grace said, 'I've learned from my last experience. I'll never ever cling to anyone again!'

Her words were a springboard for Cory to launch into a review of the importance of independence and assertiveness. Grace obliged, pointing out examples of her growth.

'Before therapy, I'd never ask anyone for a

favor, afraid they'd be angry at me, but today I did,' Grace said, toward the conclusion of the session. 'You'll be pleased to know my appetite returned and I'm sleeping better, too.' She hesitated. 'I wish my aunt was like you.'

Cory, struck by Grace's words; a similar lament repeated many times to therapists, wanted to keep the boundaries clear for herself and for Grace. 'When we don't have adequate parenting, we must learn to do it for ourselves,' she said.

After Grace left, Cory had an uncomfortable feeling, like an itch she couldn't locate. Was it a trick of the devil wind, or intuition gnawing at her warning that something was amiss?

2

Mallory's team had just won the volleyball tournament. Jubilant flushed faces, tanned bodies glistening in the fading sun, they linked arms and formed a circle. 'Yea!' they shouted, jumping about on the beach kicking up sand.

'Let's all go to El Torito for Happy Hour,' a teammate suggested.

Mallory checked her watch. It was almost four o'clock and she expected a call from her phone pal at five. Torn with conflict, she wanted to celebrate the victory with her friends, but did not want to disappoint Nick. He was oh, so sweet. She wondered when they would actually meet. Brazenly, she had suggested an innocent coffee date at a popular café, but he had declined. He said he was sorry to disappoint her, but a social meeting in a public place made him uncomfortable.

'I'm painfully shy,' he had said. 'I've never joined colleagues for lunch or after work activities. Never had a date, either.'

Nick was different from those macho, sure-of-themselves guys and Mallory felt sorry for him. Polite and considerate, he endeared himself to her.

At first, she had pictured him as a nerdy looking dude until he had said he was tall and muscular and considered attractive.

Mallory thought about Nick a whole lot. Too much. Sometimes her fantasies interfered with her work in the dental office. She would be off somewhere with Nick, holding hands and they would gaze into each others eyes, setting off a spark. He would take her in his arms and gently kiss her. Mallory would help him to be shy no more.

The fantasy had been interrupted by her scowling boss. 'Mallory, you've given me the wrong instrument, *again*.'

Mallory figured she had better meet Nick soon, before she got fired.

'You coming, Mallory?' Her teammate asked.

'Okay guys, but I can't stay too long.'

3

When Ann, Cory's part time receptionist who preferred the title 'Person Friday' asked to join her for lunch, Cory was apprehensive. Ann usually brown-bagged it and apart from attending an occasional psychological lecture together, they had not socialized. Cory wondered what Ann had on her mind. Given an eroding practice, she hoped Ann hadn't planned on asking for a raise.

They trooped downstairs to a café and settled at a corner table. The server took their order for veggie wraps.

Several of their fellow tenants, waiting on line for take-out service, nodded and waved to them. Ann cleared her throat. 'I need to pick your brain.'

Cory began to relax, expecting to be asked a question from one of Ann's psych classes.

'I'm having second thoughts about a psychology career. I can't see how I'll support my family.'

Cory stared at Ann's furrowed brow. 'That's true if you start private practice right away, but you can work at a clinic.'

'That's what you think. Those jobs are hard

to find. I'm considering quitting the doctoral program.'

'Oh, no! Not after all you've invested,' Cory said, as the harried server rushed toward them with their meals. Cory shook her head. 'I understand. Managed Care has made it hard to work effectively and eke out a living. If things were different, you could join my practice.'

'I'd hoped to, but now I don't know what to do.'

Cory felt sad for the woman's situation and wanted to help, but couldn't see a ready solution. 'It's frustrating. You've got the makings of a fine psychologist. Empathy, insight, dedication . . . I could go on, but it'd take too long.'

Ann smiled. Her face brightened when she told Cory about a new professor who attracted her. 'Stunning intellect. Quite handsome and a snazzy dresser, too. Distinguished. Dark hair with silver at the temples, and a cleft chin.' She paused to take a sip of water. 'I think he may be interested in me because he invited me for coffee after next class.'

'That sounds promising,' Cory said. She knew Ann hadn't dated much since her divorce. The two women had much in common. They talked about the difficulty finding suitable middle age men. Such conversation drew them closer.

Lunch finished, Ann grabbed for the check, but Cory got there first. They split it and strolled back to the office.

★　★　★

The next day, Cory came up with a solution for Ann. During a mid-morning break, they sat down over herbal tea and lemon poppy seed muffins.

'Here's an idea. Transfer to I/O. Industrial Organizational Psychology. You could use your skills in a business setting and earn a decent wage.'

Ann scowled. 'I don't know. I want to be a good therapist like you, but now intensive psychotherapy is almost extinct.' She tapped her pencil on the table. 'My social life is the pits. If I worked for a company . . . '

'You know what they say about dipping your pen into the company ink-well.'

'What an archaic expression, Cory,' she said, stuffing the muffin in her mouth.

'The concept holds true. Hey, what about your professor?'

Ann frowned. 'We had a cordial discussion after class. No hint of anything more than that.'

'Maybe he's interested in you, but makes it a policy not to date students.'

'C'mon, Cory. I'm no svelte, bubbly co-ed he could exploit.'

'You *are* bubbly,' Cory said, over the rim of her teacup.

4

Hamilton ran his fingers through the thick hair and massaged his scalp. His barber had told him the sprinkle of silver at the temples made him look distinguished as did the deep cleft in his chin. For most of his forty years his appearance was vital to him. A fine selection of well-crafted clothes enabled his stocky build to appear slimmer. Although five-ten, he wished he were taller because he thought height commanded respect. Once he had considered adding lifts to the heels of his shoes but was afraid people would notice. Footwear of the finest leather was subjected to a nightly polishing ritual. From his knowledge of psychology, he reasoned that his keen grooming was a form of competition with men stemming from anger at a father he never knew.

He suspected his mother didn't know him either. A whore, her sons in foster homes by the time they had entered elementary school, she had kept one daughter. He had not seen his brothers since childhood. Distinguished names were all that bitch gave them, he thought. On rare occasions upon receiving a birthday present from her, he destroyed it, considering it a tease, as though she said, 'Look what I'm giving you. A cheap gift. That's how little I care about you.' He wanted no reminders of her. He hated her. Hated all women. Bitches deserved punishment for spawning kids and abandoning them. Whenever he thought of it, his head hurt.

From the corner of his eye, he spied something whisk by. Small and gray, like a dust ball. A fleeting shadow. A mouse. It brought to mind Mouser, the family pet, a great hunter. His mother loved that creature more than she loved him. Of that he was positive. That miserable cat caused him to be put away in that dismal, disgusting institution, just for slashing it. An awesome sight, that blood splatter. Recalling it, his mouth grew dry. He ambled to the water cooler and drank several cups of water. He reasoned that he had sliced the cat out of curiosity, to see if its blood resembled human blood. Like the little girl's, when he had pierced her flesh. No one found out about that because she was deaf and could neither speak nor sign. Stupid kid!

Blood spilled too, when he had killed the pale one, but that had been a mistake. Not that he cared she was dead, only that cops look harder for murderers than for rapists. The terror in her eyes and the trickle of red liquid was what he had sought, but her head jerked when he sliced into her neck. With glee, he had watched the red river flow as she lay still.

But his latest escapade had tripped him up. How he wanted to see her blood gush! That damn bitch was strong. When she hit him in the gut he wanted to go after her and cut her up good, but the cops could be watching for his return. One day he would show her or another bitch like her and he would feel fantastic. Redemption would be his!

5

Later that week Cory had an odd call from Mallory Nelson, a young woman she had treated two months ago. The urgent voice, soft as a cotton wisp, didn't sound like hers. Cory gave her an appointment for the following day.

★　★　★

Cory was startled as she looked at the pale, young woman whose trembling hands clutched a steaming mug of cocoa.

She wasn't the same Mallory Nelson Cory had known.

The Mallory she had known, was self-assured and vivacious and when last seen appeared fully recovered from a broken love affair. Now, she appeared in worse shape than at her initial session.

'What happened?' Cory asked, hoping not to appear too alarmed.

Mallory rose from her chair and paced. Her straight sandy hair lay limp on her hunched shoulders. It seemed hard for her to open up. 'I've had a set-back,' she said, sliding her sunglasses on top of her head. She gazed at her therapist through blood shot eyes. 'I'm ashamed to tell you.'

'You know me, Mallory. I don't make judgments.'

Silently, the young woman stood at the window, peering out as though hunted. Several minutes passed before she spoke. 'I really messed up big time.'

Cory looked up, gesturing for her to take a seat.

Mallory slumped into a chair. 'I was raped last night,' she cried, wiping her tears with the back of her hand.

Stiffening, Cory gasped. 'Oh, my God. I'm so sorry. How did it happen?'

'Oh, man! It's so disgusting.' She bowed her head. 'It's a long story.'

'We have time, Mallory.'

'It's so horrible, I can hardly talk about it.'

'It will help,' Cory said, leaning toward her patient.

'About a month ago, this guy began phoning me. He said he'd been watching me play volleyball, but was too shy to talk to me at the beach.' She clawed the arm rests. 'He sounded real sweet and sincere. It was real cool to have a secret admirer.'

Cory nodded. 'How did he get your phone number?'

Mallory slapped her forehead. 'Oh! I'm such a flake! I figured he got it from the roster, but dumb me, I should have asked. He really seemed honest. Told me he was an accountant. And who the hell would make that up. I mean it isn't a glamorous job or anything.'

'What else did he tell you?'

'That his name is Nick. Yeah, sure!' Her voice rose. 'He's Nick — like I'm Joan of Arc! That creep conned me from the get-go. Sonofabitch said volleyball was the only social thing he did. That freaking liar called me three times a week, just to be phone friends. He handed me that line of crap to make me feel sorry for him — that bastard!'

'What a gimmick!' Cory said, shaking her head.

'Yeah. He sure as hell conned me.' Mallory drained her drink, slammed the mug on the table and paced, again. At this rate, Cory thought, by the end of the day, her shoes would be as worn out as I'm getting from watching her.

'Man, did he spoof me. He was so polite. And he spoke like a real professor. You know — big vocabulary. Made me think he was scared of women — said he drops out of the game when they play with his team — pretends he twisted his ankle.'

Cory rolled her eyes. 'He's twisted, all right.'

'You've got that right! The more he told me about how he wanted a woman friend, the more I felt bad for him. Finally, I invited him over. Can you imagine! I invited a rapist into my apartment!' She stamped her foot with a force that shook the sturdy table. The mug fell, but she caught it mid-air, her victorious smile lightening the mood.

'Quick reflex, Mallory.'

'Cory, I am sooo stupid!'

'No. Naïve. He took advantage. It's useless blaming yourself now. You've suffered enough already.'

'It's so crazy. I can't believe I fell for it. Dumb me. I'm so mad at myself. Damn, damn, damn! As soon as I let him in, I realized I'd made a big, big mistake. Didn't expect him to be dressed in sweats and to look like he did. He had this big ole black beard and jet black hair. Yuk! May that freak rot in hell,' she shrieked. 'I'd like to scare the shit out of him. If I ever see him again — I swear I'll kill him!' She dropped to her knees, placed her palms together in prayer position and stared at the ceiling. 'I promise to God, I will!'

'Most victims feel as you do, Mallory.'

'Dear God, I want to rip his balls off.'

The words, like an ice cube rolling down Cory's back, chilled her. They were the same she'd used many years ago. Anger, rage, long ago put to rest, now resurfaced.

'I know how you feel, Mallory,' she said.

'You couldn't. The way he grabbed me by my hair and shoved me on the floor. Man, was I scared! No one could understand what I went through.'

'I can. I've been there too,' Cory said. 'I was raped and nearly murdered a long time ago. I was terrified — then furious. And like you, felt powerless and wanted to lash out.'

Mallory stared at her. 'You too? You — you were raped?'

Cory nodded.

'Oh, God! How did it happen?'

'This is your session, not mine, Mallory. I told you because I want you to know I do understand. I recovered from it, and so will you.'

'Then you'll know how disgusting I felt at the hospital. There's that special unit for rape victims — where they poke around inside you for semen samples. Oh, man, it was so gross! And so embarrassing.' She plopped into the chair, folded her arms around her long legs and rocked. 'The staff tried to be nice, but the whole thing was awful. They bagged all the clothes I'd worn when it happened.'

Mallory buried her face in her hands. 'I never want to see those dirty things ever again, anyway. It'd remind me of the worst night in my life.'

Cory slipped her arm around Mallory's trembling shoulders.

'A police artist drew my description of the pervert. She didn't get it exact, but I swear, I'll never, ever forget what he looks like! Those mean, beady eyes. Yuk! The thought of him makes me sick. They'd better catch that freak soon, before . . . '

'Before . . . what?'

'Damn it! Before he comes after me.'

'Rapists usually don't do that. They're afraid the police are watching the victim's house.'

'You don't understand. I pissed him off. You see, after he . . . he did it to me, I punched him real hard in the stomach. Knocked the wind out of him. Then I ran to my neighbor's and . . . freaked out.'

Mallory began to hyperventilate. Cory directed her patient's breathing pattern until the young woman calmed down.

'My neighbor called the cops. They got there pretty fast, searched for him, but of course, he split. The cops had me grab a change of clothes, then drove me to the hospital. Have you ever sat in the back of one of them cop cars? It stinks. I mean really stinks like a sewer. I felt like a dirty criminal.'

'I can imagine, but they were trying to help. Did they offer to protect you?' Cory thought of how little the police had done after her assault, but fortunately times had changed and now most law enforcement agencies required officers to take sensitivity courses.

'No. They go, 'stay with a friend,' so I went to my neighbor, again. I didn't want to because I felt in the way.' Shivering, she rubbed her hands along her arms. 'What the hell should I do?'

Briefly tempted to offer shelter, Cory dismissed the notion as improper. 'Is there somewhere — away from here, you may feel safer? Someone you can live with for awhile?'

Mallory held her head in her hands. Rings of sweat darkened the armpits of her white shirt. 'I think I can stay with Mom's cousin in Palm Springs. She's got a Rottweiler, so I'd feel secure.'

'It sounds like a fine idea for now. What about your job? Does your boss know what happened?'

'Yeah. I called in today. He told me to take a few weeks off. His wife'll fill in for me. She's cool, used to be a dental assistant, like me.'

'Good. The D.A.'s office near Palm Springs has a crime victim program. They'll refer you to a therapist. Maybe some of your teammates can stay with you while you make arrangements to leave.'

'That sure would help,' she said, tears rolling down her cheeks. Cory handed her a tissue. 'Trouble is, I can't stop thinking about it.'

'After what you went through, Mallory, it's expected. You can't prevent thoughts from coming, but can stop them when they do. Like switching a TV channel. Think of something pleasant. An event you're looking forward to — whatever. Keep busy so you won't dwell on it.'

'But the nightmares . . . I can't sleep.'

'In time, they'll stop'

'Food makes me sick. I don't want to waste away.'

Cory rifled through the desk, pulled out a handout of coping tips for trauma victims and slid it to her.

Mallory skimmed it and shook her head. 'Thanks, but it's hard to concentrate now.' She stashed the paper in her backpack.

When the session ended, the young woman stood at the door, her shoulders stooped. Her despair and vulnerability cried out. Mallory needed more than support and empathy. She needed time. She needed *and* Cory needed the menace to be put away.

'Please keep in touch with me and let the police and D.A. know where you are, too.' Cory stretched her arms toward Mallory. The young woman sobbed on her shoulder.

'Thanks,' Mallory mumbled, mopping her eyes.

She left Cory to her own memories and fear for her patient's safety.

6

Mallory's session alarmed Cory — for her and for Grace whose new phone pal had given her a similar pitch. She called Grace's office to warn her, but she was out-of-town on business. Cory left an urgent message.

Glad for a long break between patients, Cory grabbed her running gear from the bottom desk drawer and slipped on her new maroon and gold Brooklyn College T-shirt. When she had purchased it at her recent twenty-fifth reunion, she recalled the good undergraduate years and the rape hadn't entered her mind. She thought she had successfully put aside those frightening years. Mallory's rape convinced her that if the rapist had been imprisoned, her fear of further attacks would have dissipated.

On her way out of the office, she caught a whiff of pink and yellow roses that Ann had grown in her garden and was arranging in a vase. 'Sweet and lovely,' Cory sang out.

Ann looked up with her large brown eyes. 'Ouch,' she said, pricked by a thorn. 'I should know better. Roses, like some people, are pretty, but should be handled with caution.'

'Right. Band-Aids and peroxide are in my top desk drawer, Ann. Let me help.'

'No, thanks. I can do it. This is worse than a paper cut,' she said, sucking the droplets of blood from her index finger. I don't want to play Mom to you, Cory, but sometimes you're too zealous in your beach runs. You come back here exhausted.'

'No. Exhilarated. Try it sometime.'

Ann frowned. 'Remember, you have a full schedule today.'

'It's why I've got you to remind me.' She patted Ann's shoulder.

Cool air fanned Cory's back as she jogged along the foot path of the coast highway to Del Mar beach. Sun warmed her face. Tugging the bill of her red cap down closer to her eyes, she imagined how silly she appeared in clashing colors. She arrived at the shore line where a few surfers awaited big waves. A regiment of sandpipers lined like Air Force cadets ready for the leader to start their flight while seagulls dove into the Pacific for their catch. Cory sprinted past a volleyball net and wondered if the rapist actually had seen Mallory playing volleyball. If he hadn't, how did he target her? Was he the same man who phoned Grace? Thank goodness she's safe at her seminar, Cory thought.

Like a movie playing in Cory's head,

Mallory's rape and fear of reprisal resurrected vivid, painful memories:

Brooklyn, New York. September, 1965

It's early evening. She walks to the bus stop on the way to a lecture. Suddenly, someone grabs her arm from behind. She whirls around to face a man in his twenties wearing a brown leather bomber jacket with a furry collar. His greasy hair is dark, his lips crooked. A blade in his hand glitters in the street light. 'See this? I'm gonna use it on ya. I'll fuck you and then I'm gonna stab ya all over and watch ya bleed. Is ya blood yella? I'll slice off ya arms and legs, ya Nip.' His shrill laughter a cacophony, 'Hah, hah, hah. I'm gonna cut off ya head too. I'll bury it. Hah, hah, hah.' Her heart races. She screams, but there's no one to help.

Though it's night, everything seems so clear. Unlike death's eternal darkness. Is death waiting to take her away to nothingness? She wonders. No! It's too soon. She must find a way out. She glimpses a blur of yellow. A cab approaches. 'Help!' she screams, but it whizzes by.

The man's arm encircles her waist. He drags her into a vacant lot, partially sheltered by tall weeds. The damp ground sucks at her feet. She struggles to escape, but he's strong and has the cold knife-blade on her cheek. He slides it down her chin and neck. She wants to grab it, but is afraid he'll slit her throat. He faces her now, holds her in a tight grip. She has an urge to bite, scratch, spit, but is terrified. Oh, God. If only I can delay him, maybe someone will pass this way and see or hear me, she thinks. Maybe I'll live after all. He pushes her to the muddy ground. She's on her back. He lifts her skirt. Rips off her panties. Her arms and legs flail about and she kicks him. He laughs that hideous laugh again. Horrified, she stiffens. Her heart plays a pounding rhythm as she listens to his shrill laughter and the repetition of his threats. Frozen in terror now, but her mind clear, she watches him. He unzips his pants and pulls out a pinkie-size penis. She is surprised at the small size of his organ. Maybe it won't hurt so much. He straddles her and bounces up and down. A rancid, oily smell from his hair sickens her, makes her want to vomit. She feels a piercing pain as his tiny, but fierce organ thrusts and rips through her. Liquid runs down her crotch and thighs. She knows it's her blood. He shrieks like a banshee. Then . . . sticky stuff — his semen. Panting, he shuts his eyes and rolls off her. A slip of *paper falls from his pocket on to the ground. Quickly, she snatches it and stuffs it up her sleeve. Within his reach, the knife glitters on the ground. Can she shove it into the mud — bury it before he sees? Should she grab it and run? She's about to go for it, but he opens his eyes. Aloud, she prays, 'Dear God, please save me. I promise I'll do everything to be worthy. I'll help everyone. I'll be the best person I can. I'm so young, please don't let me die. Please, dear God, please.' He is panting now.*

She catches a glimpse of a yellow cab driving slowly up the street. 'Help, help!' she screams. The taxi edges closer and stops. The driver flings open the passenger door. She breaks away and jumps in — grateful to the angel who whisks her to safety.

After all the flashback-free years, Cory thought it wouldn't happen again, but her night of terror had just streaked before her. To rid herself of the venomous memories, she ran as though chased. Faster and faster — until she felt as if a fire raged inside her lungs. Slowing her pace, she cooled down and began to breathe normally.

Her response to Mallory's rape surprised her because hers happened so long ago. But her patient's words of vengeance had been

Cory's mantra after her assault.

She hiked up the ramp from the beach and walked through Seagrove Park. Apart from a few squirrels, Cory was the sole occupant. A rare occurrence. Alone and feeling vulnerable, she ran across the street to the popular Del Mar Plaza. From the balcony, lined with bright yellow and white mums in large earthen pots, she gazed at the ocean and heard the romantic hoot of the train sweeping the coast. When she had first arrived in California from a cold, gray New York winter, she fell for perpetual spring-time, clear skies, and the blue Pacific. People and places, like some easy chairs, have a way of telling you it's where you belong. Where you'll feel comfortable, she thought.

She strolled to Esmeralda's Bookstore–Cafe and eyed the display of management's recommended list. At a table overlooking the patio, she lunched on a naked bagel and fresh orange juice. Skimming through the newspaper, her eyes focused on a headline:

BEACH RAPIST STRIKES AGAIN

Several rapes occurring in the homes of beach area residents have been recently reported to the police. Women are urged to lock all doors and windows and report suspicious strangers. Neighborhood watch groups are being formed.

Times have changed, Cory thought. Now police take rape seriously.

Descending the stairs of the plaza, she bumped into an Asian woman about her mother's age. Cory smiled at her, but the woman, probably a tourist who considered eye-contact rude, looked away. Shading her sudden tearful eyes under dark glasses, Cory walked briskly to her office. Here I am, she said to herself, a well-trained, analyzed psychologist and still holding on to my old sack of woes. Every time I see an Asian woman my mother's age, I get an impulse to know her, to really look inside her. How could she leave me forever? Cory was grateful to her grandmother for parenting her and for the closeness they had shared. Nevertheless, abandonment by the woman in whose womb she was nourished hurt her deeply. Cory's efforts to be the best parent to her children helped make up for the emptiness she often experienced. Her work with patients had a similar effect, but she had to tread cautiously and monitor her counter transference. Her boundaries.

The consulting room — Cory's sanctuary brimmed with books, plants, comfortable chairs and a multitude of left-over memories. A place of pain and resolution. Prints of Claude Monet's 'Japanese Footbridge' and Van Gogh's 'Drawbridge' hung in the reception room. They symbolized psycho-therapy — a bridge over troubled waters.

Cory peeled off her running gear, showered and changed clothes. She felt privileged to have an office with kitchen and bath amenities. Privileged in many ways: To be alive, to have escaped a sadistic attack long ago. Her concern for Mallory heightened. Cory squeezed her eyes shut, hoping the young woman would be okay.

7

After a week had passed with no word from Mallory, Cory figured it was a good sign. Probably her patient had connected with a crime victim counselor, and given ample time, should get better.

Ann had been grumpy lately and Cory understood what the woman was going through. Today, Cory detected an improvement. Ann whistled as she scrambled around decorating the reception room with an expanse of flowers. Cory loved the splash of color and scent, but thought it too celebratory. Rather than offending Ann, she said she would like to take some blossoms home.

'Sure. As you can see, I'm in a great mood.'

'Glad to hear it. What's happened?'

'I have an interview for a clinical internship. The job starts next year.'

Cory expected Ann would leave after graduation. 'That's great! Where?'

'Orange County Mental Health. I wouldn't have to move.'

'I'll miss you, Ann, but for your sake, I hope you get it,' Cory said, hugging her.

She retreated into her consulting room to

write progress notes in her patients' charts. At her desk, Cory couldn't concentrate on the charts. She valued Ann for the comfort and support she provided. Although her tasks were limited, she always did more than was required. A quality any employer would welcome. The office was always tidy. The daily fresh flowers were a bit much, but Cory appreciated Ann's home-grown pesticide-free produce. Most of all, Cory enjoyed Ann's company.

A clinical internship meant the woman wouldn't have to chart a new course in an allied field. Confident Ann would do well at the interview, Cory took out a pen and stationery and wrote a glowing recommendation.

She placed it on Ann's desk, just as the phone rang.

Ann's bright voice announced, 'Rachel's on the phone.'

Cory flinched. Something must be wrong, she thought, dashing into the consulting room. She picked up the receiver.

'Hi, sweetie.'

'Hi, Mom. Figured I'd catch you between sessions.'

'What's wrong, Rachel?'

'Nothing . . . but I think I should come home.'

'Why? What is it?'

'I miss you, Mom. And my friends. Noah is off on his own and Grandpa's busy, too. And learning Hebrew is hard.'

'Miss you too, pussy-cat. I don't want you to be unhappy, but you might feel worse if you leave ahead of time. Think about it?'

'It was fun meeting interesting people and seeing the sights, but the kibbutz is boring now.'

'How are you getting along with Grandpa and Noah?'

An expensive long pause. 'Uh, okay. Like I said, they're busy doing their own stuff.'

'Like what?'

'Females.'

This surprised Cory. 'Israeli guys are dynamite, aren't they Rachel?'

'I wouldn't know,' she said.

'Stick it out for another week or so. See about a tutor. If things don't improve, come home. I'd love to see you.'

'It's good to hear your voice, Mom. Will you call next week the usual time, please?'

'Of course. I love you, baby. Say hello to Grandpa and Noah.'

Damn! Her kid's pain became hers. From a built-in Parents Manual, she gave Rachel the same *shpiel* she had given Noah the first time he went away to camp and had begged to come home.

Cory had an impulse to fly off to Israel, but she considered the effects of her precipitous two-week vacation on patients. She thumbed through the pages of her appointment book; the concrete evidence of the downward spiral of her practice, mirroring that of her colleagues.

'Rape by managed care!' she muttered.

Cory had anticipated problems. Motivated by profit, a non-professional dictated health care decisions. She had tried to steer psychologists away from joining panels, but like consumers, they accepted the hype that it would be beneficial. Some had tried to start their own panel, but could not compete with rich corporations armed with a highly paid sales force and advertising executives.

Now, checking her roster, she did not expect her travel plans would harm anyone, and she could rely on her usual back-up.

Cory pulled out her check book, examined the account balance and phoned a travel agent. She figured on taking off within a few weeks.

8

Dusk, Hamilton's favorite time, found him seated behind his desk in his private office, everyone else having left for the day. He draped his beige cashmere jacket on the back of his chair, loosened his brown paisley silk tie and slipped off his shoes.

Several colleagues had invited him to Happy Hour, but as usual he declined. If they only knew what he was up to. A broad grin crossed his face.

Thriving on privacy, he enjoyed hiding behind his shield of a hard-working, polished professional and allowed no one to get close.

Except that one time when a psychologist had tested him as a youth, stirring his imagination and challenging him, piercing his privacy. Hamilton had been duped. Now he was in a position to deny psychologists' requests to test patients. That's justice!

He recalled the late winter afternoon in his youth when he had broken into the clinic after hours. Although confident he would not be caught, he had an excuse. He would say he came back in search of a lost house key. He sprung the lock of the rickety office door with a paper-clip. Heart racing, he heard the door creak. A sliver of sunlight shone on the floor. Thumbing through the unlocked file cabinet, he noticed dust particles flew in the air accompanied by a musty odor. Funny the senses his memory stored, like the cheap texture of the folders. He reached the letter 'P' and there it was. Stashing the flimsy folder between the pages of his school notebook, he hurried to the university library to figure out the contents of his file.

Hamilton committed to memory, the psychological evaluation summary:

'This adolescent of superior intelligence, attempts to present a pleasant façade which conceals a rich fantasy life. He is suspicious, narcissistic, socially isolated with obsessive compulsive, claustrophobic and strong psychopathic tendencies. Diagnosis: Potentially dangerous character disorder.'

Hell, he knew that already anyway. His last foster mother had told him he was a wicked boy, unfit to live with others.

To this day, the young woman social worker who had tried to befriend him starred in his rape-slash fantasies The bitch tried to penetrate his mind, with a bribe of cheap tootsie rolls, but he refused.

He had memorized her report, too. She stated Hamilton was a difficult infant who screamed when anyone touched him. His developmental milestones indicated advanced physical and intellectual abilities, but social immaturity. Lashing out at other children, he preferred to play alone. She described his refusal of the candy and his preference to sit far from her.

What she had not known was that he was afraid he would kill her if he got any closer. Hamilton would have enjoyed it, but feared the consequences of the crime.

How convenient for the psychologist and social worker to have been in the county car when it exploded — just before they were to present his case before the juvenile authorities. Yes, he knew how to protect himself. Too bad theirs was not a slow death that he could have witnessed with relish.

Although he had stolen the case file, he felt threatened that copies existed and someone could be privy to this incriminating information.

Whenever he reviewed that time of his life, his head throbbed, but he had a compulsion to continue the replays to prove to himself how far he had come from those miserable years.

9

Erin Caldwell would be the bane of any psychologist's existence. Such patients rarely got better and angered most people they encountered. Trying hard, Cory found little about her appealing. That very fact made her feel sorry for the young woman. Sorry for her self-inflicted misery.

Defensive, Erin refused to accept her husband's concerns, but agreed to therapy as a last resort, hoping he would change so she wouldn't have to.

In their first therapy session last week, she presented herself as a young mother desperate for a reconciliation with her estranged husband. She spewed relentless criticism of him and everyone else including Cory whom she called a phony because her name didn't match her appearance:

'Dr. Cory Cohen. Hah! You have a Jewish name so people will think you're smart, when you're from some God-forsaken Oriental place.'

There were times when Cory thought someone had some cockamamie idea like that about her, but was too polite to voice it. She was glad her children had watered down Asian genes and wouldn't experience racial bigotry. It was hard enough being Jewish and having an absent father.

Erin's husband had blurted out, 'Erin, don't be so damn blunt!'

Stifling her urge to laugh, Cory had said, 'Well, Erin, you're honest. You do say what you think.'

Cory recalled Erin's face turning crimson, making the freckles that sprinkled across her light complexion disappear.

★　★　★

That was last week. Now, Erin sat opposite Cory, pouting. 'Why can't you make him come back to me?'

'That's not my task, Erin. With all his faults, why do you want him?'

She shook her head. A long braid of carrot color hair danced from shoulder to shoulder. 'Because I'm alone. I hate it.' Sniffling, she wiped her moist eyes and small up-turned nose with the last tissue in the box.

Cory pulled out a fresh box, and slid it towards her.

'Do you have friends, Erin?'

The young woman looked down and studied her shoes as if considering whether they'd do with a polishing. Cory waited for a response, figuring the question made Erin uncomfortable.

'I've no chums here. Seldyn was all I needed. Now he's gone. I don't know what I did to deserve it,' she whimpered.

'He'd prefer you were with him because you love him, not because you're lonely.' Although convinced her remark was valid, Cory questioned her motivation for stating it so bluntly. She wondered if she was cutting to the chase, or getting even for the patient's cruel words about her last session.

Erin's green eyes flashed, 'How dare you! I do love him.'

'How do you show him?'

She narrowed her eyes. 'I'm loyal, dependable, a good housekeeper and mother.' Rubbing her hands on the arms of the chair, she muttered, 'He's a lousy lover — only thinks about satisfying himself.'

'A lousy lover who fails to pick up after himself, dresses poorly, doesn't earn enough to buy you presents. So why do you want him?' Cory wondered how many times she'd need to go over this terrain.

'It's simply dreadful the way you take Seldyn's side. Just help me get him back,' she sobbed.

Cory folded her hands on her lap. 'Okay,

Erin. If you want him back so much, you'll have to change. Even then, there's no guarantee.'

'I don't want to be alone. I'll do anything. Tell me,' she pleaded.

'Stop trying to change him.'

'Oh, so you think I'm all wrong and he's the right one — just like my parents. I was always the one wrong. My brothers and sisters were always right. Well, that's a bloody lie.' She hung her head and cried into her hands. 'Nobody understands me. Not here, not anywhere.'

'Erin, I know this is hard for you. I didn't say all your complaints weren't valid, but you can't force him to be the way you want.'

'Why not? If he loved me, he'd do it for me.'

'Maybe he thinks if you loved him, you'd accept the way he is.'

Erin sprung from her chair, hands on her hips and glared at the therapist. 'You're wrong and I'm right,' she whined.

For a moment Cory saw Erin as a little girl. A little girl who needed to grow up. She half-expected her to stick her tongue out. 'Okay, Erin. Would you rather be right than happy?'

The young woman plopped into the chair and stared at the wall. She cupped her chin and said, 'I'll have to think about that.'

47

10

Cory was busily making plans for her trip to Israel when Ann buzzed.

'Steve Glass on the phone. It sounds urgent,' she said.

Cory picked up the receiver.

'Hi, Steve. What's up?'

'Serious business. I need to talk to you about one of my patients. Have you time today?'

A glance at her appointment book showed two free consecutive hours.

'Sure — from one to three. Want to eat lunch here?'

'If it's okay, I'd prefer outdoors at Torrey Pines, I'll bring food and pick you up at one o'clock, okay?'

'Sounds like a winner.'

For Cory, supervising Steve was a joy. They learned from each other. She got a kick out of the way he reasoned like a rabbi, framing statements as questions and answering them. He had taught Hebrew for twenty years before becoming a psychologist three years ago. A studious and religious man, Steve guided Cory through parts of the Talmud

48

— the commentaries on the Bible, written during the Jews exile in Babylon. Those talks brought pleasant memories of her grandfather, a biblical scholar who had made her feel she could be anything she wanted. Steve peppered his language with Yiddish, making Cory feel at home. His serious problem aroused her concern.

She rang Ann on the intercom. 'I'll be out of the office for a couple of hours.'

Cory changed into yellow sweats and was tying her shoelaces when Steve arrived.

A red and blue yarmulke fastened with two bobby pins, perched on top of his dark curls. Silver threads sprinkled his trim beard. He appeared tense and pale.

'Are you feeling okay, Steve?'

'I'm fine. It's this gray sweatshirt. Miriam says it fades my skin. Let's head for my car and I'll tell you why I had to see you,' he said, waving to Ann as they left the office.

'How are the kids? Still traveling with their grandpa?' Steve asked.

The mention of her children brought a painful reminder of her longing for them. Cory wanted her children to be independent, to enjoy their travels with their grandfather and profit from consistent male companionship, absent for much of their lives. She realized her presence in Israel would intrude on their special time. She chided herself for considering her patients before her family and decided she would cancel the trip.

'They're having a blast, staying at a kibbutz for six months. How's your family?'

'All is well, but poor Miriam works so hard in that school and they pay her *bobkes*.'

'The fun in helping kids is a wage supplement, huh?'

He sighed. 'Well . . . we manage.'

They rode a short distance in Steve's old Volvo, and were approaching the entrance to Torrey Pines Reserve, when he began to tell her about his patient, Roz, a newcomer from Australia. Nervous, he drifted into a lane, nearly sideswiping a car.

'Maybe we should wait to talk outside,' Cory cautioned.

Steve nodded.

He parked and they stepped out of the car, the crunch of eucalyptus leaves underfoot. They hiked a trail near the indigenous red rock, an area her son, Noah, called his spiritual sanctuary where he enjoyed snapping photos.

Steve and Cory settled themselves on a bench, enveloped in the scent of sage and pine. From a brown paper bag he handed her a neatly wrapped warm pita sandwich and a large napkin. 'Now about Roz. For being only twenty, she had *chutzpah* to come here alone, not knowing a soul in this country. A new experience, she wanted. And what happened to her? No one should know from it.' He shook his head.

'So tell me, already.'

'A couple of nights ago, the poor kid was raped.'

Cory winced. Oh my God! Raped. Like Mallory. 'Where did it happen?' she sputtered, almost choking on the falafel cucumber. She wiped her chin with the paper napkin.

'In her own house. I'm telling you, it's a real *shanda*.'

'I know. It's a shame. How . . . ?'

'This character, a real *momzer*, had been calling her for a few weeks. Told her he was shy and wanted to be phone friends. She was impressed by his intelligence. Go know what he was. She was lonely, so . . . she invited him over for coffee. Only to meet him, that's all. But when he arrived, he attacked her. Threatened her with a knife. Thank the Almighty, she wasn't killed.'

Chilled by his words, Cory rubbed her arms. 'He's a *momzer*, all right. A real bastard!

'If only I . . . '

'You . . . what, Steve?'

'Go know what would be. Maybe I could have stopped it.'

'How?'

'If only she'd talked to me before she decided to invite him over.'

'Look, we can't be there all the time to help patients make good choices.'

'I didn't anticipate this. I was happy for her that she had someone apart from me to talk to. I've a lot to learn, yes?'

'We all do.'

'And here we are enjoying lunch in this peaceful spot while a rapist goes free!' He held his head in his hands.

'Whoa. What's with this self-imposed guilt, anyway? This isn't the Day of Atonement. You don't have to beat your chest and feel responsible for the sins of others.'

'I never can get over the words that come from your mouth, Cory. You're so Jewish and yet . . .'

'Yeah, I know. It's funny, I don't look it.'

Steve flinched, probably sorry he had struck her Achilles heel. He flashed a sad knowing smile.

'Look, Steve. This is too coincidental. Last week, the same thing happened to one of my patients. What a scheme! Someone's found a way to get to vulnerable women.'

'Is it possible he follows women from our offices?'

'Could be. Let's check it out with other

psychologists. If that's the case, we've got to figure out how to handle it. Has your patient notified the police, or was she too ashamed?'

Steve bowed his head. Guilt, like a shroud, seemed to have enveloped him.

'I feel like a *shmuck*. When she told me, I pictured what she went through and was so upset, I couldn't think of anything else.'

'Roz was shook up and no doubt embarrassed at her mistake. Dealing with her feelings took priority, but you can help her to face the police, now.'

'That's right. I'll do it at her session, today. Thanks for not reading me the riot act. I'm going to see if any of the guys at the office are familiar with this scam.'

'I'll check around, too,' Cory said.

'You're looking at Rosalind's only emotional support here, Cory.' He poked his chest with his thumb.

'It's time for her to join a group.'

'Good idea. He dipped his hand into the paper sack. 'Orange or carrot juice?'

'Don't give me such big decisions, Steve.'

He tossed her a chilled plastic bottle.

'They say rape victims do better with women therapists. Should I refer her?'

'Usually, it's easier for women to talk to other women about it, but you're a kind, gentle man — a *mensch*. It's clear you care about her and she needs you,' she said, recalling the support given by her male friends in the aftermath of her rape. 'Besides, she might feel rejected.'

'Ah-hah,' he replied.

After lunch, they trekked above the cliffs that dropped about two hundred feet over treacherous paths leading to the beach. How strange it felt to calmly talk about therapy for rape victims here, in a deserted area like where her own rape had taken place, she thought.

They strolled to the parking lot and Steve drove Cory back to the office.

'Thanks. It's better we talked,' he said.

'Lunch was delicious. And I loved the restaurant. Such ambiance!'

He laughed. 'The best! Be well.'

'Regards to the family,' Cory said, shutting the car door.

Hoping the attacks on Roz and Mallory weren't epidemic, she flew upstairs to her office to leave phone messages for colleagues.

11

Marge Abbott, a forty-one year old widow with three teenage children and few office skills had been seeking full-time employment for several years to no avail. Despite her prudent life-style, her husband's insurance was almost drained and left her desperate. Her part-time housekeeping jobs were demeaning and exhausting. When Superior Health Care moved to San Diego and increased their subscribers ten-fold, they hired her on the spot. She was ecstatic. The wage was two dollars above the minimum, but she was promised an increase and health insurance after a three month probationary period.

Marge, the quintessential mother and housekeeper, had paid little attention to her appearance, but working in an office forced her to shop for a wardrobe. Her fashion conscious seventeen year old daughter, Ellen, accompanied her on a shopping spree. From off a rack, she pulled out a stylish suit and examined the price tag.

'Mom, you'd look super in this outfit and it's on sale. It's just right for an office.'

'The skirt is much too short. I couldn't cross my legs comfortably and I don't want to appear seductive.'

'But it's the style. All the women wear this. Here, look.' Ellen whipped out a magazine she had stashed in her backpack, flipped the pages and pointed. 'See. Lawyers, stock-brokers, just about everyone your age wears this stuff. And besides, it wouldn't hurt to attract a guy. Maybe you'll have an office romance. You should date, now. Dad's been gone for five years. Don't you ever get lonely?'

'Lonely? I have you and your brothers.'

Ellen rolled her eyes. 'C'mon Mom, you can't depend on us. We have our own lives, now.'

The thought of dating filled Marge with anxiety. Her life with Paul had been good. They had known each other since high school and married soon after graduation. He had joined the police force and she had taken a job as a nanny until her eighth month of pregnancy. She had never known another man and was content to live with fading memories. Now she wondered how long that could nourish her.

'I have an idea Mom. I'll show you how to use makeup, and that discount beauty salon in our neighborhood can cover your gray hair.

You'll look younger. How about it?'

'I'll take you up on the makeup, but we can't afford the salon.'

'But Mom, you look older than you are. It shouldn't, but it does make a difference in career advancement.'

Conscientious and a quick learner, Marge had felt assured of her potential for job promotion. It hurt to think her premature gray hair could bar her from it.

'What kind of a big career do you think I can have, Ellen?' She scowled.

'You graduated with honors from high school, but preferred working at home to college. Do you still feel the same way?'

Marge smiled at her clever daughter. 'No, honey. I think I'm a bit burned out.'

'Understood. Now that you're not needed so much at home, you can attend college. Maybe we'll graduate together.'

'It's not too late for me?'

'Of course not. Don't let that gray hair fool you. You're still young. C'mon, Mom. My treat at the salon. I got a big tip for staying late on that baby-sitting job last Saturday.'

Marge, filled with appreciation, felt her eyes well up with tears. Figuring with her first real pay-check she would make it up to Ellen, she agreed.

In a few hours, the women headed home,

arms filled with packages, Marge's hair tinted a warm hazelnut brown. Quietly, they sneaked into Marge's bedroom to complete the task.

After Ellen stepped back to examine the fruits of her make-up tricks, Marge checked her reflection in the mirror. Facial lines earned from a hard life seemed to have evaporated. She smiled at her daughter. Giggling, Ellen hugged her. 'Tomorrow, we'll have another makeup lesson,' she said. 'I'll coach you while you put it on by yourself.'

Their laughter carried through the house and brought the boys bounding into their mother's bedroom where they faced her.

Wide-eyed, the younger one whistled.

'Awesome!' said her older son.

12

Humiliated at the loss of his last job, Hamilton had contemplated revenge, but before he had time to plan it, he interviewed Behavioral Health and was accepted for a position as case manager. A degree wasn't required and they probably hadn't checked his references. His experience as an aide in a psychiatric facility qualified him. Now, he was a big shot, just as a man with his ability should be — with power.

Power in a burgeoning managed care industry. Managing mental health benefits was a new field, designed to keep costs down. Subscribers flocked to buy the cheap insurance, unaware that mental health coverage was limited to specific diagnoses, usually crisis situations and only for a few sessions. Working in an industry that devised such a clever scheme thrilled him.

Behavioral handled those benefits and was devoured by Superior, an industry leader. As contracts grew, the company expanded and with it, his duties. Now an executive, he commanded the largest section of the company, employing forty permanent employees and from time to time several part-time data entry people. He made sure his staff certified the minimum sessions and didn't fall for any crybaby stuff.

His ambition was to become Chief Executive Officer either at Superior or one of its competitors. A perfect job for him, a man who understood the goal — to generate profits for shareholders and officers at the expense of consumers. The less the corporation paid out for health care, the more profit it made. At the helm, salaries were substantial. As CEO, he would have wealth and control over others.

It was he who specified to doctors the kind of treatment to perform, and the drugs to prescribe. The generic ones in which his company had a financial interest. He loved the authority to make health care decisions. His only tool, a case manager's reference manual lay on his desk. He caressed the index with his finger.

He spread the batch of new treatment reports in front of him, carefully reading the identifying data:

NAME / ADDRESS / BIRTH DATE / MARITALSTATUS /PRESENTING PROBLEM

From one batch he created two by sorting through the reports and stacking his selections in a short pile. Panting, he became aware that sweat moistened his shirt and underwear as he read:

Ida Murphy, age 39, single, presenting problem: depression and anxiety due to break-up with boyfriend.
Too old. He tossed the report on the larger stack.

Sara Dawson, age 27, single, presenting problem: depression result of marital dissolution.
This is a good one. On the shorter stack it went.

Jennifer Slovak, age 25, divorced, husband left for another woman, sad, lonely, depressed.
Not another Jennifer like that bitch, Jennifer D'Amico. She was bad news. When she'd howled and kicked, it scared him. He hadn't intended to stab her so many times, just enough to terrify her and watch her blood spurt. No. He would not pick another Jennifer.
Beads of sweat accumulated on his forehead and drew wet rings at the arm pits of his shirt sleeves. The heat of his body made him feel alive. He tossed Jennifer Slovak's report on the larger pile.

Tammy Belvedere, age 30, single, boy-friend left for another man, feelings of betrayal, abandonment and loneliness.

She merited the shorter stack.

Erin Caldwell, age 28, isolated, no friends, family support in Ireland. Estranged from husband. Desperate. Fear of being alone.

Running his tongue across his dry, cracked, lips, he clutched the report in his hand and began to pant. An easy mark. The others can wait. He grinned in anticipation. He loved the feeling of a full bladder so he held back on voiding and drank two more cups of water.

From his desk drawer, he slid a legal-size yellow pad and a ruler and neatly drew columns. From his polished black attache case, he withdrew a large leather notebook containing copious notes of nearby beach communities he had researched before settling in San Diego. He had explored thoroughly, the grounds and facilities of each apartment house and condo facility, making maps of exits and entrances of those with no guards or security gates. He coded the secure complexes, 'Off limits.' His collection was designed with purpose and exactitude.

On his yellow pad he wrote down Erin's address and located it in his notebook. She lived in a large resort-type condo with recreational amenities. In order to approach her with a credible story, he needed to scope her out at her place. Snooping was a role he had enjoyed since childhood.

He drove home, changed into jeans, a gray sweat shirt and baseball cap and jogged to Erin's complex, pretending to be a prospective tenant. Passing a McDonald's, he stopped for a Big Mac, large fries and a coke and stuffed several packs of ketchup in the bag. When he arrived back, he consumed the contents of the bag. Satiated, he stretched out in his Eames chair.

Hamilton remembered an Irish priest whose sermons were filled with rolling R's. After rehearsing his pitch, he punched in Erin's phone number. Imitating the lilting Irish speech, he said, 'Hello, Erin, this is Patrick. I've noticed you at the condo and admired your lovely Irish looks. I was too shy to approach you. I hope I'm not bothering you now.'

13

Cory drummed her fingers on the desk while waiting for Grace who was usually punctual for her session. After ten minutes, she called the young woman's home. A man answered, startling her.

'May I please speak with Grace. This is Dr. Cohen.'

'Ah, yes. I'm sorry she won't be able to keep her appointment with you today.'

'Who are you?' Cory asked in a hoarse voice.

'Detective Sharpley.'

A detective? 'What happened?' Her heart went into fast mode.

'I'll explain at your office. I'm on my way,' he said.

Like an anxious parent whose child was late coming home from school, Cory waited for the detective. Within ten minutes, he arrived, gawking at her. Here we go again! That familiar look of surprise when people first met her. For some, her name conjured up an image of a short man with glasses, not a tall woman with an Asian face, she thought.

'Well, I'm surprised to see you, too,' she

said staring back at the detective, a man of average height, clean-shaven, with brown hair and eyes. A generic guy. Probably of middle age. Someone who would neither attract nor repel. Indistinct. A good trait for a detective, she figured.

'Ma'am, I'm Detective Sharpley, San Diego Police,' he said, pulling out his ID.

She read the card and stiffened. 'Homicide? Oh, my God! Was Grace murdered?'

'Seems so, Ma'am. I know Ms. Myles was your patient because your name appears in her appointment book at the same time each week for some time now. What can you tell me about her?'

With no time to process the impact of Grace's murder, Cory reflected on a response. Once upon a time, confidentiality was sacred in therapy, but now many insurance companies required treatment reports, blurring the issue. This tempted her to drop professional ethics and tell all, but she knew it wasn't appropriate.

'Although I'd like to, unfortunately, I can't show you her file without a court order,' she said, folding her quivering hands.

Blood rushed to the detective's face. 'For God's sake! This is a homicide investigation, and you have to stick by the rules?'

Cory shrugged. 'I'm really sorry.'

'I'll be back soon,' he snarled.

Ann tapped on the consulting room door and entered. 'Are you okay? That detective was from homicide. Can you talk about it?'

'Grace was murdered,' Cory blurted out.

'Oh, no!' Ann wrapped her arms around Cory. 'How awful. She was such a sweet thing. And so young.' Tears rolled down her cheeks, wetting Cory's neck.

Cory clutched her churning stomach. After her rape, she'd developed a spastic colon and whenever she was under stress, it acted up.

'I'll get you something,' Ann said, dashing out.

She returned with two cups of peppermint tea.

Cory had curled up on the couch, her eyes hot and wet. She pulled up her knees, making room for Ann at the edge. The two women tried to comfort each other. Finally, Ann left to greet the next patient.

With little time to cry, Cory swallowed her bitter tasting tears. She washed her face, brushed color on her lips and porcelain cheeks, and tried to focus on her work.

A few hours later, Cory met Detective Sharpley in the reception room. His eyes were watery and his nose, red. She figured he must have an allergy. He sauntered into her office, slapped the court order on her desk and said,

'Let's go, Ma'am.'

She slid Grace's chart to him. He yanked out his pen and a little notebook and began to write.

'No need. I'll make a copy of this for you, Detective. Unfortunately, it's probably not much more than you have.'

He flipped through her notes. 'Is this all?' he asked, frowning.

'I wish I had more. I knew her a short time. Too short. Grace transferred here from the L.A. branch of a law firm. Her office manager suggested therapy.'

'Why?' he asked.

'Grace was depressed over the end of her affair with one of the partners. She had trouble eating and sleeping, lost weight and energy. That's why her boss suggested the move here. She'd started to brighten and felt hopeful. Began sketching, again. Her talent was a good outlet.'

'What else can you tell me?' the detective asked.

'Let's see. Oh! A man claiming to be a client of her firm where he said he'd noticed her, began to call her at home often.'

'Got a name?'

'No. The attention probably helped her feel better about herself, although all he seemed to want was phone friendship.' A flash went on in Cory's head. 'Oh, my God! That's the same scenario of two recent rape victims.'

'What? Who?'

'The police know about one. The other is my friend's patient. I'm sure you'll hear about it soon. Please tell me what happened to Grace?' Stifling her tears, Cory felt a wad in her throat.

'When Ms. Myles didn't show up for work today, the office manager called us. He thought she may have committed suicide, but that wasn't the case. Upon entering her apartment, the officers found multiple bruises and her jugular vein had been cut.'

Imagining Grace's terrifying ordeal, Cory shivered and tightened her jacket around herself.

'The medical examiner estimates time of death around nine o'clock last night.' The detective's nasal voice was matter-of-fact.

'Was she raped, too?'

'It looks that way, Ma'am.'

'Grace must have come home from the seminar last night and missed the message I'd left at her office. I wanted to warn her about the rapist. Damn!' Cory punched her fist on the arm of the chair. 'I should have called her at home.'

Ann knocked on the door, entering with

two steaming mugs of chamomile tea. Cory handed her Grace's chart to copy.

A few minutes later Ann returned with copies in an envelope.

'Much obliged, Ma'am,' the detective said.

'Sergeant, if you let me go through her appointment book, maybe it'll trigger a clue — a reminder of something she'd mentioned.'

He stared at Cory over the rim of the mug. 'Thanks, but investigation is my job.'

Cory leaned forward. 'It's mine, too, Detective. Psychotherapy *is* investigation and Grace Myles was *my* patient. I want her killer found before he strikes again.' Cory's voice echoed in her ears. 'Two recent rapes. Now a rape *and* a murder. If it's the same guy, he's on a rampage. He's getting worse. Can't you see. I'd do anything to prevent that! *Please* let me help.'

The detective glanced at the framed diplomas and certificates on her wall. He disliked people who thought they knew everything, just because they had earned those stupid pieces of paper. If they were so smart, why couldn't they make a pill to cure his allergies? He wrote this one off as another hysterical broad. A-pain-in-the-ass.

★   ★   ★

'If you think of anything more, Ma'am, call me.' He plopped his card on her desk and abruptly left.

'Detective Sergeant William Sharpley, Homicide Unit, San Diego Police Department.' Another *shmuck*. Just like Detective Ryan, N.Y.P.D who had discounted her when she was a young college student, Cory thought. Now she was a mature professional woman, and still discounted. Was it her gender? Were cops on a power trip?

She recalled that terrible period in her life, over thirty years ago, when Detective Ryan said he didn't need her help and ignored the significance of the slip of paper she'd snatched when it had fallen from the pocket of the rapist — a bill from a hotel in Montreal. A police artist should have sketched her description of the rapist and sent it to the hotel in Montreal for identification, but, no. Their meager effort consisted of showing her a photo album of bad guys.

She had never understood how an incompetent man like Ryan became a detective. He wouldn't follow her common sense suggestions and smirked when she'd asked him about footprints and fingerprints in the muddy area where she'd been attacked. He told her she didn't know what she was talking about. Rape crimes seemed inconsequential to the N.Y.P.D. at that time.

Now, it haunted her again:

Brooklyn, New York. October, 1965

She lifts the hood of her fuchsia wool coat and ties the string to keep the cool blast of Atlantic wind away from her body. Shuffling school books, she jams her chilled hands in her pockets and starts toward campus, her philosophy assignment on her mind. She's a few steps from her apartment building when her thoughts about Existentialism are shattered by shouts of a neighbor from his open window, 'Hey, Cory! Get into the lobby. Quick!' She freezes. He yells again, 'Hurry!' Dashing inside, she hears a noise. A car backfiring? A dark car speeds away. Mr. Levin runs breathlessly into the lobby. 'Are you lucky I saw the car crawl up Ocean Avenue behind you. Some meshugener with his head out the window had a gun pointing at you! What's going on?'

Cory shivers. Feels faint. Mr. Levin grabs her shoulders. 'Cory, I'm a witness. You'd better call the police right now.'

Still stunned, she clings to him for a moment, then nods. She races upstairs, two steps at a time and hollers, 'Thanks, Mr.

Levin, thanks. Thanks a lot.'

Her hands shaking, she unlocks the apartment door, kicks it shut and hooks the chain lock. She grabs the phone and dials the police precinct. Detective Ryan, assigned to her rape case, is out on an investigation. She gives the report to the dispatcher.

'Yeah, yeah, I'll tell him. Come on. You didn't actually see the guy shoot at you.'

'No, but my neighbor saw it from his window.'

'Sure. Sure he did.'

Cory's heart pounds with a rhythm matching one beginning in her head. 'How dare you? My neighbor, Mr. Levin is a retired gentleman. He wouldn't make this up. Wait until the chief hears about this call.' But there's only a dial tone on the other end. Cory trembles with fear and rage. 'That lousy sonofabitch!' she yells.

Not only was she raped at knife point by a stranger a few weeks ago, but she's totally dismissed by the New York City Police Department with little attention given to her case. She could help find the rapist, but they won't listen to her. Why don't I matter? She wonders.

The rape and the attempt on her life are intolerable. She must do something.

She blows money taking cabs to school.

Tries to focus on classes, but intrusive thoughts about the rape interfere with concentration. When someone enters the room, she jumps. To protect herself, she registers for karate. From her teacher — her Sensei, she learns she must understand people and be aware of her surroundings. Vigilance becomes her style. Self-defense, her power. The discipline and exercise appeal to her and provide a sense of control she thought the rape had taken from her.

After the second attempt on her life, for a brief period, Ryan had escorted Cory to and from school in his battered old Ford. Ten years older than the students, with none of the earmarks of a professor, he had seemed out of place on the small Brooklyn College campus, where everyone else toted books and no one wore unfashionable crumpled suits and neckties. A self-involved co-ed, Cory was unconcerned about how awkward he may have felt when her classmates stared at them, but rather how it increased her feelings of being different.

Ann poked her head in Cory's office. 'Ready to leave?'

Looking at Ann's guileless face with its delicate features, Cory felt protective of her.

'We've got to be cautious, Ann. Promise me

you won't let a stranger into your house. Not for any reason. Please!' She knew she sounded like a worried parent, but like most people from small towns, Ann was trusting. Divorced, with grown children, she was in her late forties. Like Cory, she too, lived alone.

Ann smiled. She didn't mind Cory's harangue. 'Don't worry about me. I live in a secure complex. There's a gate and a guard. I'm cautious. You be careful, too.'

Cory grabbed her purse and briefcase before Ann locked the door behind them. They stepped downstairs to the dimly lit garage where flickering lights cast scary shadows. Overwrought with Grace's brutal murder, Cory tensed, imagined someone hiding behind a car. Expecting to spot a security guard who usually started his rounds at this hour, she scanned the area.

Ann had parked her silver Toyota Camry next to Cory's old white BMW.

'I wish you'd take some self defense classes, Ann.'

'I know karate is important to you, Cory, but it's not my thing. School and work are enough right now.'

'Just give it a try,' Cory pleaded. 'Self defense empowers people.'

The movement of the security guard

checking a door upstairs caught her glance and she relaxed.

'Would you feel better if I had a gun?' Ann shoved her hand into her pocket.

Cory gazed at her in disbelief, expecting her to pull out a small revolver. 'No. Do you?'

Ann whipped out her keys. 'I'm thinking about it. Would you have one?' she asked.

'No! I hate weapons.'

Ann opened the door to her Camry. 'You are such a Jewish mother, Cory.'

Cory started to climb into her BMW. 'Look who's talking. You feed the patients chicken soup.'

'Only in winter.' She grinned. 'Wait a minute. How about joining me for dinner tonight, Cory? Grace's murder is a horrible shock and we can use a nice break.'

Still stunned over the loss, Cory tried not to dwell on the young woman, but the mention of her name made her throat constrict.

Dining with Ann gave Cory an excuse to skip a karate workout where she would probably run into Ron. Every time she saw the young man, she felt vulnerable. She marveled at herself, a middle-age woman who felt like a teenager with a crush, ashamed he would sense her attraction to him. She wasn't ready for that, now.

'Sure. Where to?'

'L'Auberge. Nice atmosphere, good food, classical music and ample parking.'

The women drove a short distance, parked, and traipsed into the sedate restaurant. They passed through the bar where a tuxedo clad pianist was playing a Strauss Waltz. The host escorted them to a rear table overlooking a lighted garden.

Cory settled into the tapestry upholstered chair. 'The crab cakes are delicious, Ann. Made from real crabs.'

'I didn't know you went for that stuff.'

'I don't keep kosher.'

Ann's curly blonde hair bounced as she turned her head to scan the commodious room. 'Speaking of crabs, I thought I saw that professor I told you about.'

'Maybe it's because you'd like to see him.'

'That's what you think. I'm no longer interested in him. Oh, I can see by that look on your face — you think it's sour grapes. Well, it isn't. He's weird. There's something about him — I don't know. He gives me a sick feeling.'

'Suddenly — just like that, Ann?'

'Last night a student asked him a question that he'd answered earlier. The way he glared and gritted his teeth at the guy, you'd need a sledgehammer to cut through the tension in the air.'

Ann's description of the man reminded Cory of her ex-husband. Without obvious provocation, Geoff would leer at her in a terrifying manner and then sulk into morose silence. She had begged him to explain what had set him off, but he refused. Such episodes eroded the marriage. 'I know what you mean,' she said. 'That kind of behavior puts you on edge, because you don't know what's coming.'

'Exactly. It looked like he was going to smash the student. And he's so damn pedantic. I'm pretty literate, but sometimes he uses words I've never heard. Probably showing off — compensating for insecurity. I think he hates people. Some psychologist, huh? It's good he's only part-time faculty. I'd hate to have him for another course.'

'What does he teach?'

'Statistics.'

'No comment.'

The server took their order. They'd split a glass of Merlot. Halibut smothered in a citrus and ginger sauce for Ann, and Cory, with no appetite, would have the crab cake appetizer.

'Want to talk about Grace, Cory?'

'All I can say is I cared a lot for her and am obviously furious at her murderer. It's awful that she had such a short life — that ended in terror.' Cory was tempted to discuss her guilt for not calling Grace at home to warn her of potential danger, but it wasn't appropriate to tell her receptionist. Ann wasn't a full fledged colleague.

Cory often had to remind herself of boundaries. The emotional intimacy her patients shared with her was a privilege and not a two way street, and she could only share her professional life in a consultative capacity.

The two women, usually vivacious, dined shrouded in silence.

'There's an operatic group singing arias in the hotel lobby. Can you stay for awhile?' Cory asked, after paying her portion of the bill.

'Sure. We can do with some cheer.'

They seated themselves on a crimson velvet couch facing a large window. Clouds shredded the moon, but a few stars could be seen in the dark sky above a lighted swimming pool area. Cory and Ann enjoyed the music until a well-dressed group of rowdy people interfered.

'Time to go,' Ann announced.

They headed for the garage. 'Nice evening, Ann. Thanks for suggesting it.'

'I know you can't tell me much, Cory, but please remember that I'm here for you.'

'Just being with you is supportive.'

Cory drove home, tears pouring down her cheeks. Her thoughts shifted to Ann's Statistics professor. The malevolent pedant. Ann and Cory shared a similar temperament and each found such a man attractive. At least in Ann's case, the relationship hadn't developed.

14

Two days later, Ann, her face flushed had news to share with Cory. 'You won't believe what happened. Last night I told that miscreant professor I'd have to skip class because of my internship interview which I couldn't rearrange. Guess what he said?'

'Good luck?'

'Hardly. He threatened to fail anyone who missed more than two classes. No exceptions and no make-ups. That power hungry freak!'

'Yeah, with an erratic emotional thermostat.' Just like my ex, Cory thought. 'That guy is sadistic. As part-time faculty, he probably hasn't too much clout. Appeal to administration,' Cory said. 'If that doesn't work, circulate a petition and submit it to the department head.'

'They could kick me out.'

'And ruin their image?'

'C'mon Cory. It's not worthy of the back page. Anyhow, with the number of desperate students scrambling around for grad school admission, a scandal would be meaningless.'

'It's frustrating, but you're not totally impotent. Ask advice from administration and don't anticipate a negative response.'

The phone rang, interrupting their conversation. A call from Steve.

'What's up, doc,' Cory said into the receiver.

'I canvassed the guys here. So far, none have patients reporting a phone pal.'

'I haven't had a response from my calls, yet. Talk later, Steve.'

Cory enjoyed the fully packed day — each session a gem — the fruits of her therapeutic work. At the close of her last session, she packed her briefcase and looked forward to two favorite pastimes; music and a good read.

'I took your suggestion and made an appointment at school for tonight,' Ann said, locking the door behind them.

'I'm figuring on a good response,' Cory said, starting her car.

Emerging from the parking structure into a tangerine sunset, Cory drove toward home watching the sky change from orange to purple. Distracted, she'd nearly forgotten the karate class. She knew what stopped her: Anxiety over seeing Ron. Cory had urged Ann to be strong. Taking her own advice, she braced herself and changed course.

The Karate Institute was in a strip mall with a nail salon, a shoe repair shop and a hardware store. All the stores closed at six. It was six-fifteen and Cory was late. The only place open for business would be the karate studio, but the interior was dark. No cars in the parking lot. Street lamps were dim, but lights from the shopping center across the street provided good visibility to the studio.

Not a soul there. Usually Monday evenings brought the regulars, two women and three men. Where were they? Cory drove closer to the door of the studio and squinted into the darkness. No message on the door. She sensed something was wrong.

15

Hamilton hated many things in his life, like the suffering he endured when everyone compared him unfavorably to his two older brothers, Jefferson and Madison. What a joke his mother played on them, giving them such names to make her family sound distinguished when she was nothing but poor white trash! Now, Hamilton paced his office, stamped his foot and shouted, 'To hell with my bastard brothers!' He despised them because they were older, stronger, smarter with better nicknames than his: 'Jeff' for Jefferson, 'Maddy' for Madison and his was 'Ham,' but the kids called him 'Pig.' Now he understood why he was fastidious in his appearance.

Hamilton had been subjected to daily comparisons of his 'devilish' behavior and that of his brothers. Ridiculed and scorned for wetting his bed until he was eight years old, he had retaliated by secretly urinating on Jeff's bed and at times in Maddy's underwear drawer. Sometimes he hid a favorite toy of Jeff's in Maddy's closet, joyfully watching the resultant fights.

He didn't need a psychologist-nerd to explain this behavior. He understood that he was pissed off.

Mastery of his bladder was important. An adult, now, he drank excessive volumes of water to fill his bladder. His delayed urination brought him great satisfaction — proof of his excellent control. He was proud of his achievements: Getting even without getting caught.

16

Marge Abbott prided herself on the rate with which she learned new tasks. The job at Superior was not complicated and she was well prepared. Her thirteen year old computer savvy son had been delighted to instruct his mother on the fundamentals. He was proud of his mother's speed and accuracy on the keyboard.

Armed with basic knowledge, Marge learned how to enter data on the computer quickly. She enjoyed the hectic office atmosphere and her thickly carpeted cubicle, a change from her domestic routine.

Well accepted by her co-workers, Marge looked forward to staff luncheons. She began to make office friends and occasionally played cards or mahjong on the weekend with some of them. Apart from strange feelings of discomfort whenever she encountered Mr. Pope, one of the executives, she was generally happy. She could not explain the sinister quality she found in him, but she felt frightened in his presence.

It was her turn for the mahjong game on

Sunday. The children helped tidy the house before the family left for church.

When they came home Marge set the bridge table on her small patio in preparation for her three co-workers. She placed bowls of snacks on the table and filled a pitcher with raspberry tea.

During the lively game, talk turned to office gossip.

'Rumor has it that we're going to be sold to a larger company,' one of the women said.

Startled, Marge was afraid she could lose her job. She reminded herself not to jump to conclusions. 'What will happen to us?' she asked, a tremor in her voice.

'Oh, don't worry, Marge. You won't get fired. I doubt any of us will. They'll probably need more help. They're growing. Probably the take-over will be good for us. Maybe even give us promotions.'

'I don't know where they'd put me, but I sure as heck don't want it anywhere near that Mr. Pope,' Marge said.

'He gives me the creeps, too,' the woman said. 'He never looks anyone in the eye. That stuffed shirt wouldn't lower himself to join the staff at Happy Hour.'

'Yeah, I know, he keeps to himself. A regular recluse. They say he has no family and from the looks of it, no friends. No one at Superior likes him. He's too intimidating.'

The talk validated Marge's feelings about Hamilton Pope.

17

Cory raced home, activated the security system and grabbed the phone directory. She called Oliver Baxter, an advanced student who worked at the Karate Institute.

'Hi, Olie. This is Cory. I've just come from the studio. It was dark. What's up?'

'Beats me. I was helping my dad at the hotel so I wasn't at the studio all day. When I got there — must have been close to six, it was shut,' he said. 'Uh, first time this ever happened. I didn't have the key so I watched the door from the coffee shop across the street, but no one came to open it.'

'No one showed up?'

'Uh, a few of the regulars, but they split when they couldn't get in. I waited there until the coffee shop closed. Must have been close to six-fifteen.'

'Did you call anyone about it?'

'Yeah, I did. All I got was answering machines.'

'This could be serious, Olie. Maybe someone's hurt or in danger. Who was supposed to open today?'

'Jennifer.'

'What's her number, please. Her address, too.'

'I don't have it, but I know where she lives. I'll go with you.'

After giving Olie directions to her house, Cory called the sheriff dispatcher, supplied her name and address and explained the need for a security check of the studio. About fifteen minutes later, Olie arrived at Cory's door followed by two uniformed officers who announced the Karate Institute was secure. She told them that Jennifer hadn't missed work, before. The deputies agreed to check her house with Olie as navigator and Cory as support.

Her pulse beat a fast rhythm. Jennifer could be dead or unconscious. How? Why? Could it be the same guy who killed Grace? Gripping Cory's hand, Olie called out directions to Jennifer's place.

'There could be many reasons why she didn't open the studio,' Cory said. Given recent events, she expected the worst.

Shortly, they arrived at Jennifer's Solana Beach secluded condo. The officers asked them to knock at the door. Olie pounded, but no one answered. He swiveled the door-knob. It was unlocked.

'Don't go in,' the deputy cautioned. 'Wait in the car, please.'

She watched his partner circle the periphery of the house, checking windows. When he returned, he called out, 'No forced entry. Let's go in.'

The officer pushed open the door. 'This is the police. Anyone hurt? We're coming in,' he shouted.

Within minutes, the shriek of an approaching ambulance grew louder until it stopped a few feet from them. Carting medical paraphernalia, the paramedics ran into the house.

A few moments later they came out carrying Jennifer on a stretcher.

The officer beckoned Olie and Cory and they ran towards her.

'Is this your friend?' he asked.

Gasping, Cory stared at Jennifer's puffy face and nodded. A white blanket covered her body and dried blood was visible on her neck.

The ambulance sped away. The officers drove them back to Cory's house.

'What should we do,' Olie said, trembling.

'I'll drive us to the hospital,' Cory answered.

While Jennifer was treated in the emergency room, they paced the corridor until they found seats in the crowded reception area.

Olie sat on a bench, clutching his head. 'Of

all people — how could this have happened to Jen?' he asked.

'I don't know, Olie. The front door was unlocked. Why would she let someone in, unless she knew him? Who could do this to her?'

'Beats me. She's not stupid. And she's not rich. I don't know anyone who hates her.'

'Let's hope she'll be able to explain it, soon, Olie.'

Hospital waiting rooms changed their perception of time — a minute felt like an hour. Cory scanned the visitor's gray faces and puffy eyes that telegraphed dread and turned to Olie.

A sweet young man about her son's age, Olie aspired to become a 'sensei,' a teacher with his own studio. He was proud of his trophies displayed in the Karate Institute foyer.

Jennifer was in her mid to late thirties, single. Worked two jobs, waitress and karate instructor. Cory had learned a lot from her, but little about her. Olie knew more and Cory pumped him.

'Jen's a nice chick but hard to get to know. She had a boyfriend recently, but he dumped her. I think she did everything to get him back, but it was no go.'

It was late and the waiting room had

emptied, so they walked through the swinging doors to the emergency room corridor. A full bosomed, middle-aged nurse with sparkling blue eyes and curly brown hair that framed a friendly face, bounced to her duties like a child's rubber ball. Her badge read, 'Tanya Rifkin, R.N.'

'I'm Dr. Cohen, and this is Mr. Baxter. We're friends of Jennifer D'Amico. How is she?'

'We've just taken her to the Intensive Care Unit. Just a precaution. Because she was knocked unconscious, she's had x-rays. There's no fracture, but she needs to be monitored.'

'Why? What's wrong with her?' Olie asked.

'The doctor will explain,' she said, pointing to a thin, pale, young man wearing a white coat, stethoscope and thick glasses who approached them.

'You're the ones who sounded the alarm for Jennifer D'Amico, yes?'

They nodded.

'Well, it was good you helped get her here in time. She's had superficial slashing and lost some blood, but didn't need a transfusion. We sutured her. Lucky, she's an athlete, because her neck muscles were so thick they protected her. Lucky too, he didn't cut a major vessel. You know that would have been fatal.'

Cory gasped.

'Because she lapses in and out of consciousness we need to monitor her for an epidural or subdural hematoma. The lapses raise the possibility of a subdural hematoma.' His pager beeped and he glanced at it. 'Over the next twelve hours if her sensorium is cleared completely, she can be discharged, but she should be observed.'

'Uh, what does that mean?' Olie shrugged. 'I'm not a doctor.'

'Oh. I thought *you* were Dr. Cohen. The nurse will explain it.' The busy doctor waved his hand and hurried down the hall.

'It means she's bleeding under or inside the skull compressing the brain which causes lapses of consciousness. A hematoma means a blood clot. If it grows she'll need surgery to remove the clot,' the nurse said. 'That's why she must be monitored. If she doesn't go into a coma, isn't drowsy, stays aware and alert, she can leave the hospital after twelve hours with continued observation.'

'What's her condition now?' Cory asked.

'Guarded. Don't worry. I think she'll be fine.' The nurse's smile was broad and reassuring. She seemed experienced and remarkably fresh for the time of night, probably had just started the evening shift.

'When can we see her?'

'I suggest you wait until tomorrow. She's talked to the police and is exhausted.'

'Thank you,' Cory said.

'Are you sure she's okay?' Olie asked.

'Well, as okay as she can be under the circumstances.' Cory liked Tanya Rifkin's gentle voice and the competent way she handled her tasks.

Olie and Cory returned to her house. She felt they weren't ready to be by themselves and invited him inside for cider.

'Thanks for asking me in, Cory. I really didn't get all that gobble-de-gook at the hospital. I feel awful about Jen. She's such a swell person.'

'Jennifer was hit on the head and her neck was cut, Olie. She lost blood and they stitched her up.' Cory didn't repeat the part about the possibility of surgery for a blood clot on her brain.

'I hope she's not in danger. I . . . well . . . never mind.'

They sat opposite each other in Cory's den sipping warm drinks. The warmth and the cinnamon scent began to soothe them.

'Would you like more than friendship with her?' Cory asked.

He poured himself another helping from the carafe. 'Yeah, I guess I would. If I were older, maybe she'd go for me.' His dark eyes seemed sad.

'If older men find younger women desirable, Olie, why shouldn't older women find younger men acceptable, too?' Her thoughts wandered to Ron, a dozen years younger than she, who inhabited her fantasies.

'Yeah, why not?' he asked.

The grandfather clock chimed ten and Cory yawned.

'Guess I should go now,' Olie said.

He'd been through a lot tonight and Cory felt protective of him. She jotted down her number on a slip of paper. 'If you want to talk, I'll be here until ten-thirty tomorrow morning.'

She watched him walk to his car. Tall, lean, with light hair and broad shoulders, he reminded her of her son. A sudden pang of lonesomeness struck her. So many emotions converged on Cory at once. Love. Rage. Fear. Her stomach responded as though to a bad combination of food.

It was hard to accept that Jennifer, an inspiring karate teacher, was in such a predicament. Cory shuddered to think the woman could need brain surgery. Strong and capable, how could this happen to her?

18

The cold blade pressed against her neck. She strained to scream, but no sound came. Trembling in terror, her breath raced. She bolted upright in bed, awakened from a nightmare in which she was a composite of Mallory, Grace and Jennifer.

Her throat felt sore from tension. She sat at the edge of the bed and rocked. To reassure herself that it was only a bad dream, she peered around the room. Digital clock read 6:10. Security switch on. Nothing amiss. No one had broken in. She rolled off the bed and opened the shutters to pale rays of early morning sunlight. The garden appeared untrampled, and the street beyond it — innocent. Cory hopped into the shower to revive.

She tried to push thoughts of Grace away, but memories of her made tears spill from the corners of her eyes. She wished she could set the clock back so Grace would still be alive. Snippets of her therapy sessions replayed:

' . . . aunt and uncle never hugged or kissed me . . . dressed me up to show off at church to make themselves look good . . . didn't *really care about me . . . that I was too thin. Never fed me anything I liked.'*

'Do you think you're still too thin?'

'Yes. I'd like to gain a few pounds.'

But it was too late, now! That bastard snuffed out her young life, took away her chance to flourish. A person who had endeared herself to Cory was dead and she yearned to lash out at the killer. She had visions of stomping on his face. Grinding her heel into his eyes. And she was ashamed of not being ashamed.

Grace haunted her. When Cory saw other beautiful, blonde young women, they reminded her of Grace. She resembled a Scandinavian beauty contestant. Now, no more. The only way to keep her alive was to remember her. Cory hoped she wasn't the only one with tender memories.

To distract herself, she switched on the radio. KFSD played the last movement of Beethoven's Ninth. She marched to the doorstep, scooped up the newspaper and took a deep breath of early morning fog — a welcome relief from the Santa Ana. The thermometer outside registered a cool sixty degrees — a fine day for gray wool slacks and an electric blue sweater. She propped the newspaper on the dining table and poured a glass of orange juice. Nibbling an oat bran muffin, she nearly choked when she read a chilling description of the assault. The Solana Beach rape victim was not identified, but Cory knew the woman was Jennifer.

The rapist had struck in beach areas a few miles apart. Mallory in Pacific Beach. Steve's patient, Rosalind, and Grace in La Jolla. Jennifer in Solana Beach. All within days of each other. The monster was slithering up the coast in a state of mania. Each victim young, lonely or depressed over a broken relationship. Vulnerable women. Even Jennifer, a black belt!

A knife was used to terrorize Rosalind and to kill Grace. Had he meant to kill Jennifer, too? Did Mallory avert a slashing by knocking the wind out of him before she fled? Were these attacks made by different people or by the same man growing more vicious? Who would he strike next?

She called Memorial, relieved to find Jennifer's condition upgraded to satisfactory and she could receive visitors. Cory had time to see her before work. She phoned Olie at the studio. He assured her he was okay and planned to see Jennifer soon. Better for him to go alone, Cory figured.

On the drive to the hospital, Cory rolled down her window to buy fresh flowers at a corner stand from a man wearing a sombrero. Although she wasn't a steady customer, he remembered her preference for yellow chrysanthemums and handed her a bunch. Driving away, she wondered if she'd impressed him because of her friendliness or her unusual looks.

Cruising down the Coast Highway, an ocean breeze swept her hair. On KLON, Chet Baker's mellow trumpet crooned, 'Autumn in New York.' Cory missed the cool, crisp season — leaves turning colors, the aroma of burning wood and camphor scented winter clothes. Fall's subtle changes offered no reference point here, fading the time line of memories. A reasonable price for eternal spring.

In ten minutes she reached the hospital's crowded parking lot. Her search for a slot subtracted time from the visit. Tempted to use the doctor's area, she imagined her beloved grandmother shaking her finger. Someone pulled out from visitors parking and Cory zipped in.

She located Jennifer in the Intensive Care Unit. Sheets the color of her pale face covered her body, and an IV was attached to her hand. She smiled, nodding at the flowers. Cory held her free hand. 'I'll stay a short time. If there's anything you want, please let me know.'

Jennifer whispered, 'All I want is to get the bastard.'

A doctor about Jennifer's age, attractive, tall, thin with a dimpled smile entered the room. Cory rose to leave. 'No, it's quite all right. I'm only looking in for a moment. Your friend is fortunate. No vital organ or major vessel was punctured. She lost a lot of blood, but she's healthy.' He patted her head. 'Nice hard skull.' His accent suggested South Africa. Sun-streaked blonde hair and tanned complexion suggested outdoor interests. 'I'll pop in again this afternoon,' he said, rushing out the door. Jennifer blushed. Poor Oliver didn't stand a chance if Cory picked up the vibes correctly.

'What a way to meet a man!' she teased.

'So you know,' Jennifer replied.

'Know what?'

'How this happened to me.'

'No. I was thinking about the doctor.' Cory grinned.

'I meant how I got hurt. Everyone must wonder how this happened to me — not supposed to — not to a black belt. Moon Kim taught me to be alert — but I sure blew it.'

'Karate also teaches that we can't always protect ourselves, Jennifer.'

'True, but I wasn't cautious when I

should've been. That's going to be hard to get over. I'll have to go back to my shrink. Maybe you know her — Betty Pepper?'

'Betty? Sure. We're friends.'

'I needed more therapy, but my stingy health plan wouldn't allow it. So we wrapped it up. Now, I've got to go back.'

Jennifer appeared so frail in the hospital bed. So unlike the Jennifer Cory worked out with.

'Maybe Betty'll visit you here.'

Jennifer's face brightened. 'Good deal! Would you call her?'

'Right away. If there's anything else, please get in touch.' Cory scrawled her home phone number on the back of her card and placed it on the little table next to Jennifer's bed. 'Your sessions with Betty are confidential, so don't worry about that. I'll tell her I know you from karate.'

'I'm not ashamed of seeing Betty. Just felt like crap when my boyfriend bailed me — had a hard time accepting it. Hard for me to accept a lot of things.' A tear ran down her cheek. Cory dabbed it with a tissue.

'That's a good reason for therapy.'

'Yeah. Thought I was over it, but still felt lonely. Christ — I was needy. I wanted to meet someone new. Hell, I missed sex. When this guy called at the studio and told me he'd watched me work and found me appealing, I was stoked. I told him we ought to meet, but he kept canceling out on me. So annoying. He said he was too shy to meet me just yet, and wanted to be phone buds first — like he had to warm up. I pushed him into a date. When he came over, he seemed okay — nothing special except his hair looked tinted black. I don't go for hairy guys and this creep had a lot of hair — a dark beard and mustache.'

Flinching, Cory thought, oh, no, not again!

'Even though I wasn't attracted to him, I was so damn hard up, any stud would do. All I wanted was a quickie, then off to work I'd go.'

Cory raised her eyebrows.

'Yeah, you got my drift. I put sex first. Betty understands. It was stupid. I should've thought about what I was getting into. Anyway, we started to make out real fast. Man, it'd been such a long time since I'd been with a guy — I was willing to get off with this hairy stranger.' She gasped. 'Then . . . when he started to take off my sweat shirt . . . and it covered my head, he shocked me by twisting and tying the sleeves together so I couldn't move my arms. I couldn't believe it. It happened so fast. Man, I was trapped! Couldn't wriggle free. He got on top of me. I kicked, but it didn't do any damn good — he sat his heavy butt on my legs. That crazy man's ass weighed a ton. Imagine how I felt! I couldn't do anything except brace myself and yell.'

Cory stroked Jennifer's brow. 'Horrible . . . just horrible!'

'You've heard my shouts at the studio. They're damn loud. But my sweat shirt muffled them. I couldn't stop him . . . but it was all I could do.' Her chin quivered. 'I wanted sex, not rape!'

'I can imagine what you went through.'

'He must have hit me on the head with something hard. Maybe his fist. Wow, was he strong! I blacked out. The cops told me it was you who called them, Cory. He slashed me pretty bad and I could have bled to death if they hadn't gotten there in time. Thank God for you.'

Cory shuddered. 'Your story is like one I heard recently from another woman. You're not the only one who fell for it, Jennifer. He's very convincing.'

'He's got to be stopped!' she shouted.

Cory left the hospital with graphic images of Jennifer's horrific experience. Because the insurance had refused additional sessions, Jennifer's therapy had ended prematurely. Cory felt the muscles in the corners of her mouth twitch. She called Betty and arranged a lunch meeting.

19

A six-foot high metal sculpture resembling tree limbs stood inside the entry of Thai Haven. Upon close inspection, the Indonesian depiction was of three erect phalluses. It surprised Cory that she had not recognized it before.

She spotted Betty seated in a quiet corner. A Rita Hayworth look-alike, long, wavy copper hair caressed her shoulders. Warm and inviting as a spa on a cool day, it was easy to understand why she was the most popular psychologist in town. Empathy and humor combined with professional training was an elixir. She always welcomed Cory with a sweet smile, a comforting word, and a warm embrace. Today was no different.

They had first connected at a group of women psychologists, a few months after Cory left her husband and Betty was newly divorced. She invited Cory and her children to her house for dinner — whipped up a tasty meal and fussed over them. Her kids had baked cookies in their honor, and picked flowers for the table. That day was etched in Cory's memory. It was the first time since her grandmother had died that she had felt nurtured.

Neither of the women had siblings, nor family nearby. Their friendship, created out of mutual need and respect for each other, gave their children an extended family. Aunt Cory and Aunt Betty. They celebrated holidays and birthdays together. As the years passed and their lives grew busier, they saw less of each other, but in tough times, support was there.

Betty greeted Cory with a surprise.

'Did you hear the news about your rabbi, Cory?'

'What news?'

'He was arrested for trespassing.'

Cory stared at her. 'Oh, no! Where?'

'Fishing on private property.'

Puzzled, Cory said, 'The rabbi trespassed?'

'Yeah. When he went to court, the judge asked him if he'd read the sign. The rabbi said, 'Certainly, your honor.'

'You read it, yet you disobeyed? What did it say?'

'Trespassing Prohibited? No! Fishing Allowed.'

Giggling, Cory realized how much she had missed Betty. 'Thanks. I needed that. We should get together more.'

'I've tried, but you — you're too busy for a social life.'

'You know I'm there for you, Betty. In the

little free time after work, I schedule karate and jam when I can.'

'I know how you spend your time, Cory. You haven't dated a guy in years.'

Cory thought of the many times after Betty had ended a relationship, she would seek Cory's comfort. 'True, but maybe you date too much, huh?'

'It beats loneliness. Sometimes you're so damn critical.' Betty shook her finger at Cory.

'Sorry. Don't worry about my poor social life. I'm not lonely, but I've missed you. Listen, I had to see you, today.'

Pressed for time, Betty had ordered in advance for them. The server brought spicy eggplant salads on brightly colored platters and they dug in.

'Oh, so it took something urgent to meet me?' Leaning back in the peach colored velvet booth, she pouted, feigning disappointment.

'I'd have called you soon anyway, but this pushed me.'

'So what is it?' She furrowed her brow.

'I just visited someone from karate in the hospital. She's a patient of yours. The stabbing victim.'

'Oh, my God, Jennifer — a black belt like you!' Betty's shrill voice drew the attention of diners.

Cory lowered her tone and leaned forward.

'She was sexually assaulted. That's why her name wasn't in the paper. She needs to see you.'

Betty's voice cracked. 'Of course. Which hospital?'

'Memorial, La Jolla — ICU.'

'What's her condition? How did it happen?'

'Satisfactory. She'll give you the gory details. There's a serial rapist and murderer on the loose, Betty. Probably the one who raped one of my patients. One of Steve's too. Murdered another. I think I know how he operates,' Cory whispered.

'Damn!' She glared. 'How?'

'Maybe he hangs around outside therapy offices, stalking young women on their way out. Sees where they go. Where they work. Where they live. Targets those with no social life.'

'Then what?'

'He phones them. Pretends he knows them from somewhere. Tells them he's shy and just wants to be phone friends.' Cory pushed her salad aside. 'He gains their confidence. Because they're needy and naïve, they invite him over.' Cory looked down at the table and noticed she'd torn the pink paper napkin to shreds.

Betty cupped her flawless face in her hands. 'Now I *am* worried,' she said. 'I treat a lot of women with those symptoms. Not only that, but Marjorie just told me she has two patients who developed phone friendships. She thought it was coincidental. I thought it was practicing safe sex.' Her usual cheerful face turned tense. The tiny lines around her eyes and mouth appeared deeper. 'So what do we do?'

Gazing at the dessert on the table, Cory didn't remember its arrival.

'Warn women.'

'How? Call the cops and the media?'

'No. We can't give out patient's names.' Cory poked her spoon into the lime mush of the melted sundae, tasted its sweet flavor, and became nauseated. 'For now, let's inform therapists and patients.'

'I know — a phone tree! Divide the calling among psychologists in different areas. Want me to take care of it?' She plunged her hands into her purse. Rooting out a pad and pen, she scribbled.

'Good idea, Betty.'

'Let's have a meeting at my house. How's Sunday at noon?'

'Probably too short notice. The following week, okay?'

'But, Cory, it's an emergency!'

'I know. Try. If we can't get enough people, make it next week.'

Betty glanced at her watch. 'Sorry, I've got to run. I'll see Jennifer after work. I'll make calls tonight and phone you as soon as I set it up.'

'Great. Uh-oh! Don't look now. You have an admirer. The guy sitting at the entrance. His eyes are glued on you and he looks about to drool.'

'You mean the bald guy with a strand of hair twirled around his head?'

Cory nodded.

'Oh God!' She turned and smiled in his direction.

'Betty, what *are* you doing?'

'Just a habit.'

Cory shook her head at her flirtatious friend. They paid the bill, hugged and left for work.

Would their warning come on time?

20

'Cory, listen to what I heard through the grapevine,' Betty said over the phone. 'Norma has patients who received those friendly calls from a stranger. Thank God, nothing has happened so far.'

'Has she warned them?'

'Not yet. She doesn't want to be an alarmist.'

'What? She'd rather risk their lives?' Cory banged her fist on the cluttered desk in her den. Papers flew, but it didn't matter. She saved paper shuffling for a rainy day and there were few of those.

'Listen, I know how you feel. I'm disgusted too. And it's a bitch trying to pull this meeting off. I've had only a few positive responses for this week, so we'll do it next Sunday. In the meantime, I'm going to push Norma.'

Cory had visions of pushing her, too. Smashing was more like it. 'If she doesn't bend, I'll try. Tell me, after you smiled at Baldy, what happened?'

'Oh, the guy at the Thai restaurant? Well, after what you'd told me — I was spooked.

He tried to pick me up. I told him to leave me alone, that my husband's a very jealous man. You know, Cory, I actually like bald guys.'

'Yeah, Betty. You like *guys*.'

'Not those who twirl their sparse hair around their head. Anyway, he apologized and walked away. It's going to be hard for me to date now. I'm going to be super cautious — like you. Talk to you soon.'

Several colleagues called back, but none knew of any patient who received calls from a stranger wanting phone friendship.

★   ★   ★

The next week Ann had her appointment with a university administrator. She arrived at work, smiling. 'He was encouraging. He told me not to worry and that he'd speak to my professor.'

'I'm pleased for you, Ann.'

Things were looking up. Cory spent the balance of the week without reports of phone pals until her session with Erin.

Radiant, her face aglow and her lustrous wavy red hair pushed back with a green velvet ribbon, she was decked out in school-girl attire. Erin bent down to adjust her knee socks and loafers. Folding her green plaid skirt under her knees, she smiled. 'I don't need Seldyn after all, because I've made a new chum.'

'How nice. Who?'

'A chap called Patrick Callahan.' Blushing, she fingered the collar of her starched white blouse.

'Well, he's had a nice effect on you. You look lovely today, Erin. I like the way you put your ensemble together.' Cory wished the young woman would do as well with her emotions.

'Thank you.' She smiled.

'Are you meeting him today?'

'Oh, no. In fact I haven't met him yet, but he's rung up several times to chat. He's full of compliments — said my lovely Irish looks and brogue remind him of his family in County Cork. Isn't that grand?' Erin stroked the arms of the chair. 'We have so much in common. We both enjoy shooting pool. He's quite shy . . . has no chums, either.'

The hair on the back of Cory's neck rose.

'He rarely speaks to anyone. He's really quite sweet. I'm so happy now.' She grinned like a contented child.

Her innocence troubled the therapist.

'Do you know how he got your number — where he lives — what his phone number is?' Cory's questions shot out like a verbal machine gun.

'Hold it, Dr. Cohen. You're coming at me too fast. It sounds like you don't care for me to have a new friend.'

'I'm sorry, Erin, but that's not it. I'm concerned because of the rapes and slashings which you may've read about. They were preceded by phone calls to the victims from a man who knew a bit about them. Like Patrick, he was polite and told them he's lonely and shy. Can you see why I'm concerned?'

'Rubbish,' she said, rubbing her hands on the folds of her skirt. 'I haven't read anything of the sort. I think you're making it up to frighten me away from having a chum so I'll stay miserable and need therapy.' Her face flushed. 'That's how you make your money, isn't it?'

Cory gulped. 'It hasn't been reported to the media.'

'So how come you know about it?' Erin's freckled hands jabbed at her waist.

'I know some of the victims.'

'How ridiculous! Patrick isn't a slasher or a rapist. He simply can't be!' Her bottom lip jutted out. 'He's right as rain.'

'Listen Erin,' Cory leaned forward. 'I know how disappointing this is, but it's better to be safe. If you prefer to believe him, it's your choice, but *please* just let it remain a phone friendship. Don't meet him anywhere, and for heaven's sake, don't let him into your house. If the rapist gets caught and it isn't Patrick, we'll be glad.'

Erin sniffled, tears streaming down her rosy cheeks. Cory touched her shoulder, but the angry woman shrugged away.

'You're upset with me because I burst your bubble. I'm sorry, but it was necessary to protect you.'

Erin's face flushed. 'I don't need your bloody protection. You have no right. Absolutely no right. I'm leaving!' she yelled, pushing away from her chair. 'And I don't need you anymore. You didn't help me get Seldyn back. Now you're trying to scare me away from a fine chap. Patrick thinks shrinks are in it only for the money. They pretend to care, but they don't. Not really.'

Cory was frustrated and upset, not so much by the accusation, but because she feared Erin's neediness and naïveté could be the young woman's undoing. Cory felt powerless to stop it.

21

After several attempts to reach the unreachable Detective Sharpley, Cory phoned the local newspaper.

'San Diego Union-Tribune. For classified ads press one. For sports press two. For news desk press — '

Cory slammed down the phone. Drumming her fingers, she settled on giving Shitty Sharpley another chance before she'd call the media. She phoned Betty for support and to plan Sunday's agenda. They made a dinner date.

★   ★   ★

Sorrento's Trattoria was dolled up with red and white checkered tablecloths and lit candles dripping wax on raffia covered Chianti bottles. Italian travel posters plastered the walls, but the decor failed to provide Cory the illusion of Italy.

She easily spotted Betty who looked as if she had stepped out of *Vogue*, coifed and manicured, wearing a stunning form-fitting blue silk dress. Sometimes the stark contrast between Cory's utilitarian look and Betty's fashionable one made her uncomfortable, but not enough to do something about it. At times Cory enjoyed being invisible.

Before Cory launched into her *shpiel*, Betty pitched one of her own.

'Cory, I'm upset over that cold, mean spirited Norma Rogers. I tried convincing her, but she refused to warn her patients. Can you imagine? She said it's not her place.'

'What? Where's her conscience? She's icy cold. I would never want her for a therapist.'

'Who would? Norma doesn't have to worry about being a good psychologist. Under managed care, patients have no choice. Our reputations are meaningless.'

'Sickening. Norma probably became a therapist because she's a *yenta*. She likes getting attention from her juicy stories so much that she'll spill privileged information.'

'She's a wart on therapy,' Betty said.

'More like flatulence in a restaurant.'

'Cory! That's disgusting.' She hid her mouth behind a napkin.

'So why are you laughing?'

'You like to shock people, huh?'

'Not really, only when I'm miffed. I'd better call the wart, or fart, while I'm in the mood.' Punctuating her statement, Cory banged her water glass on the table. In response, the server snapped to attention to take Cory's special order for pasta with marinara sauce, extra garlic and steamed vegetables.

Betty rolled her eyes. 'I'm surprised you don't march into the kitchen and show the chef how to do it.'

Bracelets jangling on her slim wrists, she dug into her purse to fetch Norma's number. 'Be my guest,' she said, handing over Norma's card.

'Is that thing you carry, your home away from home?' Cory pointed at her friend's enormous purse that doubled as a briefcase. 'Are you expecting an emergency get-away?'

'Tit for tat, huh?' She stuck her tongue out at Cory.

'That dumb detective doesn't return my calls. I'm furious, Betty.'

'Sure. Who wants to feel discounted? Maybe he's sick.'

'Yeah, in the head. Maybe heart, too.'

'If he doesn't call today, contact the media.'

'That's my plan. Now, what about Sunday's meeting?'

'Okay. I've asked everyone to make lists. In the first column are the initials of the women receiving the calls. Next columns are work and home addresses, followed by places they play — like tennis or gyms or whatever, and

117

then the names of their physicians and dentists. If there are commonalities, we can narrow down suspects.' She slid a yellow legal-size paper to Cory on which she'd labeled five columns.

'You are so well organized, Betty.' Cory smiled approval. 'I must tell you, I'm starting to overreact. I feel desperate and want to go after that pervert myself.' Cory sucked her lower lip. 'When I called Grace at her office to warn her, I was told she was away on business for a few days. So I left a message, but neglected to call her home. Now she's dead. Damn! I feel so guilty.' Cory buried her face in her hands.

'It's not your fault. Most of us would have done that.'

'But I don't have to do what most people do. I should do better.'

'Ah, hah! I don't have to ask where that reasoning comes from — Grandma and Grandpa Cohen.'

The mention of Cory's grandparents triggered her early memories.

She recalled one early morning when she was about eight years old. Her grandfather, a tall, vigorous man, lost in reverie, unaware of Cory, was preparing for his morning prayers. He donned his prayer shawl — the *tallit*. Usually when she approached him, he would collect her in his strong arms and propel her high. She would touch the ceiling and they would laugh. But that morning, he thought he was alone with his Maker. Prayer, a private time for him, a spiritual, meditative moment which Cory knew she should not disturb.

She had watched him don *tephillin*, the leather phylacteries, religious objects wound around the arm and hand and placed on the forehead at the start of morning prayers. When he finished, she wanted to copy him and feel the softness of the leather against her skin and feel its magic, but Grandpa told her it was only for men.

'It's not fair,' she'd said.

He swooped her to his lap, caressed her hair and explained the importance of women's role in Judaism. Even then, Cory had doubts. She had the notion that men needed something special to get closer to God because women were already there. It was her initiation into feminism.

★   ★   ★

'Cory, you're daydreaming. This situation is playing havoc with you. Seems you don't want consolation. You'd rather punish your-self.'

'Yes, doctor. Maybe I need to feel bad to

vindicate myself. Not that it's possible,' she muttered.

'I don't like the sound of that. You'd better be careful, Cory.'

'Don't worry. I don't take chances.'

22

On the drive home, Cory listened to a Bill Evans tape, enjoying the pleasant dialogue between piano and bass while thinking of Betty. The rich, calming melody of 'Someday My Prince Will Come,' could be her friend's theme song. How different they were! Betty dated almost every man she met, while Cory seldom dated since her divorce eight years ago. Despite Cory's repeated warnings to her friend, Betty's sweet and hopeful serial infatuations turned to sour disappointment and despair. Three months was the average life of her affairs. Where men were concerned, unfulfilled expectation was her hallmark. For a long time Betty had known that if her doting dad hadn't died when she was seven, she wouldn't search for inordinate male approval. But insight wasn't enough.

Flipping the tape to the other side, Cory heard a mournful, 'Every time We Say Goodbye' and hoped that soon, Betty's prince would come.

Friendship with Betty was a privilege. Her concern that Cory was becoming too involved with the case, warmed Cory. Betty thought

Cory needed to spice up her social life and wouldn't accept the fact that her friend was afraid of repeating a mistake. Betty was not the only psychologist who had sold herself short.

When it came to sizing up a potential mate, Cory's hasty marriage in graduate school proved her lapse of judgment. Charmed by intellect and good looks, she had failed to consider character. Her husband had punctured every pleasure with relentless ridicule. He was adept at plunging the depths of her psyche, surfacing with a fistful of her self-doubts, making her believe his criticisms were justified. To that quintessential macho jock, her lack of interest in competitive sports, apart from karate, proved her clumsiness. She was no tennis match for him and he was the wrong match for her. Later, she realized he was jealous of her black belt.

In his mission to tear her down and change her appearance, he commanded her to wear make-up and exotic clothing, reinforcing her poor self-image. She hoped if she changed, so would he.

'Why did you marry me?' she had asked.

'Because I hate you,' he had jeered.

Miserable, she went for therapy and concluded her marriage depended on compromising her integrity. She regained her self respect and left a tumultuous union.

Marriage to a tyrant was the poorest decision she had made, divorce, the wisest. Betty often had to remind her that her judgment was restored. Nevertheless, Cory chose a safe, celibate life and wished the same for her friend. At least the safe part.

Cory parked the car and heard the phone ringing. Fumbling for the key, she raced into the house and heard the answering machine click off. Hoping it was the detective, she hit the play back button. To her delight, it was Ron Miller.

'Hi, Cory, missed you at karate, just calling to see if you're okay.' He left the numbers of his pager and home phone.

She replayed the message, enjoying the sound of his voice.

Duty before fun, she spoke to Norma Rogers' voice mail.

To feel comfortable when she spoke with Ron, she changed into red sweats and tied her hair in a pony tail. Sitting cross legged on the bed, she punched in his phone number. He picked up after the first ring.

'Hi, Ron. It's Cory. How're you?'

'Fine. You haven't been at the studio. I called to see if everything's okay.'

'Thanks for your concern. I've been too busy for karate lately. It's good to hear from you.'

'The place isn't the same without you and Jennifer.'

'So it's just the generic feminine presence you miss. How disappointing!' Cory couldn't believe her own forwardness for which she'd thank Betty.

'No. I missed *you*.'

Her heart did cartwheels. 'Oh! I'm pleased to hear that.'

'Well, that's good to know,' he said in a deep soothing voice.

She wanted to prolong the conversation. 'I'm really happy you called.' She pinched her thigh to caution herself against being aggressive.

'In that case, how would you like to meet me for dinner this Saturday?'

She could feel herself growing moist. 'I'd love to. Where?'

'If it's okay with you, I'd like to check out the new vegetarian place near the studio. They're featuring a jazz combo that plays standards. My sources tell me it's a new group from L.A. that really swings. If we get there at seven, we'll have time to talk before the set.'

His interest in jazz surprised and delighted her. 'Great. I dig jazz and hate when people gawk at the musicians and talk during the set.'

'Cool. I figured you were hip. I play sax with some great guys.'

'Really! I come from a family of musicians — classical, but I gravitated to jazz. I play a little percussion — timbales, conga, bongos.'

'Well . . . then you'll really dig this group.'

Grandma — the voice of her conscience intruded. *'Cory, be cautious. What are you doing going out with such a young man? It's a shanda, an absolute shame.'*

'Just a date. Just friends. That's all I want.'

'But what of him? What does he want? At his age, he might want kids. If not now, later. Then what. Someone's going to be hurt.'

'It's only a date. Why can't I have a young man for a friend?'

'Because he may expect more.'

Cory was not sure if it was her conflict over dating a younger man, or her ruminating about the rapist and Grace's brutal murder that kept her from falling asleep. Probably, all. It was hard to get a good night's rest with anxiety as a bed companion.

23

Strauss Pharmaceuticals wanted to buy Superior. A conference was scheduled in ten minutes in the office of Robert Russell, Chief Executive Officer of Superior.

Hamilton had always hated meetings and preferred working alone. The prospect of mingling with others and making small talk filled him with apprehension, causing him to perspire. Concerned over the outcome of the meeting, he reminded himself that when Superior merged with Behavioral Health it had advanced his career. This acquisition may do the same — or could dash it, since with many take-overs, heads roll.

The possibility of losing his position enraged him. Clenching his fists, he felt his face grow hot. He mopped his brow and reached for the empty water decanter on his desk. Livid, he marched to the water cooler, passing his staff and ignoring greetings. Hamilton filled his pitcher to the brim and carried it into his office, water sloshing on the floor. Closing the door behind him, he drank two full glasses in rapid succession, then burped. His temper began to cool.

Hamilton thought if Russell moved on, or died, he could be next in line. In small doses, he could put on a suitable façade. For a few minutes, he closed his eyes and breathed deeply.

Relaxed, he sauntered into Russell's office, arriving before the others.

Russell stepped from behind the desk, walked towards him, extending his hand. Although Hamilton despised being touched, he forced himself not to cringe as he clasped his boss's hand.

Lionel Jones, a large impeccably dressed man with mocha colored skin, arrived next. Prior to his job at Superior, he had been a social worker. Lionel was known for his brief stint as a professional football player. His reputation, academic degrees and appearance made him a formidable rival.

A striking contrast to Lionel was Hugh Morris who entered next. His small stature, light hair and complexion gave him a meek appearance. Both men were about forty. Hugh's business background could have made him a competitor for the coveted position, but a man wearing frayed cuffs and a wrinkled suit was not appropriate for such a position.

After exchanging greetings, Russell walked to the head of the ebony conference table, motioning them to join him.

The ample space between chairs pleased Hamilton. Physical proximity to others made him uneasy — he had to control the urge to strike whoever came too close.

A secretary appeared with a platter of pastries and a carafe of coffee on a silver tray. A clerk placed crystal mugs and purple linen napkins on the table. Russell examined his Piaget watch. 'The meeting will start as soon as the VIPs from Strauss Pharmaceuticals are here. They're a conglomerate manufacturing most of the drugs prescribed for mental conditions. Their gross sales of medication for depression, anxiety and obsessive compulsive disorders yield over a billion dollars a year. We can make their earnings soar higher.' Reaching for the coffee, he poured himself a mug. 'Anyone want some?'

No one moved.

Hamilton spoke first. 'We can help their business, but what's in it for us?'

'Our company is worth a lot to Strauss,' Russell answered.

'That's obvious. Shareholders will make a profit, but what about us?' Hamilton persisted.

'We're proposing a profit-sharing plan,' Russell said.

'And if they don't go for it?' Hugh pressed,

rising to pour his coffee.

'That's what we're negotiating.'

'And what about personnel changes?' Hamilton probed.

'With more funds to market our product, we'll need additional staff to accomodate expansion.'

Lionel, the sole mental health professional at Superior, shook his head and mumbled, 'Product?'

'Product. Service. It's semantics. We're in business. You knew that when you left social work, Lionel,' Russell answered.

'Can't help being affected by my training. I had the mistaken notion we'd offer low-cost service to people needing therapy.'

'We are, Lionel. We monitor it. Time and money aren't wasted on cry-babies.'

Lionel's face darkened. His mouth opened and quickly closed. Hamilton knew the Joneses were expecting their third child.

Hamilton heard a tap at the door before Russell's secretary ushered in four men and one woman, all in expensive dark suits. The white haired, regal men resembled pall bearers. When Dr. Higushi, in charge of Research and Development, was introduced, Hamilton had an urge to slash the pompous man. Good that he had locked the knife in his briefcase, he told himself, as he listened to

Higushi discuss the profits to be made from his fancy new drugs.

Hamilton addressed the scientist, 'What other mental health management companies are you considering?'

The woman replied, 'Preferred Providers because they contract all over the United States. Frankly, we're most interested in Superior because California is a large state with ninety-three percent of your population in managed care programs. You lead the nation in innovation. We believe that with our resources, your contracts can expand to other states.'

Blonde, beautiful, bright and powerful, she irritated Hamilton. Women had no right to high positions. Bad enough they had the right to bear children, he thought. He yearned to watch terror escalate in her young steel-gray eyes, and blood gush down her white silk shirt. The vivid image made him pant. Fearful of drooling, he drank dark coffee, ate a lemon-filled pastry, and carefully wiped his mouth with a napkin. The uncomfortable feeling remained.

After they left, Russell said, 'They're eager for us. We're in the driver's seat — we can call the shots. No problem.'

Hamilton was not so sure.

24

It's called cross-training, but Cory called it monotony prevention. A perfect way to start the day, a ride on Rachel's bike. Seated where her daughter's little tush had been, she caressed the handlebars and felt closer to her. She pictured Rachel the day she'd taken her first two-wheeler ride. Noah's intense look of big-brotherly pride was etched in her memory. It touched her because like most siblings, they fought a lot.

'*Mommy, Mommy, Noah has Teddy and he won't give him back!*'

'*Rachel scratched me on purpose, Mommy.*'

Now, young adults, they still kicked each other under the table. Cory bet they didn't do it when she wasn't around. With only one available parent, they vied for her attention. This year they were independent and Cory was free, but longed for them. A layer of tears waited behind her eyes.

Sniffling, she pedaled uphill and coasted downhill for two hours. She returned exhausted, gulped sixteen ounces of water and collapsed on the couch.

Just as Grandma had done, Cory kept personal correspondence in shoe boxes. She withdrew the ones marked Rachel and Noah and re-read their letters. His made her laugh. Hers were thought provoking. Rachel was compiling a family history and wanted to know more about her great-grandparents.

Memories moistened Cory's eyes. The smell of chicken soup on Friday nights. The glow of Sabbath candles. Her sensible shoes, his old violin. She choked back tears. Crying came too easily for her. At inconvenient times. When the misery of patients was discussed at conferences, Cory's frequent nose blowing caused unwanted attention. Sentimental commercials made her gush. She was a sap for the maudlin.

E-mail, free and efficient, doesn't beat holding the paper in your hand, written by a loved one. Cory spent the balance of her free time writing individual letters to her family.

In the shower, she shifted gears. She hadn't heard from that *shlemiel*, Sharpley. She quickly dried off and punched in the familiar number.

A woman answered, 'Investigations.'

'May I please speak with Detective Sharpley. This is urgent.'

'Sorry, he's in the field. If this is an emergency, I can give you his pager number or would you like his voice mail?'

For all the good she expected it to do, Cory left another message, this time stating she had new information and that if she didn't hear from him today, she would submit it to the media.

She had zipped up her slacks when the phone rang.

'Sergeant Sharpley, here.'

Cory felt a twinge of relief.

'Ma'am, I don't appreciate your threats. What do you want?'

'I'm not threatening you. You've ignored my previous calls, although I said it was urgent.'

'All my calls are urgent.'

Frustrated, she gave the phone an obscene finger gesture. 'I have a theory about the rapist and slasher. It's too coincidental that three of the victims were lonely, vulnerable patients. I suspect he tails young women when they leave psychotherapy offices. He sees where they go, how they spend their time. Then he calls and cons them into feeling sorry for him. Says he just wants to be phone friends.'

'Really?' The detective said. His tone dripped with mockery. Cory stuck her tongue out at the phone.

'Yes. He exploits their neediness. After a

few weeks of calls, he manipulates an invitation, wangles his way into their homes and does his horrible deed.'

'So that's what you think is so urgent?'

His nasal contemptuous voice irritated her. That unsympathetic sonofabitch made no effort to appease, she thought. She wanted to curse him and hang up. Instead she reverted to her best professional tone, 'To prevent another crime, this scheme merits publicity.'

'Ma'am, you only suspect. You have no proof.'

'Oh, but I do. Several victims told me how it happened.'

'Who are they?'

'One rape was already reported. The victim fled in fear. I'll ask the others to call you . . . if that'd do any good,' she muttered. 'What about Grace, whose homicide, I *assume* you're investigating. I suppose you've checked out her ex-boyfriend.'

'Of course. He has a perfect alibi. At the time of the murder, he was on a plane returning from a trial accompanied by witnesses.'

'Well, I really didn't suspect him anyway,' Cory said.

'Despite what you may think, Ma'am, I haven't ignored you. I've taken into account that Grace told you she was phoned by a client of the law firm where she worked. We're investigating everyone with connections there. This takes considerable time.'

'I appreciate your efforts and am not implying that you're idle, Sergeant, but please consider that all the victims were psychotherapy patients. I've canvassed several therapists and learned that some of their patients received such calls. I bet from Grace's killer.'

'Now is that right? How would he know they were lonely?'

His derision tried Cory's patience. She clenched her jaw. 'I told you. He shadowed them from therapists' offices. Maybe for weeks. Saw none of them had any social life.'

'He must be a busy guy,' he said, chuckling.

Contemplating her next words to this awful man, she bit her lip. She realized she had to be polite. 'I know it seems incredible, but there must be a connection. It sounds like you don't believe me.'

'Well, Ma'am, it does seem improbable. Listen. We look for patterns. We interview victims several times to see if there's a commonality between them. You're telling me that they are all psychotherapy patients. So what? Many young, single women are in therapy and lonely. Now, if they used the same psychologist, we'd have a pattern. If they went to the same gym, it'd be something to go on, but the victims we've interviewed don't resemble each another or have anything in common. I assure you, Ma'am, we don't sit still. If there's more . . . give it to me. Without names, I'm stuck. Have those patients contact me. I'll get the phone company to put traps on their phones so we can trace the calls. Okay?'

'Fine. After the psych meeting this Sunday, you'll have a list. In the meantime, I've asked colleagues to warn women about the calls. For your information, another patient received one. Since nothing about this scheme appeared in the paper, she didn't believe me.'

'Too bad.'

Cory wasn't sure if he was serious or sarcastic. Her reaction to his attitude struck like an invasion of marching storm-troopers in her gut. She closed her eyes and breathed deeply until the pain faded. 'Look, Sergeant, I'm trying to help, but it seems you think I'm a nuisance.'

'Well, you only have a theory, and honestly, Ma'am, it seems unlikely. Furthermore, I don't want any interference with my investigation since you have nothing concrete to offer apart from speculation. Sometimes when outsiders try to help, they mess things up. It's not personal.' A pinprick of softness poked through his police armor, as his voice fell. 'Call me after you get your data, but it will be useless without names.'

'Since you're hard to reach, call me. I'll be home after the meeting on Sunday.'

'I'll try to do that, Ma'am.'

'I hate the word *try*. It's meaningless to me, Detective Sharpley.'

'I'll call.'

Cory wouldn't bet on it.

★   ★   ★

When she arrived at the office at one o'clock, a new patient with a one-thirty appointment waited in the reception room. Ann, flashing a smile, handed Cory a batch of phone messages, a new case folder and nodded in the woman's direction.

The last time Cory had seen her friend, Dr. Harold Greenwald, he had joked that he related patients' diagnoses to arrival for appointments. 'Patients who come early are anxious. Late arrivals are hostile. Those on time are compulsive,' he had said. His remark had merit. When she finished returning phone calls, she fetched the new patient.

Paige Warren, a petite, young woman was a

study in beige. Her short, dark blonde hair faded into a pale complexion. Tortoise-shell glasses framed her clear hazel eyes. Sitting at the edge of the seat, she folded her hands on top of her lap. Suspenders attached to flared trousered legs concealed her waistline. Chunky shoes completed the ensemble. Paige's attire may have looked attractive on a tall woman.

'Behavioral Health referred me to you because I've recently developed insomnia. I'm irritable and can't function well.'

Paige appeared well-organized and rehearsed. Her voice, soft as a meow reflected shyness. Cory had to lean forward to hear her.

'How long has this been going on?' Pen and note-pad poised, Cory looked up.

Studying the floor, Paige said, 'It started about the time of my promotion to supervisor. It's really hard for me. I don't want to be critical and I don't know how to motivate my staff.'

'Did you want this promotion?' Cory underlined *job* in her notes.

'Good question. I wanted recognition for my hard work, but prefer working with technical problems. That's my strength. I really don't like supervising people.' When she reached for a tissue, her beige satin blouse clung like jelly on a donut, emphasizing her flat chest.

Cory fantasized sending her to Betty for a make-over. 'What's the worst thing about your job?' she asked.

Toying with a Phi Beta Kappa key hanging from her gold necklace, Paige said, 'I'm afraid my staff won't like me if I tell them what to do.'

'I understand, but they expect you to tell them.'

'So if I don't tell them — they won't like me?'

'That's close. You learn fast, Paige. I don't know that they won't like *you*, but they may not like *it*.'

'Uh . . . I have another problem. I'm shy . . . I'd like to have friends, but I'm afraid of rejection. I'm twenty-nine, and would you believe I've never had a boyfriend?' Her large sad eyes blinked. If she were an animal, she'd be a fawn.

'Your fear of rejection affects your work and your social life?'

Paige took off her glasses and wiped her eyes. 'Exactly. And I'm so lonely. Work is all I have.'

Cory shook her head. 'And rewarded for it with a job you don't like. Are you angry at that?'

'Well . . . sort of.' She squirmed, checked her watch, looked at the door, seemingly eager for the session to end.

Cory told her she would fax a request to Behavioral Health for an additional five sessions above the three authorized. Paige agreed and they made an appointment for the following week.

Maybe eight would be her lucky number.

Another lonely young woman. Maybe Sharpley was right, after all.

25

Lights were on in Suite 200. With his tie loosened, jacket and shoes off, Hamilton padded towards the fax machine when the security guard opened the door with a key. Startled by the presence of the uniformed man, he shouted, 'What the hell are you doing here?'

'I saw the lights on, sir. I'm supposed to check all the offices in the building and switch off the lights. I didn't know anyone was still here.'

'Don't you know I work late?' he barked. 'It's not necessary to come in here. What happened to the other guard?'

'There's been a change in the company, sir.'

'Tell your people I don't want to be disturbed when I'm working.'

'Yes, sir.'

Violated, he was tempted to punch the snoop, but realized the mess it would cause.

Hamilton grabbed the treatment reports faxed from Behavioral Health. The company was in the process of completing business in northern California. The merger with Superior had afforded the promotion that brought him to San Diego. And what a good thing it was.

Anonymity wasn't possible in the small town in which he had lived. He was glad to move away from the danger of his mounting deeds coming to light.

Hamilton recalled delicious pleasure after discarding other's treasured items. When he clipped the parakeet's wings and cat's whiskers, they went wild. Call me a devil, I'll show you what a devil is, he thought when he put his foster-mother's cat in the dryer. She cared more about that cat than anyone or anything. Bitch!

He couldn't remember the order of these events, but knew the window curtains aflame had caused an awesome sight, too. The foster mother had screamed, 'You're out of here!' After that came the group home where he hoped to be free of ridicule, but unable to tolerate close quarters, he hyperventilated.

Recalling that feeling, he felt himself on the verge of panic again. Taking deep, slow breaths as the psychologist had instructed, he reminded himself that now, he was in a different time and place, in his own opulent office with windows and a door.

Maybe there was something to it when the psychologist asked him if he was ever confined in a closet, or a locked room, or felt suffocated by a blanket, but he had no such memory.

On that basis, Hamilton theorized that his mother, saddled with two other boys, didn't want him and tried to snuff out his life when he was an infant. A reason for his hatred of women. His sister had remained with their mother and the boys placed in foster care. Females stuck together. Bunch of bitches.

Torturing his sister and mother, was a favorite, repetitive fantasy. His brothers weren't worth the trouble.

It had been easy to find his mother, but his sister eluded him. She had probably left the area she grew up in, went to school out of town or married young and took her husband's family name. One day he would find her, and then . . .

26

Why Detective Sharpley ignored the compelling fact that *all* the victims were psychotherapy patients puzzled Cory. She hoped the meeting on Sunday would bring clues and warning calls to potential targets. She also hoped a better detective would be assigned to the case. May as well hope for eternal peace and harmony in the world, she thought.

Angry enough to give her lungs a workout, she drove to the karate studio where for one hour, she released some of the tension sparked by the conversation with Sharpley. She made a lot of noise, yelling, 'KIAI' in a feverish pitch until her throat and chest were sore.

Arriving home drenched, Cory popped into the shower. Tingling from the endorphin rush, she felt better physically, but frustration lingered. While toweling off, she noticed the blinking red light on the answering machine. She punched the replay button and learned that Norma Rogers had called. She phoned her, but the woman wasn't there. Funny the way things work: An entire day would pass with no calls until several came one after the other, or it would be a telephone tag day. It seemed today was destined to be the latter, bound to add to her annoyance. A stroll on the beach would be a good cure, she thought.

Weekend surfers, joggers and volleyball players crowded the Del Mar beach. The sight of frolicking, bikini clad nubiles with fresh faces was like sand stinging her face. She realized the sad fact that her age could quell a relationship with Ron, but not necessarily. In her work with younger men involved with older women, age didn't appear to be a problem. Ageism, like sexism, had begun to occupy her thoughts.

Cory was in business to cope with problems, not create them. She knew it was useless to ruminate about the prospects of a long-term relationship with Ron, when she didn't know him well and perhaps neither of them would want more than friendship, but her concern lurked like a stalker.

She left the beach and ambled along Camino Del Mar past shops and outdoor cafés brimming with robust looking people. She played a game with herself, scanning the crowd to pick out tourists from residents and wondered whether a murderer was in the midst. He could be the man at that table drinking a café latte, or that fellow under the palm tree eating yogurt. The guy tying his shoelace wore black sweats and had a beard and a mustache, just as Jennifer and Mallory had said.

Clues were sparse. She wanted to know about his speech pattern. Did he have an accent? For the victims to notice subtleties was probably too much to expect, but she planned to inquire.

Cory approached the Farmer's Market, an outdoor Saturday happening. Bustling with shoppers, lush produce and colorful fresh flowers, the scene had a European flavor, the ecology minded carrying their purchases in net sacks. A lean man wearing a straw hat and Hawaiian shirt played a ukulele.

She dawdled at a vegetable stand. A wafer thin, young, blonde woman clad in a familiar blue denim dress approached, smiling at her.

Cory gasped. Oh my God! Grace! Was it really her? But she was dead! She felt the blood drain from her face. The woman's greeting startled her.

'Are you okay?' the young woman asked, removing her dark sunglasses. You look like you've seen a ghost.'

Jittery, Cory nodded to the woman, a librarian with whom she had spoken many times. 'For a moment, I thought you were someone else.'

'Oh, I hope she's nice.' She nodded and resumed her shopping.

Unshed tears constricted Cory's throat. She watched the Grace look-alike for a few seconds realizing the resemblance was superficial, but she had wished and willed her to be Grace. Funny what the mind can do.

In haste, Cory bought vegetables and hurried home with a sinking feeling for young Grace, here no more.

Plopping on the couch, Cory wept for her. The tightness in her throat dissolved.

To relax, she ran a bath, added herbal salts and soaked for twenty minutes, listening to a Chopin piano concerto.

The time for her date with Ron approached and she felt as excited as a teenager. She took time applying make-up and chose her most flattering outfit — a dark purple wool dress with a green leather belt that emphasized her small waist and high breasts. She stared at her reflection in the mirror and heard Grandma's wise words: 'Beauty lives in the soul.' She had referred to Cory as a *goota n'shuma*. A good soul. She said her Asian looks made her special. *A shaina maidel*. A pretty girl. That's why people stared at her. But Cory hated standing out from her peers. She wanted to fit in and look like everyone else. Grandma had tried too hard to convince her that she was pretty. Cory hoped her character compensated. Betty had said Cory came across as Goodie-Two Shoes to conceal her base, evil side that crept out now and then. She agreed Cory was not pretty, but strikingly attractive, especially when she made the effort. Cory thought Betty tried to be kind.

★　★　★

Cory arrived at The Vegan a few minutes early, where she found Ron pacing at the entrance. He caught sight of her, smiled and grasped her hand. His touch charged her like an erotic current and she imagined his strong, but gentle hands on her body. Ashamed that her stored up sexual energy would surface, she hid behind innocuous chatter.

Colorful photographs of apples, carrots and eggplant decorated the walls of the café. Live plants hung everywhere. A guitarist strummed softly in the corner. Anticipating music, she cocked her head, but only heard chords. Background for conversation.

At first, their meeting seemed like a fact-finding trip. She learned Ron hadn't married, was an only child of loving parents who lived near Sacramento. Devoted to them, he visited monthly.

'You're quite a find, Cory. Easy to talk to *and* a knockout. A dynamite lady.'

She felt herself blush. 'Thank you.'

This was the first time she had seen him outside karate. She admired his style. His red cotton sweater and khaki slacks looked great on his trim, athletic frame. Long tawny hair gave him a boyish appearance, but his eyes, the color of the noon sky, appeared wise. A doctor, he had seen much.

A server took their orders for steamed vegetables in oriental sauce. Shortly, their dinners arrived. The scent of garlic and ginger tempted her, but Ron was a greater temptation. When Cory was young and single, on a dinner date with someone special, she would pick at her food. And so it was again. Feasting her eyes on Ron satiated her. She grew warm in the wool dress.

Choosing a life free from the risk of romance, Cory lived vicariously through the adventures of patients and friends. Now, she wasn't sure whether the absence of her children liberated her libido or whether it was this particular guy whose touch made her sizzle. She sensed an undercurrent of sexual excitement in the way he gazed at her. Long, lingering. The magnetic attraction had begun at the karate studio. She was a psychologist, not a mind-reader, but how she wished she could read his thoughts. Embarrassed at the prospect he could read hers, she hoped chitchat would disguise her lust — until she felt safe.

'Jen told me what happened. Glad to see her back after what she's gone through,' he said.

Cory had almost forgotten the recent rapes, until the turn in conversation.

'What kind of creep would do that?' he asked, shaking his head.

Cory didn't want to think about it and spoil the evening, but she answered, 'A psychopath.'

'Any experience with such patients?'

'Some. Usually they're sent by the court, or a relative. Few choose therapy on their own.' She poked at the heap of brown rice on her plate. 'Often they try to con the therapist. Sometimes it works.' More often than she cared to say.

'Yeah. They're con artists.'

'They can charm the pants off a confirmed virgin.'

'Or con a rabbi into eating pork.' Ron grinned.

'Champions of deception. Charisma is their camouflage.' Stop being a show-off, she cautioned herself. This isn't *Dinner with Andre*.

'Yeah, I know. I've met my share.' He smiled a quality smile, like a toothpaste ad.

Cory wondered if Ron's conversation was a cover-up for what she thought she read in his eyes. Was she detecting a Let's-Go-To-Bed look? Or was it her fanciful thinking? She shifted in her chair.

'Most of us have, but they're not easy to detect, Ron. They're sly. The last one I had as a patient was a pleasant, charming fellow until it came time to pay his bill.'

Ron chuckled. 'I know the sort.'

'Another didn't even bother to hide it. Beating up his girl friend was no big deal to him. He warned me that if I dared suggest she leave him, he'd beat me, too. That jerk was on steroids. A body builder.' Still not hungry, she twirled her fork and wondered about how Ron's body would feel against hers.

'Some guys get violent on that drug. Your job can be dangerous, Cory.' He shook his head and a strand of hair fell over one eye. She resisted the urge to fix it.

'Not usually. I avoid such patients because I can't be effective with people I don't like.'

'It's refreshing to hear you say that. Most psychologists defend them.'

'Those that do, are idealistic. Naïve. Instead of blaming the criminal they condemn his environment. They forget that many folks with terrible lives don't take it out on others.'

'They really think they can cure these guys?'

'Hah! Frankly, Ron, I think criminal behavior is intractable, and to portray psychopaths as victims gives them an excuse to be cruel.' Her face and neck heated with anger.

'You sound like you were burned. Even worse than not getting your bill paid.'

Ron was right. Because Cory was a victim, she had a different perspective. She wouldn't forgive a sadist. If she wouldn't forgive, she wouldn't forget, but she didn't feel like explaining this to him, yet. She preferred a romantic interlude.

She stared at her plate and thought about changing the unpleasant subject.

'You're not eating,' Ron said, touching her arm.

Again, his gesture made her dizzy with desire. She didn't want him to think she had anorexia like some of the women he may have known. 'The food is tasty, but the subject put me off.'

'I'm sorry.'

'Do you ever worry about treating a patient with a contagious disease?'

'Nah, I'm cautious, Cory. Some docs think

they're immune and others are hypochondri-acs.' He shoveled a scoop of rice onto his fork.

It reminded her of someone she knew who ate his lunch while watching an autopsy.

'Why did you choose medicine, Ron?' She studied his hands as he clicked table utensils. Smooth, tanned with long fingers and neatly clipped nails. The hands she yearned to caress her hidden places.

'It's a Miller thing. My father, grandfather and great-grandfather. It was expected.'

'Was that okay with you?'

Ron's face darkened. 'Don't psychoanalyze me, Cory.'

She stiffened. 'Sorry.'

Having hit a sore spot, Cory changed the subject to fluff. Fillers. It had been so long since she had a date with someone she had the hots for, she was ashamed her awkward-ness showed.

When the trio played — fresh, uncluttered, she got into it. Harmony and percussion weaved in a bright, bouncy way. Her foot tapped the rhythm to a rendition of 'Satin Doll.' Ron's head bobbed to the beat. Apart from the few musicians Cory knew, she had no one to share her passion for jazz. To do so with someone who turned her on, heightened the thrill. Much too soon they were the last patrons in the restaurant.

A server brought the bill. She opened her purse.

'No, I invited you.'

'Thanks, Ron. I had a great time.'

'Me, too. I'll call next time we jam. You can sit in or just hang out,' he said as he walked Cory to her car.

That night before going to sleep she thought of Ron. Will he call? When? She liked much about him, but he was a tinge too touchy. She had hit a raw nerve. Maybe he would have preferred music to medicine. Damn! If things were perfect he would be her age, forty-eight, or she would be his — thirty-six, she thought, dozing off.

27

Hamilton leaned back in the leather office chair, his muscular arms crossed over his wide chest. Smug, independent, he trusted no one and didn't give a damn about anyone. Why the hell should he? No one cared about him. Licking his dry lips, he surveyed the physical material of his achievements — the fine furniture and wood paneled walls. Nothing like the clinic office where he was forced to visit as a young patient.

Hamilton caressed the faxed reports. Yanking his engagement calendar from his attache case, he opened to current entries:

Wednesday, Nov. 2, 5:30 P.M. Erin #1 Her phone number appeared next. In the remaining space before 6:30 he wrote: *Shoots pool/Ireland. Cnty Cork, G*; the letter he had assigned to her building.

At six-thirty, he called Sara for the first time. Unresponsive. He scratched her name out on the yellow pad.

Three minutes later, he made his first call to Tammy, gave her his customary ten minute pitch, made his usual entries and wrote her in as a *phone call appointment for Friday, Nov. 4 at 6:33.*

Taking pride in his efficiency, he asked each woman a set of questions and noted her responses. Quickly, he rejected dog owners.

Hamilton phoned the same women regularly at the same time, but couldn't predict the number of calls he'd need before he could elicit an invitation. Sometimes it took a dozen in a space of a month. Unpredictability annoyed him, but it was worth it because the stalking and planning excited him. The attack was almost an anti-climax. A way of completing business. The power he felt when he saw fear in his victim's eyes made him ecstatic. Hamilton thought he loved it all equally.

Stretching in his chair, he leaned the back of his head in his hands and sighed.

He covered only two prospects this week — Erin and Tammy. Each time he had tried Linda, her answering machine picked up. Too much trouble, he thought, tossing her report onto the larger stack.

He sifted through the faxed requests until he came across one with Paige Warren's name. Scanning it, he became excited. He researched her address in his notebook. Familiar with her beach condo, he smiled, imagining the final scene — the thrill of overpowering her — fucking her. The wonderful release afterwards. One more for his fantasy reruns. He drank his customary two cups of water. When he felt the pressure of a full bladder, he punched in her phone number.

28

The big day arrived. The meeting Betty and Cory had planned would take place this afternoon under a cloudless azure sky. A day in paradise for others, but not for Cory. Her failure to warn Grace clawed at her like a cat scratching on a tree. She expected guilt, anger and fear, her constant companions, would stay until she avenged her patient. Now she went through the motions of living.

Pacing through the patch she generously called her garden, she swept leaves, plucked an orange from the tree and replenished the humming-bird feeder that hung from a bottle-brush tree. A tiny bird landed, twittering. Its relentless movements like a nervous child's. Wings fluttered as it ate and drank. After watering the grass and the potted yellow mums, Cory jumped rope for fifteen minutes.

Friends often caught up with her at Milton's, a neighborhood deli where Sunday's at ten, seated in her usual spot at a back booth, she breakfasted on bagel and lox. But not today. She zapped a bran muffin in the microwave and peeled the orange. Under a green and blue striped umbrella table, she read the newspaper. No reports of rape. Breathing a sigh of relief, she took a bite of the muffin and pushed it aside. Nutrients would have to come from the vitamin pill she popped with the fruit segment.

The New York Times lay on the kitchen counter like a treasured dessert to savor after the meeting at Betty's.

In the shower, her thoughts turned to the crimes. It was her job to make sense of the seemingly senseless.

Was it rotten genes or a rotten life that drove people to do savage things? She had treated various law-abiding patients who had horrible experiences as youngsters. Many remembered someone who gave them emotional goodies. A grandparent, teacher, neighbor or therapist. But some had no such memory.

Cory thought of the many parents she knew who made hardy efforts to raise fine children, yet spawned deviant offspring. She had examined other influences in their child's life and rarely could account for the behavior. Perhaps one day, a 'conscience' gene would be discovered.

She did a lot of thinking in the shower — a place her son Noah had labeled, 'The H.C.' The hydrotherapy closet. In bare feet and towel, Cory padded to the wardrobe and selected jeans, a red silk blouse and loafers. Threading a red silk ribbon through her long braid, she admired her handiwork. The application of lipstick and blush gave her a cheerful appearance.

Humming a refrain from 'I Don't Know Why,' she prepared a platter for the meeting — a colorful splash of broccoli, carrots and cherry tomatoes.

Sunday traffic was sparse on Interstate 5 south. Opening the sunroof of her BMW, she heard a noisy chorus of honks from a flock of geese. To add to the crap around me, they'd probably bomb me, she thought, closing the sunroof. Cory opened the windows, admitting a warm gentle breeze. She sailed down the freeway, the radio tuned to Jazz 88. A Billie Holliday recording of 'Lover Man' came on. Joining the raspy voice, Cory kept the tune. Much to her surprise, her mood lifted.

Few places in the San Diego area are more than fifteen minutes away from wherever you start your journey. Fourteen minutes later she arrived at Mission Hills, a neighborhood reminiscent of where she had grown up near Brooklyn College. Stately old homes with front lawns, mature foliage, sidewalks and the absence of tract houses gave it character. A few remodeled homes added interest.

Betty's house was one of those — a curved contemporary white stucco structure with glass block windows of art deco style. Like its inhabitant, the interior was attractive, warm and inviting. She greeted Cory with a hug. 'Could hardly wait for today. I hope something good comes of this.'

'Me too. I've been anxious all week.'

'Hang loose, Cory. You're tense,' Betty said, massaging her shoulders.

Cory heaved a grateful sigh. 'Thanks.'

They placed the food, drinks and utensils on the garden table under an enormous lemon and pink floral umbrella. The scent of chocolate raspberry coffee permeated the air. Betty filled two mugs, handing one to her. Cory spared no detail about her date. Grinning, Betty gave her a big hug. Cory was moved by Betty's genuine friendship.

Before the others arrived, Cory strolled inside to freshen up. She passed several small rooms. One with the door ajar served as a walk-in closet and dressing room. Each time Betty changed the man in her life, she bought a new garment. Cory hoped her concern with the dangerous man on the loose would change her dating pattern. She would be safer and have a less crowded closet.

Many of Cory's patients had 'come out of

the closet' and now she had the urge to hide in one. To lose herself among Betty's soft silk fabrics. To make believe she was a kid again, playing grown up as she did with Grandma's finery. To forget her mission. To feel safe, she thought. Safety, paramount in her life, prevented her from taking risks. Usually.

Scattered on the hardwood floors, rare in this part of the country, lay several white furry Afghanistan rugs. Sensual, like Betty. Four comfortable sofas facing each other were suggestive of group therapy. Cory resisted the temptation to lie down and escape into sleep. Although she wanted the meeting, she was nervous about the outcome.

On the patio beside the lush garden they arranged white plastic chairs in a large semi-circle and a small table in front of the chair for Betty. Fragrant honeysuckle and tall golden rain trees grew on the periphery. A breeze fanned the leaves and sun rays danced like strobe lights through lace. The calm setting, a striking contrast to the agenda.

Twelve psychologists arrived. After mingling and refreshments, they took seats. Attention was drawn to Betty, her copper curls glistening in the sun.

'I'll get straight to the point. Someone is phoning single women psychotherapy patients and conning them into thinking all

162

he wants is phone friendship. Once he has appealed to their sympathy with a sob story that he's painfully shy, they invite him over. He rapes and slashes,' her voice rose. 'And in one case murdered Cory's patient.'

A woman gasped. 'Oh, dear Lord!'

'We're here to plan a course of action. I've asked you to list where your patients who have received such calls work, play and live and their doctor's names,' Betty said. 'We're looking for commonalities.'

A few latecomers stood in the back. Betty beckoned them to take the lined note paper she held up in her hand.

'There are five columns, but I've just thought of a sixth. Their occupations. Perhaps he met them professionally,' she said.

About fifteen minutes later, they passed the papers to her. Conversation hummed in the background while Betty examined the entries, pushed buttons on her calculator and scribbled on a writing pad.

Looking up from her notations, she said, 'There's no obvious commonality. These women neither live nor work in the same buildings. Their occupations vary — three lawyers, one accountant, two computer programmers, one admin secretary, three teachers, three research scientists, one sales rep. As far as recreation, nothing of statistical significance here. Few play at all. One plays volleyball. Another keeps horses in Ramona and someone else boards hers in Del Mar. All these women use different physicians. Any ideas?'

Tom stood, a vein in his forehead throbbing. 'This devil could be an eavesdropping hairdresser.'

'True. These women could have been overheard talking to someone in a personal service industry,' Cory said.

'Sure, but we don't have time or resources to check these possibilities. We know all these women are psychotherapy patients, so it's likely the caller learns about them by stalking them after they leave our offices,' Betty said, pushing her note pad aside.

'He must be incredibly active, because from what I heard, at least fourteen women were called. And he must have a lot of free time,' John said.

'What do you expect of us?' Norma asked.

'Warn patients,' Betty shouted.

'I refuse to compound the problems of my patients by frightening them,' Norma said. 'Besides it would deter people from therapy.'

'You'd rather they be raped or murdered?' Cory asked. If Norma was a tin can, Cory would have kicked her over the garden wall.

'It's not my job. I think it's unethical to interfere.'

'Me, too,' piped Harriet.

Steve stood grabbing his yarmulke caught by the wind. 'Ethics, shmethics. This is a moral issue. Already one of my patients was raped. We must warn all of them.'

Cory gestured thumbs up to Steve. She glared at Harriet and Norma who sat next to each other.

'It's a police matter,' Norma said.

'It is, but they won't do anything until recipients of the calls notify them. That's the purpose of this meeting,' Cory said. 'We must warn patients, if contacted by the caller, they should report it to Detective Sharpley at once.'

'Well, I'm not going to get involved,' Norma said.

'How would you feel if one of your patients is raped or murdered when you could have prevented it?' Cory said. She wanted to express how she felt after failing to warn Grace, but shame stopped her. Betty shot her a knowing glance.

'That isn't our responsibility,' Norma answered.

Tom rolled his eyes.

'What?' Cory yelled.

Norma had the compassion of a flea, Cory

thought, her face flushing as her anger spiraled. For a moment she imagined Norma as a rape victim. Perhaps then she would realize — and care — if that was in her repertoire. Although others showed concern, Cory suspected her feelings were more intense because of her personal experience. So much time had passed, yet the feelings resurfaced. She wondered if revenge would offer an antidote.

Cory glanced around, checking the responses to Norma's flagrant irresponsibility. Steve shrugged. Ginger lifted an eyebrow and John raised the palms of his hands.

With the exception of Harriet and Norma, the psychologists agreed to warn patients.

Her mind whirling, Cory took a deep breath and inhaled the sweet scent of gardenias. Suddenly pieces snapped together and she blurted out, 'John's right. It's unlikely he'd have time to stalk fourteen women. These women have nothing in common apart from their diagnosis, so the pervert must have another way of learning about them. Let's figure this out. Who else knows intimate details about our patients besides us?'

Bewildered faces flashed at her.

'Someone reading treatment requests,' Cory bellowed.

'Of course!' Betty said. 'We're the only ones who can write them. They're not seen until they reach a managed care company.'

'Oh damn! What a disgusting violation!' A woman shouted.

'Egregious!' hollered another.

The furor that erupted was unprecedented in a psychology meeting.

'Hold it! Two patients on my list are from different companies.' Tom frowned.

'Which?' Cory asked.

'Behavioral Health in northern California so that rules them out, and Superior in San Diego.'

'Let's take a few minutes to go through our cases. Then we'll see what we have,' Betty said, her voice shaky.

Papers rustled as people shuffled notes.

They concluded of the total fourteen targeted patients, ten were from Behavioral Health, and four from Superior. Definitely of statistical significance.

'Would the same case manager handle Behavioral and Superior? It makes no sense,' Tom said, scratching his salt and pepper beard.

'Wait a minute,' Vince said, 'The Wall Street Journal had an article on the health care industry. I think Superior and Behavioral Health merged.'

167

'You're not sure,' shot Harriet.

'Stop! He's right. A pharmaceutical company bought some of the largest managed health care companies,' Tom said, 'Superior, Behavioral and Better Care are now owned by . . . Damn! I can't remember.'

'No wonder when I asked Behavioral for more sessions, I was told to send the patient for medication,' Vince said. 'I protested that he had a history of prescription drug addiction and medication could inflame his problem, but the case manager ignored it.'

'If Behavioral is owned by a pharmaceutical company, they'd profit from prescribing drugs,' Marjorie said.

'Look. There are many other single vulnerable young women on other managed care programs who haven't received calls from the rapist,' John said. 'So we're sure the problem comes from Behavioral and Superior. Their merger suggests they have installed some deviate worker here.'

'Let's warn Superior of our suspicions,' Steve suggested.

'And risk being dropped from the provider panel? My practice is down two-thirds already. I can't afford to close shop,' Ginger said. 'I've got kids in college.'

'We shouldn't think only of ourselves.' Steve shouted.

'Shut up and sit down,' Norma yelled. Turning to Harriet, she said in a stage whisper, 'Moralistic *putz!*'

Well respected with a practice spanning three decades, Tom's face reddened. 'Managed care! What a misnomer,' he boomed. 'They manage benefits, not care. They don't give a rat's ass about patients and dole out precious few sessions for people who need more. And now this!' He flung up his arms.

Charged by frustration with managed care, everyone had a horror tale:

'I saw a suicidal man whose boss assured him insurance would cover his health needs. They were misinformed,' Vince said. 'The plan authorized three sessions, max. I called the case manager, but the voice mail-box was full and I couldn't reach a live person,' he scowled. 'That poor guy had no resources.'

'So what did you do?' Steve asked.

'Sent him to County Mental Health. They're overcrowded and it was a pain to get him admitted.'

'I know how you feel,' Ginger said. 'I had a young woman recently diagnosed with cancer. She was depressed and needed emotional support, but the case manager recommended Prozac and *no* sessions. Can you imagine!'

John nodded. 'We spend more time on

stupid clerical details than therapy. It's an elaborate scheme to discourage us from giving effective care. The divine buck is all they care about.'

'Cook-book brief therapy for serious situations,' Cory said. 'All those years of training and experience — useless. We're generic shrinks. One size fits all. Let's *kvetch* another time. Let's prepare to make it a long weekend. For now, let's stick with our agenda and figure out what to do about the phone-caller.'

'Right. When a new patient is a likely target for the rapist, how should we word a report?' Ginger asked.

'Up to three sessions are allowed before an additional treatment request is due. Delay submissions,' Betty replied.

Norma stood, hands on hips. 'That's ridiculous. We may have to wait months for an authorization. We'll lose money.'

'Work pro-bono for a few sessions,' Cory said.

'You can't expect us to work for nothing,' Norma said.

No wonder many psychologists disliked her. Self serving, she thought everyone else was too.

'To protect a life, I believe we would,' Cory said.

Everybody, but Norma nodded. Harriet had the good sense to keep quiet.

'Okay. Let's send a letter to Superior about our suspicions?' Marjorie suggested.

'I bet anyone who signs it will be blacklisted and out of business. If those two companies merged, they have most of the health care contracts in the state.' Tom shook his head.

'Enough already,' Cory blurted out. 'I'll call Superior.'

No one talked her out of it, but Betty shook her head.

29

Lost in the magazine section of the New York Times, the phone jolted Cory out of nostalgic reverie. She half expected it to be one of her old college friends, but Ron's voice brought her to the present.

'Hi Cory. We're jamming tonight. How about it?'

'Great. Where shall we meet?'

'How about a walk on the beach, first?'

'Sure. Where and when?'

'Is four at the Del Mar post office okay? We'll catch the sunset.'

'I'll bring my bongos.'

'Better leave them in the car or we'll draw a crowd.'

'Hah! See you later.'

Cory dashed into the shower, French-braided her hair and dressed in tights and a long, loose cotton shirt. Mild southern California winters were not warm enough for cotton at night, but when she drummed, she heated up. Off tune, she hummed a romantic refrain from 'Moonlight in Vermont.' At least I've got rhythm, she thought, tossing a royal blue sweatshirt around her shoulders.

* ★ *

With growing irritation, Ron, seated on a bench watched the passing crowd and checked his watch. Two minutes before four. Where was she? A former girlfriend had often protested that he was impatient and rigid and expected too much of others. Perhaps she was right.

At four, he spotted Cory heading toward him. She smiled and his heart bounced. Her long limbs, her lithe body. Good God, what a turn on!

'Glad to see you, Ron,' she said, reaching for his hand. The softness of her skin aroused him. He fought an urge to draw her to his lips, but let go of her hand instead. This was no place to get a hard on. To distract himself, he studied the surroundings.

Up ahead, a crowd had gathered at the park overlooking the ocean. They ambled toward it. A photographer was posing a wedding party whose formal attire appeared incongruous in a setting of beachgoers.

Ron and Cory carefully stepped over the railroad tracks on the way to the shore. They stopped to slip off their shoes. Ron rolled up his khaki pants cuffs. Cory zipped her sweatshirt. They pranced to the water's edge.

He gazed at her, but she looked distant as though she had transported herself to another time, another place. Perhaps another romance.

He touched her arm. 'You look distracted. Anything wrong?'

At first she didn't speak, then slowly she told him about the meeting.

'What a drag. In medicine, we expect managed care to deny needed services. It's frustrating, but we work around it as best we can. In your work, confidentiality is more crucial.'

'I'm glad you called me. It's good to be here with you,' she said.

On the cliff above them, the northbound coaster train whizzed by, interrupting the conversation.

They walked a few miles toward La Jolla. At the shoreline, cool and wet beneath their bare feet, joggers slick with sweat wove around them.

Gradually, the pink and lavender sky darkened to variegated shades of purple, colors merging as the golden sun slipped into the sea.

By the time they abandoned the beach, the moon was full, the sky ablaze with stars, and they had unremitting hots for each other.

She followed his late model red BMW in

her old white one to a two-story pink stucco house with a tile roof, high on a hill off Carmel Valley Road. Ron pressed a code to open the ornate gate. Four cars were parked in the massive circular driveway.

They carried their instruments into the house. Sixteen foot ceilings, antique furniture, ornamental framed Japanese paintings greeted them behind the host, a short man with a gray goatee and long gray hair. He wore a blue mechanic-style jumpsuit and sandals. Shades of the sixties.

'Come on in. I'm Harvey, your host. Glad you brought your bongos, we're out a drummer tonight,' he said to Cory.

Ron introduced Cory to the guys. The blonde long-haired thin young man tinkling the keys of an electric piano was a local named Matt.

'Hi. I'm not a professional. I teach elementary school,' he said.

Roberto, the guitarist, from Puerto Rico, tuning up, grinned. 'Matt likes to surprise people. He's a great musician. But me, I'm a television technician during the day.'

'Harvey's a semi-retired ophthalmologist. A fine bassist,' Ron said.

Damon, a tall man from Philadelphia with skin the color of milk chocolate played vibes. She said she recognized him. A professional

175

musician who recorded with well-known jazz groups, Damon's presence was a compliment to the group.

'I must confess, guys. I'm rusty and nervous about playing with you.'

Compatible musicians on the same wavelength, they improvised and played a fine repertoire of Latin jazz and standards. Cory carried the rhythm backed by Harvey. Cory sizzled. An incredible, natural high.

They drifted into a Bossa Nova mode and played the lyrical, rhythmic melodies of Luiz Bonfa and Antonio Carlo Jobim. Heaven! Roberto's pizzicatto guitar, delicate and rhythmic, as Bonfa intended.

When Ron took a sax solo on 'Manha de Carnival,' Cory fell in love. Passionately. He played tenor sax in the soft, warm way of Stan Getz, yet fresh. Roberto backed him ever so sweetly and Damon, fantastic on vibes, added a vocal melody — similar in effect to Torme or Gilberto. Perfect.

The huge grandfather clock chimed eleven, but Cory, grateful that the music had given her a chance to get out of her head and into her senses, didn't want to leave. She thought they could have played all night.

Everyone gathered at Harvey's kitchen counter where he had prepared a tureen of scrambled eggs. Musician fare.

'You were great, Cory. Thanks for coming. Do it again next week, okay?' Roberto asked. Harvey hugged her. Damon smiled and nodded to Ron, 'Great chick, great drummer.' Cory stifled a feminist retort and allowed herself to bask in his compliment.

'Thanks for asking me. What a high, jamming with you guys!'

In the parking area beneath the star-studded velvet sky, after the others left, Ron and Cory reached out to each other. She didn't want to let go. More than arousal, she felt comfort in his strong arms. 'Ooo this feels so good,' they said in unison.

A short distance away, waves caressed the shore as Ron and Cory kissed. She hoped it was a prelude to more.

'I'll call soon,' he whispered.

Cory followed him to the freeway accompanied by an assaulting put-put sound of a low flying helicopter — its search beam, probably surveying the canyons for illegal immigrants.

Music nourished her soul, whether she played or listened, like her son, Noah's love of nature. Spiritual. It separated Cory from the troubles of the day and the portent of danger ahead.

30

Cory arrived home eager to shower, slip into bed and dream of Ron, but the red light on her answering machine blinked. She punched the playback button and heard a tremulous voice: 'This is Norma. You don't have to call me back. My patient was raped tonight. She was one of the women who had received the calls. I've notified the others.'

Cory hoped Norma wouldn't sleep well. Grandma, the guardian of her morals intruded, '*Cory, it's not good to wish bad things on people, even if you think they deserve it. Let the Almighty take care of it.*'

'*Grandma, wishing doesn't harm anyone.*'

'*Cory, it harms the wisher. You can't think too well of yourself.*'

'*Some people deserve to be punished.*'

'*Disciplined.*'

Grandma was true to herself. She never punished. She disciplined. Even from her grave.

Cory hoped beyond belief that the helicopter she had heard earlier had caught the rapist.

Detective Sharpley, as she expected, did

not call. His meager mentality probably pegged her as hysterical, and as an Asian woman, not a force to worry about. Except for the Dragon Lady. Her new role model.

★ ★ ★

The next day Cory phoned Superior Health. Placed on hold, she doodled on a piece of paper while having to listen to canned music on the line that sounded like rain dripping into a tin bucket. Finally a wine commercial interrupted. How incongruous on a mental health and alcohol abuse line! She would mention that, too. With each wasted minute, her anger multiplied.

After an eternity, and three more pages of doodles, Ann knocked on the door.

'Steve Glass is here waiting to speak to you. He said it's important.'

Relieved to hang up, Cory invited Steve in.

He slouched on the chair, dropping his briefcase on the floor.

'I was in the neighborhood so I took a chance you'd be free. Wasn't that some meeting yesterday? I shouldn't say anything bad about anyone, but that Norma Rogers is deprived of a conscience.'

'She sure proved that. But, she's recanted. One of her patients was raped and she's

179

notified the ones who were called.'

'Not another rape!'

'Proves how much we needed that meeting. I was on hold with Superior half a morning when you showed up.'

Steve scowled. 'Listen, Cory. There's an interesting development with Rosalind, the rape victim. I was right about her. She's a *shtarkeh*. A real strong person. She's willing to go public.'

'Good for her.'

'Well . . . when she told her family in Australia what happened, they pleaded with her to go home. Who'd blame them? But she refused. So they came here. We had quite a productive family session today.'

'That's good, Steve.'

'You'd be proud. I supported her parents. Suggested she'd be safer with them, but Roz wouldn't budge. They hollered so, I'm glad we have a sound screen. Can you believe it! They blamed her for the rape.' He banged his fist on the desk. 'I said it wasn't her fault that several women have recently had the same experience. They've hired a top personal security firm to guard her and to find the bastard.'

'Great idea.'

'What a job to get Rosalind to agree. Is she trying to prove she's some kind of martyr?'

He stroked his beard. 'Better she should be protected, no? She's only a kid. Knows from nothing. Dealing with her resistance to a detective following her around, is like talking to the wall. Worse. Banging your head against it.'

'She's ashamed. Tell her P.I.'s can be discrete, and if he makes her parents feel secure, they'll be less likely to pester her to go home.'

'I'm telling you, Cory, Roz has screwed up priorities. We have to work on a control issue with her parents.'

'You bet. It's great they can afford a personal security service.'

'Have you heard of Harry Hornsby?'

'No, but he's bound to be better than the police.'

'From your mouth to God's ears. Anything new with the cops?'

'No, the sergeant thinks I'm *meshuge*.'

Steve shook his head. 'That's a joke. I'll vouch for your sanity. With a *schlemiel* for a sheriff, are we lucky to get a private eye! We've got to supply him with our information.'

'Of course, but first my patients must approve.'

'Let me know.'

'Sure.'

After Steve left, Cory picked up the phone and pushed the re-dial button. Within five minutes she was connected to Provider Relations. Explaining she had a matter of grave importance to discuss with the person in charge, she was transferred to Mr. Russell, Chief Executive Officer.

'Mr. Russell, this is Dr. Cohen. I have information about a possible leak of confidentiality in your organization. It may have caused a violent crime spree in San Diego.'

'You'd better speak with Mr. Pope. One moment and you'll be transferred.'

'Hamilton Pope here.'

Cory identified herself and shot off her big mouth.

'What? This is incredible!' he shouted. 'We check our case managers carefully. The leak cannot have come from here. Unless it's the security people. Ah, hah! Perhaps one of them. Our files are locked every night. I suppose a guard could come in after hours. Let's see. We've changed the security company recently. Yes, yes. That may be where it's coming from. They hire the dregs for those security jobs. I'll check on it and let you know. Thanks for calling it to my attention. By the way, do the police know of your suspicion?'

Predictably defensive, he'd rattled on

without giving Cory a chance to respond except to his question.

'Not yet. Thanks for your cooperation.'

Later, she realized she had forgotten to mention the wine ad on their telephone system, but she had alerted a jittery administrator who would take action, she thought.

31

Hamilton flung his attache case off the desk. How did he slip up? How did she figure it out? Well, at least he'd thought fast enough to point the finger at the security company.

Now, he'd have to find out about this bitch, Dr. Cory Cohen, and get her before she told the police.

Hamilton called in his efficient assistant, Jim Corita, a balding, middle-aged man.

'Jim, we must update addresses and office hours for our therapists in this area for our data base. I'd like this in a few hours. We need to weed out some providers. I'll write a letter and you send it certified to those whom I select.'

'Sure thing, sir. I'll have my people start now.'

Hamilton was a busy man. He located a form letter from the legal department that stated according to the terms of the contract, Superior could dismiss providers from the panel without reason, but was obligated to give a two month notice. He copied the letter on his computer and dated it one month earlier.

An hour later, Jim provided the list.

Hamilton checked his personal notes to insure letters would be sent to three providers whose patients he hadn't called and to all with patients he had contacted. Ten names, including Dr. Cory Cohen's, would be sent certified letters. He also knew her office hours and address.

That evening, after changing into jeans, a UCSD sweat shirt, and a baseball cap, Hamilton concealed the cleft in his chin with a Band-Aid. He stashed his knife in his pocket and drove to her office. Hamilton parked his Eldorado in the garage, and climbed the stairs to her floor. From behind a post in the shadows of the corridor, he watched the lights go off in her suite and two women leave. He figured the tall Jap was the receptionist or a patient, and the middle aged petite, curly-haired woman must be Dr. Cohen. He followed them down the steps and into the garage where they slipped into their cars.

Hamilton hopped into the Eldorado and tailed the silver Camry for six miles. He observed the woman greet the guard at the gate as she entered a secure condominium compound.

'Damn it to hell,' he said under his breath. Hamilton opened the window and spat. He drove around the corner and bought a bouquet of flowers at the supermarket. He parked his car on the street and strolled to her gate where he announced a delivery for Dr. Cory Cohen.

The guard said, 'You have the wrong address.'

Hamilton grew angrier. His head throbbed. A professional woman, Dr. Cohen probably practiced under one name, but used her husband's at home, he thought. 'Well maybe I've got the wrong name. Do you have a psychologist here named Cory?'

'I can't tell you who lives here,' the guard answered.

His mood dark, and his stomach rumbling, Hamilton drove across town to D.Z. Akins, a deli reputed to be the best in the city. He never ate in public, but would sit in a restaurant with a cup of coffee, scrutinizing the table manners of well-dressed patrons in order to learn from them.

Now, he ordered four corn beef sandwiches on rye with mustard, pickles and cole slaw and a tall cream soda. Waiting at the counter for his take-out order, he watched people place napkins on their laps and clink utensils. A man slurped soup. Hamilton had the urge to shove the old guy's head into the bowl.

'Here's your order,' the counterman

growled, handing him a large, brown paper sack.

On the way home, he consumed half the contents, planning to save the rest for the next day. He could not see what all the hype was about. To him, the food was as good as bologna on white with mayonnaise. Arriving at his condo, he changed into sweats and went to the weight room where he pumped iron for over two hours.

32

Paige looked as if she had read Cory's mind and had a fashion make-over. Eyeliner framed her sparkling hazel eyes. Her cheeks were rosy and her hair glistened. She had spritzed on a fragrant herbal scent. Decked out in a comfortable looking flared pink wool dress, she crossed her legs. Delicate pumps covered her tiny feet. Cory hoped Paige's outfit worn last session had found a new home. She wondered what had caused the transformation.

'You look great, Paige. What's happening?'

'Remember I told you I wanted a boyfriend? Surprise! My prayers are answered. Rick, a nice guy is interested in me. I haven't actually seen him, yet. He phones almost every evening. It inspired me to change my image, so I hired a personal shopper.' She rubbed her hands and smiled.

Cory gasped, clutching her head.

'What's wrong, Dr. C.?'

'Paige, did you find out how he got your number?'

'He said he's a neighbor. At first I didn't understand because I'm unlisted so I asked where he got it. He mumbled something I couldn't hear and changed the subject. I know it's odd, but he's so nice. He seems so sweet and sensitive.'

'Did he tell you he was shy and lonely?'

'Well, as a matter of fact he did. How did you know?' She twirled the charm hanging from her gold necklace.

'Oh, Paige. I'm sorry, but a dangerous con-man has been calling women giving them the same pitch. When they fall for it, he rapes them. If you call Detective Sharpley, he'll get the phone company to put a trap on your phone.' Cory reached into her desk drawer, removed the detective's card, copied it and handed it to Paige.

'And I thought he was for real!' She held her face in her hands.

'You can have a good guy in your life, Paige.'

Paige clutched a tissue in her hand and dabbed her nose. 'Well, if I make an effort, right? Anyway, I'm glad he gave me a reason to improve my appearance.'

'There you go.' The therapist smiled.

Paige was intelligent and motivated. An ideal patient. Cory expected Paige growth would be rapid.

★ ★ ★

Later in the day Cory received a certified letter from Superior Health. Dated last month, it stated her contract would officially end in two months. She examined the post-mark. Yesterday. What kind of stunt was this?

She pulled out her copy of the contract. It stipulated that a two months notice was required prior to termination. Having dealt with the notoriously ineffectual state regulatory agency, she knew reporting this violation would be futile.

Frustrated, she phoned Betty.

'Just about to call you, Cory. Superior bounced me. Norma, too, but not Harriet. What do you think of that?' Betty was breathless.

'Very interesting. Something about this isn't kosher.'

'So call Steve.' Betty chuckled. 'Maybe he has a direct line to a higher power.'

'Yeah, sure. We wish. We'll talk later.'

She clicked off and punched in Steve's number.

'Can you believe it, Cory? They bounced me off. What can we do about it? Nothing!'

'Right. The contract lets Superior dismiss providers from the panel without explanation. Let's see who got notices. We'll connect after we have this info, Steve. We'll get through this hurdle.' Cory began to feel that Superior may have done them a big favor.

She phoned ten psychologists. Of the five on Superior's list, three had patients who'd reported the calls and two of those psychologists received termination notices. The other five psychologists weren't Superior's providers. None had patients involved in strange phone calls. Ann relayed the information to Steve. Within an hour, he reported that after speaking to a dozen psychologists, his efforts yielded similar results.

Steve depended on referrals from Superior. Cory didn't want to embarrass him with an offer of a loan. She wished she was in a position to send him patients. She also wished managed care would vanish and that she had the tools to make it happen.

33

Frustrated in his efforts to kill the psychologist at her home last night, Hamilton paced his office. He would have to do it in her car when she left work. Excited by the risk, he slid his tongue over his parched lips.

Dr. Cohen posed an immediate threat, which meant he must postpone plans with the women he phoned. Infuriated, his head throbbed. He spied a potted schefflera plant. Hoisting it, he flung it across the room. It struck the wall with a resounding crash. Seconds later, Hamilton heard footsteps racing in the corridor, and then banging on his door.

'Is everything all right, sir?' Jim asked.

Through clenched teeth, Hamilton replied, 'Never mind. The plant fell. I'll take care of it.' Panting, he wiped the beads of sweat from his forehead. Slow, deep breaths calmed him. He refused to succumb to a case of nerves. With a file folder, he swept up the damage.

Back in control, he swiveled in his deep, luxurious chair, laced his hands across his large chest and relaxed.

Concern over the police intruded, making him jittery again. He reassured himself that despite all his crimes, he remained free.

What fools cops were! To think when he was a boy, he had wanted to be an ace detective with authority to arrest and overpower others. When he grew up, he realized it would be stupid to subject himself to a background check. Because he was cautious, he could have passed, but a Department of Internal Affairs could monitor him. He would not permit scrutiny. Police work required a partner. To hell with that! Outwitting law enforcement tasted delicious. He was Dr. Moriarty, but there was no Sherlock Holmes. Rubbing his pounding head, he felt feverish. His hands and feet were moist. From the crystal pitcher on the credenza behind his desk, Hamilton poured a glass of water and gulped it down. Unsaturated, he drained the pitcher into his mouth, soaking his chin. He felt the pressure from his bladder and longed to be home.

Hamilton worked long hours and deserved time off. He rang his assistant and informed him that he was leaving early because of illness, then he dragged himself out of the office.

Mission Bay Drive made the trip home pleasant. Hamilton rolled down the car windows. Though sunny, the air was crisp. The cool bay breeze evaporated his sweat. His headache subsided.

Sailboats lined the bay. Driving slowly, he studied the pleasure crafts and imagined himself captain of a yacht. Like the one he stared at . . . must be about thirty or forty . . . Suddenly a bicycle swerved in front of him. He slammed on the brakes and heard a screech. The cyclist fell. Hamilton peered around, saw no other cars and drove on.

When he arrived home, he felt better. He had battled the jitters and won.

It was time to sharpen his knife. It gleamed as he twisted and turned his hand. Hamilton caressed the blade whispering, 'Buddy.' No ordinary piece of shiny steel, but an extension of himself. He had admired it a long time before buying it, convinced by a salesman who had told him a four-and-one-half inch blade was a lawful size for a folding pocket knife. It served his purpose.

Hamilton changed into his black sweat suit and stuffed his ski mask, gloves and Buddy in the pocket of his hooded jacket. He attached a fake beard and mustache. There was no time for tinting his hair. A black seaman's cap rolled over his head would do.

He was about to leave his condo when his doorbell rang. 'Screw it,' he shouted. 'Who is it?' he barked. 'What the hell do you want?'

'I'm sorry to bother you,' a woman's voice answered. 'I'm your next door neighbor. I just moved in and wondered if I could use your phone. Mine isn't connected yet.'

Gritting his teeth, he replied, 'There's a phone in the lobby. I'm busy now.'

Hamilton waited a few minutes, his ear to the door, listening to the click of her footsteps disappear down the corridor. Squinting through the peep hole, he saw no one. He raced down the seldom used staircase to the garage.

Hamilton drove to Dr. Cohen's office and parked three blocks away. He tied his car key to the lace on his shoe and jogged to her garage. He hid behind a post until sure no one was around. He located her Camry, but it had an alarm and he couldn't break in without attracting attention. Damn! She was obsessed with security. He must be quick and kill her when she went to the car.

34

Ann locked the office behind them and they were on the stairs leading to the garage when Cory realized she had left her appointment book behind. 'I forgot something,' she said, turning on her heel.

Ann strolled ahead while Cory fumbled for the key and opened the office door. She grabbed the book and snapped the door shut.

At six o'clock, it was pitch dark outside and a little too quiet in the building, most people having left by five. Dim lights in the corridors gave an eerie quality. Cory thought she heard faint footsteps, glanced in that direction, but saw no one. She chided herself for being so jumpy. A guard was always on duty. The footsteps she heard must have been his. Tomorrow, she would request better lighting from the building manager.

Ann had reached the garage, her high heels clicking in the direction of her Camry. Rushing to catch up, Cory rounded the corner, and was about to step downstairs, when she spied a figure in black spring from behind a post. He moved towards Ann, a knife glistening in his dark gloved hand.

Tensing, Cory vaulted down the stairs and raced towards him. He grabbed Ann by the hair, yanking her head back, his blade drawn. Leaping through the air, Cory side kicked him in the ribs. The knife flew out of his hand skittering on the ground. Spinning around, she faced a heavy-set, black-bearded man, so muscular, he appeared to have no neck.

'Cory! Oh my God! Help!' Ann screamed.

The man clutched his side. Cory expected him to fall, writhing in pain, but he charged at her, grunting.

'KIAI!' she blared, side-stepping him. Sweeping his legs, she sent him tumbling down.

He sprang up and ran towards the exit.

Grasping Ann's arm, Cory pulled her towards the car. Her hand shook as she fumbled with the door lock. 'Get in,' she shouted. They jumped into the BMW. Cory switched on the ignition and sped out of the garage.

'Where are we going?' Ann's voice was weak and tremulous. Her teeth chattered. From the corner of Cory's eye, she saw the woman stiffen and grip her elbows.

'To see which way he went, so we can report it.' Seizing the cell phone, Cory punched the emergency button and relayed the information to the dispatcher.

'He ran that way.' Ann yelled, pointing to the left.

'North on 101 now,' Cory hollered into the phone.

Ann peered out the passenger side window. Cory scanned the street, but they lost sight of him.

'Hell!' Cory slammed the dashboard with her hand. 'He's gone. We'll meet the deputy at my office,' she shouted her address into the cell phone.

Cory parked next to Ann's car. Breathless, they dashed upstairs and locked the door of the suite. While awaiting the officers, Cory zapped triple strength chamomile tea in the microwave and gave Ann a cup. Her hands shaky, she spilled tea on the floor. Cory wished she had stored an emergency stash of brandy in the first aid kit.

'You've had quite a scare, Ann. How about spending the night at my house?'

'Thanks, but it's not necessary. I feel safe where I live and I'll be okay in a little while.' She wiped up the spill with a napkin.

About ten minutes later, there was a pounding on the door. Through the peep-hole, Cory spied two uniformed officers and let them in. One was a woman about five years older than her daughter Rachel, maybe twenty-five. She wore her sandy hair in a pony-tail. Her partner, a swarthy young man looked like a graduate of Golds Gym, his tan uniform snug against his biceps. Deputy Kelly opened her little notebook and scribbled Cory's statement. Kelly's partner, folding his hands across his chest, resembled a sentry with a blank expression.

'Please hurry. Let's retrieve the knife from the garage before the cleaning crew arrives,' Cory suggested. 'We'll show you where it happened.'

'Don't interrupt. I'm talking to the victim,' Deputy Kelly said, turning her back to Cory. 'Anyone want to harm you, Ms. Abrams? An ex, maybe?'

'No. I keep a low profile.'

'Please have someone look for the knife now,' Cory asked the other deputy.

No response. Cory felt as in a nightmare in which the dreamer in peril can't scream, and if she could, there was no one to listen.

'The garage is a crime scene and you're ignoring evidence. I'll speak to your supervisor about this,' Cory said.

'Just because you're a doctor, doesn't mean you know my job,' Deputy Kelly said, glaring at her. 'Listen, Ma'am. I'm in charge here,' Kelly said. 'We'll go down when I decide. Understand?'

'Apparently, you don't,' Cory barked.

The Golds Gym graduate flexed his muscles and remained silent.

Cory's rage mounted as she picked up the phone.

'Don't bother,' the deputy said, sneering. 'Administrative offices are closed until tomorrow. Pony-tail haughtily swaggered out of the office, her mute partner trailing. Of the two, Cory knew who had the brawn, but wondered who had the brain.

Ann and Cory followed the pair to the garage and pointed to where the assault had taken place. Kelly nodded and gestured to her partner. Cory and Ann watched the deputies swagger to their black and white car. Reaching inside it, Deputy Kelly hauled out a large flashlight. Without moving from her position, she switched on the torch, rotating it in circular fashion for a moment before handing it the other officer.

'Here. Bend down and search,' she commanded.

There were a few cars in the garage. Squatting, he flashed the torch under them, then stood and shook his head.

'Just as I figured,' she said smugly. 'Knew no knife would be there.' She glanced at her partner and tilted her head toward the exit. Without another word to the victims, they hopped in the car and drove away.

Ann and Cory stared at each other in disbelief. Cory repeated her invitation to the traumatized woman to come home with her, but Ann refused. It was clear from her trembling, that she wasn't in any condition to drive home alone. Feeling shaky too, she called Ron. Accustomed to emergency situations, he could help figure out what to do. Between gasps, she related the events. He instructed them to wait in the office for him. Within fifteen minutes he arrived.

'It's hard to believe, Ron, but the officers were so slow in going to the garage and made such a cursory search that maybe the mugger came back for his knife.'

'Would he have the nerve to do that?' asked Ann.

'He had the nerve to attack you in a guarded building. Unless he knew the security guard's schedule.'

'Let's go downstairs. I have a good flashlight in my car,' Ron said.

'If we get the guard to accompany us, I'd feel safer,' Ann said.

Cory poked her head out the door and saw the security man across the corridor. She motioned to him and he ran to her. After she related the incident, he called his office and reported it. He preceded them as they stepped downstairs. Ron rooted out a torch from his glove box and scooted under Ann's car. In a few seconds, he wriggled out.

'I think I see it behind the left rear tire. If I move the car, I can grab it.'

Ann handed Ron her keys. He pulled her Camry forward a few inches and turned off the ignition. He dashed to the trunk of his car, dug out a pair of surgical gloves and a plastic pouch. 'Here, Cory, fix the light on the left rear wheel. I think it's there.' He handed her the flashlight.

Crouching under the car, he pulled out a glistening steel blade and dropped it into the container. 'Let's lock it up in a safe place for now. Tomorrow, you'll give it to the sheriff.'

They headed back to the office. Cory thanked the guard and he went on his way.

Ann coughed.

'Oh, excuse me,' Cory said. 'In all this excitement, I forgot my manners. Ron, this is Ann, the person who was nearly mugged. Ron Miller, Ann Abrams.'

'If not for Cory, I hate to think what would have happened?' Ann said, quivering.

'She's impressive, huh?' Ron smiled, returning her car keys. He clasped her wrist for a pulse check. Cory watched the hue of Ann's face change from pale pink to deep rose. 'Cory, are you okay with driving Ann home in her car?'

'Sure.'

'I'll follow you and drive you back to yours.'

Despite her unsteady hands, Ann said she could drive alone, but Cory insisted on taking her home. Sighing, she tossed the keys to Cory. Ron escorted them to Ann's Camry and made sure they buckled the seat belts. Cory insisted Ann take the next day off, but she refused.

'He's very attractive. I like the way he took charge,' Ann said.

Cory thought Ann wanted to hear more about him, but was too polite to pry. She was the kind of woman Cory wanted for a friend. She hoped that when Ann completed her studies and no longer worked for her, it would occur. Cory shuddered to think of what could have happened to this woman of whom she was fond.

35

During the short drive east of Del Mar, Ann babbled about her school work, local politics and the last movie she'd seen. Anything to avoid discussing the fresh trauma. At the guarded entrance of her home, flanked by a row of palm trees, Ann told the sentry to admit the red BMW behind them. The large, white wrought iron gates swung open to the meticulous landscaped compound. Proudly she pointed out the abundance of eucalyptus trees, spacious lawns, and indigenous plants. They passed a man-made lake with a waterfall next to an olympic size swimming pool. 'Heated all year,' Ann said, sounding like a real estate agent giving a tour. The pose, Cory suspected, reinforced Ann's sense of security. Here, she didn't feel vulnerable.

'We've got everything. Tennis, golf and a state of the art gym,' she said as they passed a single story building she identified as a recreation center. 'I don't have to leave except for work and school. I feel snug here with around the clock security.' Ann shivered. 'I'm scared, Cory. The mugger could come back and hide in the building again.'

'Send a letter to the building management on my letterhead, Ann. Describe what happened. Ask them to specify the measures they'll use to beef up security. Suggest better lighting and erratic schedules for the guards. From now on, let's ask the guard to escort us to our cars.'

'Good idea. I'll compose the letter tonight.'

Cory parked Ann's car in the driveway of the small ranch house and waited until Ann switched on her house lights. She slid into Ron's BMW. Newer, but similar to hers, it made her feel right at home.

'I'll drop you at your car, then let's get a bite somewhere.'

'I'd rather fix something at home. I've got a good bottle of wine.'

'If it's no bother.' He patted her hand. 'You're some woman, stopping a mugger.'

'It was instinctive . . . after all the years of practice. I wasn't scared then, Ron, but I'm feeling it now,' she said, trembling.

'That's natural.' He squeezed her hand. 'You must have impressed the cops.'

'Not favorably. One of the officers was on a power trip with me. If they'd tried harder, they'd have found the knife.'

'It was hidden behind the tire.'

'Sure, but you found it.' She sighed. 'Am I glad you're here, Ron.' She stared at his profile. Strong features, full mouth.

'Me too. You deserve your black belt, Cory.'

'Thanks. Karate paid off.' In more ways than one, she thought.

Ron dropped Cory off at her car and tailed her home.

She dug out a bottle of Merlot from the back of a cabinet where she stored old LP records. While Ron fiddled with the corkscrew, she brought cheese and crackers and a couple of wine glasses to the coffee table.

Toasting martial arts from Aikido to Tae Kwon Do, Cory relaxed. The lessons she had learned from her *sensei*, to be alert and defend, worked. For about fifteen minutes, she basked in self confidence, until her teeth chattered.

Ron held his arms out to her and she nestled in them. 'It's okay to feel scared, Cory. Let me take care of you.'

Ron, competent and gentle, quickly endeared himself to her. Ignoring her feminist principles, she enjoyed his comforting.

'I can find my way around the kitchen, okay? You rest.'

'Thanks.'

Cory nestled on the couch, listening to the sounds from the next room: Whipping, slicing, dicing and popping. She closed her eyes and turned her attention to the stereo playing Vince Guaraldi's piano rendition of 'Since I Fell For You.' How appropriate, she thought.

Ron brought platters of toasted baguettes and vegetable omelets to the couch. Cory swallowed tears of tenderness for this caring man. They munched and drained the bottle of wine listening to the sensuous saxophone sounds of Stan Getz and Paul Desmond. Time evaporated. Ron leaned towards Cory combing her hair with his fingers. She rested her head on his shoulder. He caressed her neck and started to stroke her shoulders, but she quivered and pulled away.

'What's wrong, Cory?'

'Maybe it's the aftermath of the mugger. Or maybe . . . maybe I'm nervous about getting close to you.'

'Why?

'Well, I haven't dated much since my divorce. And that was eight years ago.'

'Single that long, huh? If you want to, you'd have someone in your life. Listen, you could do a lot worse than a guy like me. Just ask my folks.'

Cory chuckled. 'Frankly, raising my family, I didn't feel single. Did you know I've got two grown kids?'

'So what?'

'Well . . . you and I are in different places

in our lives. I don't want to get hurt. I'd like to be friends.' She sighed. 'But I'm incredibly attracted to you.'

'It's mutual, Cory.' Ron scooted to the opposite side of the couch and leaned his elbow on the arm rest. 'I understand. I've been hurt, too. Almost married a woman I knew in med school, but she dumped me for another guy. I haven't felt much for anyone, since.'

'It's hard to think of another relationship after that,' she said softly.

'Frankly, I'm not much for dating. Most of the time I prefer solitude.'

'Sounds familiar, Ron. After relating to patients all day, it's nice to have time alone.'

He nodded. 'I'd like to keep seeing you, but I can't promise much time.'

'Fine with me. I don't want a high maintenance relationship,' she said, yearning for him, wondering how long she could hold out, or if she should.

'Great,' he said, kissing her forehead. 'Listen, after what happened at your office, maybe you'd feel better if I stay here. I promise I'll be good. I can sleep on the couch.'

'Thanks, Ron. It's not necessary. The house has an alarm system. I'm safe. Besides, I don't expect the mugger to come after me.

He doesn't even know me or where I live.'

Before leaving, Ron hugged her affection-ately.

In his place were memories tossed with fantasies of what they might have done. Cory went to sleep smiling, thinking how wonder-ful that the attraction was mutual and if she could put that magical essence in bottles, she'd be a billionaire.

36

Awakening refreshed and grateful that her libido had softened the danger of last night, Cory bounced out of bed into a steaming shower. She belted out a dreadful imitation of Sarah Vaughn's 'All of Me' straining her vocal cords and not even getting close.

Deciding to forgo her exercise ritual, she dressed in black velour jeans and matching top. She tied her hair back with a black velvet ribbon. Black signaled mourning. Mourning the lost charm of elusive Detective Sharpley. She punched his number on her phone and expected to swoon in shock if he answered. Neither happened and she left a message.

Next she called the Sheriff's administrative office, got a run-around until a sergeant answered. Cory reviewed the previous night's assault and told him she had the knife. He promised to send an officer immediately.

Cory was scarfing up cottage cheese and a mango when the door-bell chimed. She was glad the sheriff responded quickly to calls from her neighborhood. From the kitchen window, she glimpsed the black and white car. She opened her door to a tan uniformed, shockingly handsome, dark complexioned green-eyed officer. She handed him the plastic pouch containing the knife. He asked questions, jotted some notes and bid her good-day. With a gorgeous cop like him, damsels in distress could easily forget why they had called.

She activated the home security and drove to the office. The flow of patients kept her mind occupied.

Taking a lunch break, she strolled to the Plaza for a salad at the market.

When she returned to her office, a middle-aged man, wearing a rumpled burgandy corduroy suit was waiting in the reception room. When Ann greeted Cory, he rose, flashed a smile and a badge identifying him as Detective Sergeant George Lewis. 'I'm here to find out more about last night,' he said.

Cory started to introduce him to Ann, but she said she had already given her statement.

He followed Cory to the consulting room, took a seat opposite her, his long legs stretched in front of him. She related the incident.

'You have the makings of a detective, you know. I bet you watch cop shows.'

She grinned. 'I used to watch *Barney Miller*. Loved it. It was fun because it took place in a precinct near Greenwich Village where I used to live. The characters were *real* characters.'

'Well, what do you know? You're a New Yorker too, huh?'

He ran long fingers through close-cropped dark hair styled in a military buzz. With Camp Pendleton nearby, Cory figured he was an ex-jughead.

'I'm from the Bronx, you know,' he said.

She liked him immediately and was impressed when he said he had graduated from Bronx High School of Science. He seemed to warm toward her, too.

'You jumped the mugger and kicked the knife from his hand? Not many people could do that, you know,' he said, raising thick dark eyebrows that framed his rich brown eyes.

Embarrassed by his compliment, she bowed her head. 'Thanks, but I'm a black belt. I did what was necessary.'

'Really? When I was in the Marines, I took Kung Fu. Later, I studied Aikido. It comes in handy, you know. Where do you work out?'

She told him about the Karate Institute. They spent a few minutes comparing notes. It turned out he and Jennifer had studied with the same masters. Cory felt comfortable enough with him to express her feelings about the deputy.

'When I asked that rude, dopey deputy to collect the knife . . . can you believe she delayed? I hope she gets in trouble.'

'You bet. She came close to suspension. She said she'd intended to go after the knife after the interview, and you were too pushy. When she got to your garage, her search was futile.'

Cory's face reddened. 'She said I was pushy, huh? Her best defense is a good offense. After she asked a couple of questions, she and her partner made a cursory search of the parking lot flashing a beam for a moment or two. They didn't even walk around to search under cars, which is where my friend found it.'

He shook his head. 'She should have secured a crime scene. Had a bad day with her boyfriend maybe. Or her girlfriend.' He laughed at his feeble attempt at cop humor.

'The knife must be important. Can't forensics tell if there's blood on it and fingerprints? Tie it to another assault?'

'Oh, sure. Thanks to you, it's being processed as we speak.'

'But if the attacker wore gloves, wouldn't it be clean of fingerprints?'

Sergeant Lewis sketched a diagram of a knife similar to the one Cory had found. 'Maybe, but we look for other things. See here,' he pointed to the diagram. 'In a Buck knife where the hinge is, no matter how you clean and sharpen the blade, blood remains. Undetected to the eye, but not to forensic specialists, you know.'

37

Hamilton felt the muscles in his face tense. His jaw hurt from clenching. He could not remember being angrier. Always careful not to make mistakes, of all the rotten luck, he had picked the wrong person.

The loss of Buddy, his trusty Buck knife, upset him, made him feel as if he had lost a vital part of himself. To find a replacement, Hamilton phoned the store where he had purchased it. The clerk said it would have to be ordered, and requested his credit card and phone numbers. Hamilton slammed down the phone. He checked his billfold to make certain he had sufficient cash.

The telephone directory listed several stores specializing in knives. After several attempts he located a shop with a knife like Buddy in stock.

Deliberately dressed in stone-washed jeans, a San Diego Chargers sweat shirt and a blue baseball cap, his mode was similar to many locals.

He drove to the shopping mall and in an effort to find parking, circled the garage several times. Damn lot wasn't large enough.

He spied a car occupying two spaces and wanted to smash into it. Selfish bastard! Finally after ten minutes, a van pulled out and he zipped in.

On a sunny weekend afternoon, the shopping center was crowded. Must be one of those advertised sales, he reasoned. Weaving through the throng of strolling shoppers, he knocked into a woman with a shopping bag. The contents fell to the ground. Ignoring the mishap, he hurried by, feeling the burn of her eyes on his back. He was a man with a mission and she, a woman of no importance.

He found a clear path, sprinted to the store and bought a replacement for Buddy. Same size, same feel, but no history, but he would take care of that.

Knife in hand, he had an irresistible urge to call Paige, Dr. Cohen's patient. To avoid a phone trace, he planned to call from a safe place. A sale on portable cassette recorders at Sears gave him an idea. He bought a package of high quality cassettes and a top-of-the-line portable recorder. Next he visited a pet store featuring a variety of birds. No customers were present and the clerk, busy opening cartons in the storage room at the rear could not observe him. Hamilton recorded the singing canaries.

A quiet parrot on a perch in a cage cocked

his head and stared at him. Infuriated, Hamilton wanted to yank the iridescent green and purple plumage, but knew the parrot could cause a ruckus.

★ ★ ★

Hamilton drove to a quiet hotel in La Jolla. The only sound he heard was the surf smashing against the shore. He located a phone booth in a remote part of the lobby, his heart dancing in anticipation. After three rings, Paige picked up her phone.

★ ★ ★

'Hi. It's Rick. I enjoyed our talk and have been thinking about you. I . . . I wondered whether you thought of me, too. You did? That's nice. It makes me feel good. Guess what? I was so lonely . . . I just bought a few canaries to keep me company. They're so pretty and sing so sweetly. Can you hear them?' Hamilton played the cassette. Within minutes, she invited him to visit that evening.

He drove home, a frozen grin smeared across his face.

Arriving hungry, he opened packages of bologna and American cheese, removed four slices from each, slapping them on a slice of

217

white bread. On another slice, he spread a thick layer of mayonnaise and pickles.

Whistling, Hamilton changed into the black sweats reserved for his rendezvous, and tinted his hair. While waiting for the tint to take effect, he munched his sandwich, mayonnaise dripping on his chin. Delicious like Mom's, before she'd sent him away.

It took longer than usual for the tint to work. He scrubbed his hands and face. Smiling at his reflection, he attached the false beard and mustache and stashed a pair of gloves and his new Buddy into the deep pockets of his hooded sweatshirt. Glancing at his Rolex, he saw it was later than expected. Cursing, he whacked his fist on the table. To insure enough time for sleep, he must be swift.

Heading towards Paige's house, nausea and anxiety overcame him. Her invitation had come too easily, after only one preceding call. That hadn't happened before. Suppose the police were on to him. Maybe Dr. Cohen and Paige had conspired with them. He should have called Erin, whom he had already called four times. A sixth sense told him not to go.

38

'We waited until eleven-thirty. He never showed up,' Paige said.

'That's a shame. It took courage, Paige. You did well.'

'I wasn't afraid, because an unmarked police car has been patrolling my neighborhood since I notified the detective. And after the call, they were ready for him.'

'I'm glad you're safe.'

'What a dull life I've had. Until now.'

Cory shifted in her chair, waiting for her patient to continue.

'I put on a good show, pretending I was eager to meet him. When I heard canaries in the background, I thought he was at home, Dr. C. I expected the police to catch him. But later I learned he called from a La Jolla hotel phone booth. Canaries in the hotel? Isn't that curious? By the time the cops arrived, he was gone.'

'Maybe he was afraid the call would be traced. Some of the posh La Jolla hotels have private phone booths. I bet he had a tape of singing canaries so you'd think he was tender-hearted.'

'How clever!' She cleared her throat. 'Dr. C., I must tell you about Detective Sharpley. He's such a nice man and very concerned about me. It's comforting. Right away, he put my office building and house under surveillance just in case Rick or what-ever-his-name is, stalks me. I really like this detective. Imagine . . . my going for a police officer!'

'Why not?' Cory toasted her with a tea mug.

'I don't know. They have a bad image.'

'People in law enforcement are like everyone else, Paige. When I was a kid, we were taught the policeman was our friend.'

'Nowadays, how many kids believe that? The media show cops in a bad light.' Paige shook her head. 'Such corruption.'

'It's universal. Politicians, attorneys, big business. Not just cops. There are rogue cops and caring ones. Could be you're making excuses. If you like him, show him you're interested.'

'Oh, no. I couldn't do that.' She shook her head. 'I'd be too embarrassed.'

'What's the worst thing that could happen?'

'He could laugh at me.' Paige studied her brown loafers.

'That's doubtful. My guess is he'd be

flattered. Although it's possible he's not available.'

'How could I find out?' She blushed.

'You could ask him if his work conflicts with family life.'

Paige smiled. 'It's fun rehearsing it.' She bounced on her chair. 'Before therapy, life was dull. I was scared of failing on my job. Now, I'm doing better.' She fidgeted with the Phi Beta Kappa key on her necklace. 'When Rick, or what-ever-his-name is, first called me, I was thrilled, but my hopes were dashed. Now, after meeting the detective, I feel more alive.'

Paige had transformed from a serious executive to an elated co-ed. That she found the nasal, contemptuous detective attractive made Cory feel Grandma was right. There is a cover for every pot.

'Would you talk with a private investigator hired by one of the victims?'

'Of course.'

★ ★ ★

Later that afternoon as Cory headed out of the office, Ron called inviting her to his house for pizza and beer. Ecstatic, she scribbled his address and rushed from the office.

She took Interstate 5 north into crawling

221

traffic. Exiting the freeway at Lomas Santa Fe, an interminable signal light confronted her. She was in the middle of a long line of cars. Behind her was a shiny black Eldorado.

After a seven minute wait, cars inched then flowed only to stop for five minutes at the railroad crossing. Her fingers drummed a fast rhythm. She glanced at the clock. Five-twenty. Ten minutes late and six miles to go. Her sweaty palms gripped the steering wheel, whitening her knuckles. She became aware that her anxiety stemmed from anticipation that Ron, like her ex-husband, would be infuriated by her lateness. No, she thought. Ron was laid-back.

Finally, she breezed along the Coast Highway, a misnomer for a two lane street with traffic signals on every corner. On one side were railroad tracks and on the other, funky shops selling vintage clothing, antiques, Mexican fast food and pizza. A few miles further, where she headed, the beach hugged the road.

Cory noticed the same black car in the rear view mirror.

She rolled down the car windows and inhaled the moist ocean breeze. Waves splashed against the shore. Cyclists sped in the bike lane and runners ran on the foot path. Two young surfers clutching their surfing paraphernalia, started to cross the street. Laughing, hair-dripping, they appeared to have enjoyed a fine surf. Cory slowed down. They moved to the side and waved her on. She heard the screech of brakes and felt her heart leap as the black Eldorado nearly rammed into her car. The driver stopped at the side of the road. Cory wondered if he was as frightened as she. Breathing deeply, she watched the sun start a slow descent. The sky glowed in shades of pink and gold. She relaxed and pulled away.

Ron's street came up faster than she expected. She made a quick turn and glimpsed the black Eldorado pass.

Ron's cottage was one block from the beach. Its vintage, probably the same as its occupant's. A surfboard and wet-suit leaned against the side of the fence that separated his house from his neighbor's. A neat rim of grass encircled the fresh painted white building. From across the street where she parked, Cory heard the croon of Ron's saxophone play 'Coming Home Baby.' He played tenor sax the way Herbie Mann played flute. Exciting, energetic. Magical. She waited for him to finish then rapped on the door. Within seconds he opened it.

Cory stared at him. A sudden thud in the

pit of her stomach signaled self-reproach. What was she getting into? At thirty-six, he looked like a teenager in tattered jeans, T-shirt and bare feet. Cory felt like a maiden aunt visiting a nephew who surfed and played sax after school.

'Great sound, Ron.'

He smiled, locking the door behind her. They stood in the small hallway. 'Glad you're here.' He motioned her to follow him into the living room.

A splash of brightly colored oriental carpets on the polished hardwood floors suggested a decorator's hand. The living room served as a music room and library. On one side, floor to ceiling built-in shelving housed a huge collection of books. A perusal of the titles reflected Ron's eclectic taste: anthropology, history, science, medicine and literature. Shelves on the opposite wall contained built in video equipment, a stereo system with multiple speakers, a large collection of compact discs, tapes and record albums, all neatly arranged.

The saxophone leaned against the pillows of a cushy black leather couch facing a large coffee table and fireplace.

'Let me show you around. I've had the kitchen and bath re-done and ordered stained glass for the front window.'

He took her into the kitchen, an operating room look-alike, antiseptic with white walls and sparkling stainless steel appliances.

She traipsed behind him into the narrow hallway where color photos of Yosemite and the Grand Canyon covered the walls. Her son, Noah, would love the collection.

'I'll show you the bedroom later. I'm starved. How does mushroom and garlic pizza sound?' he asked, picking up the phone.

Cory nodded 'yes' and went to wash up. The bathroom was as immaculate as the kitchen. A green framed abstract painting on the wall echoed the bathroom rug. With a soft blue towel from a neatly folded stack, she dried her face and hands. Noticing the calluses on her fingers, she had an urge to go home and practice to her discs of Mongo Santamaria and Tito Puente. She hadn't played conga and timbales enough. What was she doing? Here she was in the home of a guy she was dying to go to bed with, and she'd choose to practice percussion instead?

A tube of lipstick on a shelf above the sink stunned her. She decided she wasn't ready to see Ron's bedroom. Not yet.

39

Hamilton had followed her until she made the damn turn. After circling the neighborhood for several minutes, he spotted her car parked on the street, but couldn't tell which house she'd entered, or if it was her house or a friend's. In this beach community there were too many people around for him to place the bomb on her car. No telling when a biker or runner would silently come upon him.

Later that night, he returned to that neighborhood, but her car was gone.

The pain in his left eye was excruciating. When he had his last bout of iritis, the doctor warned him to get immediate medical attention if the pain reoccurred or he could lose his vision. At eleven o'clock the only place to get help would be an emergency room in a major hospital.

He was wearing sweats and it appalled him to go to a hospital looking like a slob, but he was in a hurry. Without bothering to change, he grabbed his wallet and keys and rushed to his black Eldorado. He reached into his pocket and removed Buddy, kissed the knife and placed it in the glove compartment.

In a few minutes he appeared in the waiting vestibule of the same emergency room where he figured most of his victims were treated. Angry at having to wait with all the scum bags, he paced. How dare they ignore him! Didn't they realize who he was? A man of importance. A man with the power to deny prescriptions for treatment.

Hamilton paced non-stop and figured he did the equivalent of three miles. His back seared from the stares of patients. It seemed an eternity while the pain in his eye went unattended. He felt ready to explode.

'You damn fools. I could go blind before I get help from you. I warn you. You'd better take care of me now!'

A middle-age nurse with short curly hair and a round face hurried to him and said,

'Sir, everyone here has an emergency. It's first come. I'm sorry, but you'll be seen just as soon as possible. Is there anything I can do to make you more comfortable?'

'Yes. Get an ophthalmologist for my serious eye condition. A regular doctor won't do.'

'Ordinarily, you'd have to be seen by the emergency room physician who'd make that decision. I'll see if I can pull some strings on your behalf.' She winked at him.

That patronizing bitch. She's just trying to placate me, he thought.

* * *

Tanya Rifkin, R.N. had thirty years of experience and a knack for sifting out trouble makers. Some people just had big mouths, but this guy seemed dangerous. She shared her concern with an emergency room physician who respected her judgment.

'See if you can get Dr. Weinstock to come in tonight,' he said.

Harvey Weinstock, M.D. was more than happy to accommodate Tanya. He had the hots for her for twenty years.

Nurse Rifkin escorted Hamilton Pope to the darkened Ophthalmology Clinic, flipping on lights as they entered new corridors.

After seating Hamilton in an examining chair, the nurse blushed as Dr. Weinstock arrived.

40

Marge had a moral dilemma. Initially, she had loved her job, especially making new friends, and learning office skills. The spiffy environment was a pleasurable novelty to her. Co-workers, recognizing her ability to fix a computer when it went haywire, frequently asked for her help. It made her feel good about herself and her earnings enabled her to provide more for her children. They pitched in at home and seemed pleased and proud of their working parent. Marge had become more like the mothers of her children's friends. But as she learned more about the company, she became alarmed and ashamed of working there.

Marge's primary task was to enter personal data on mental health patients into the computer. At first she was robotic about it, but as her proficiency grew she began to read the entries with interest. She chose to think she did so out of boredom for she shunned TV talk shows that ripped the human psyche wide open. Now, she was privy to information that made her very uncomfortable. Especially today when she entered the data about her next door neighbors, a childless couple she had known for many years. She was grateful to them for having incorporated her children into their lives. The couple had seemed quite ordinary, but she would not be able to look them in the face again, for now she knew they were a pair of transsexuals struggling with serious problems.

She realized the couple could not be aware that their private lives were logged into a computer for all to see. It made her ill to think she worked for a company unconcerned about the potential damage such information could cause and whose sole purpose was profit driven.

During coffee break, she decided to pump one of her friends about it.

They filled green mugs emblazoned with the company's gold logo and strolled into the courtyard. Adjacent to a sweet scented jasmine bush, they seated themselves in the partial shadow of the glass and steel structure that housed Superior Health Care.

Marge cleared her throat. 'How do you feel reading about people's private lives on the computer?'

'It's kinda fun.' The woman squinted and inched away from the glint of the sun reflecting off the building.

'Fun?' Marge raised her eyebrows. 'What if

you found out something personal about someone you knew?'

The woman hesitated and shrugged her shoulders. 'I don't know. Depends on whether it was juicy.'

Marge had an epiphany. Just because the two women shared a divider between their workstations did not mean they shared values. She shook her head. 'This stuff is too available. It's not right!'

'Yeah. None of us would use a managed care program for mental health. I wouldn't want the world to know any of my secrets. Not that I really have any.' Turning her head away from Marge, she squirmed and stared into the distance.

'I haven't been here that long, but does anyone ever gossip about their entries?'

'Sure. When it's unusual, or someone we know, we do.'

Tightening her grip on the coffee mug, Marge thought the company's logo should be a dollar sign or better yet, a skull and cross bones.

41

A lone, white crane stood at the lagoon of the bird sanctuary near Harvey's house, catching Cory's attention as she drove to the jam session. The bird's solitary, majestic appearance triggered memories of Grace's regal quality. That sweet, tender young woman with so much to live for, gone forever because Cory had failed to warn her. A bitter stew of sadness, guilt and anger stirred inside her propelling her toward action. She had to avenge her patient. She considered who and wrestled with how.

The sun peeked out from behind wispy cirrus clouds in a blue sky. Cory filled her lungs with salt air. Observing the scene, she couldn't take pleasure in it because her mind focused on Grace. It was as though the lone white crane had sent a message. Consumed by her obsession, she was about to pass Harvey's house, but the fragrance of honeysuckle blossoming in his garden, beckoned her. Cory felt unable to enjoy anything while the murderer was at large, and wondered what it would take to forgive herself. She continued the self torment until she entered the house.

She joined Ron and Harvey seated on the floor of the music room waiting for the others.

'Heard there's a traffic snarl on the freeway,' Harvey said.

'A disabled car. Don't worry. No victims,' Ron said.

'I had the weirdest patient last night,' Harvey said. 'He was aggressive in the waiting room, threatening to cause danger if he wasn't examined right away. He could do it, too. Powerfully built.'

'Did anyone call security?' Ron asked.

'They were busy with a doc locked out of his car, but my old flame Tanya Rifkin placated this odd ball. He had a miserable case of iritis.'

'What causes that?' Cory asked.

'We're not sure. The theory is it's akin to arthritis, yet many patients don't have both. Anyway, this fellow was peculiar. He acted tough, like he was used to having his orders obeyed. Instead of black sweats, he should have been wearing a military officer's uniform.'

'Black sweats?' Cory asked.

'Yes.' Harvey glanced from the grandfather clock to his watch. 'I hope these guys get here soon. Let's warm up.' Plucking the strings of his bass, he said, 'You know, come to think of it, that guy's condition may be caused by hair tint or dye. In some places it was even darker than yours, Cory. I think he's covering up the gray because the front looked darker than the back. Strange guy! He had difficulty tolerating the exam.'

'How so?' Ron asked.

'During the examination, my face gets close to the patient's. He told me to watch my distance. Said I was encroaching on him. In fact, at one point when our heads nearly touched, he shouted, 'Stop violating me.' I asked him if he'd ever had an ophthalomological exam before. He got so angry, I thought he'd have a stroke. Asked me if I thought he was a fool. He told me his doctor up north had warned him to seek emergency treatment immediately if he suspected a relapse.'

'Is that all?' Ron asked.

'I gave him some samples and wrote a prescription. Tanya was so busy, she must have slipped up because I couldn't find his chart. When I'd asked his name, he was evasive. Hemmed and hawed, but he gave it to me reluctantly. He said he had no time to go to the pharmacy and demanded extra samples.' Harvey strummed his bass. 'Stuff's expensive. Many people request more to save money so that part wasn't too unusual, but I had the impression he was concealing something. Like maybe he didn't give me the correct name and was afraid the hospital pharmacy would ask for identification. Tanya swears she remembers bringing the chart in with him. Something's peculiar. He's a good candidate for psychotherapy.'

'Some people can't tolerate physical closeness. Lucky, he doesn't have to ride the New York City subway,' she said. 'Your patient prizes his own space, probably lives alone and doesn't trust others, Harvey. He may have been physically traumatized, so he builds himself up, flexes his muscles, acts fierce. Like a jungle animal, he's aggressive to protect himself.'

'The jerk was obnoxious.' Harvey shook his head.

'Abrasive like a porcupine,' Cory said.

'Dangerous?' Ron asked.

'Possibly.'

After the others arrived, they jammed. Unnerved by the tell-tale lipstick tube at Ron's place, and tired from pretending she was Mongo Santamaria on conga and Tito Puente on timbales, Cory couldn't get into the spirit. Struck by the description of the weird patient, she wondered how to find out where he worked.

42

Sergeant Sharpley sat opposite Cory in the consulting room sipping hot cocoa. His manner had softened since their first encounter.

'Listen, Ma'am. Many men tint or dye their hair. It could be a coincidence. This business of his discomfort when people get physically close to him could also apply to others. I think you're jumping to a conclusion.'

'There are too many coincidences here, Sergeant. This man also wore black sweats, just as the two victims described.'

'But the doctor said he was beardless.' The detective's nasality remained, suggesting a permanent condition. Paige may not have noticed or cared about it, but Cory was too picky.

'True. But couldn't he wear a fake beard and mustache when he does his number?'

Sharpley inhaled the hot apple cider. 'Yes, Ma'am,' he replied.

'Since we know several of his targets were patients monitored by Superior, if we found out this particular guy works there, we'd hit the jackpot.'

'Assuming he gave the hospital his correct identity, but you said his hospital chart was missing. A guy like you describe fits the FBI profile of someone ultra-cautious.'

'You just said I jumped to a conclusion, but you seem to consider it a possibility, Sergeant.'

'I don't want to give you the wrong idea, Ma'am. There's not enough to suggest that patient is the perpetrator.' Sharpley stared at Cory as though she had a loose screw, but it failed to shake her hunch. He crossed his legs and she noticed his frayed pants and brown suede, crepe sole shoes, a throwback from the year one. Detectives seemed fashioned from second hand thrift shops. Either they couldn't afford better or they chose crummy clothes because their work would ruin fine attire, she reasoned. Unlike well-tailored FBI agents, they didn't dress to impress. That appealed to Cory.

Ann buzzed. 'Detective Lewis here to join you.'

'Please send him in.'

Lewis entered, nodded a greeting and plopped on the couch.

'Can't you investigate Superior?' Cory asked.

'We've got to get a court order which means we must have sufficient cause. Sorry, but there's not enough here to justify it. All we know from the crime lab is that hair, fiber and semen found on the victims are from the same source,' Sharpley said.

'You also know from the results of the psychologists meeting, that all the victims were Superior's patients. Isn't that enough?'

'It may seem so to you, Ma'am, but we must stick to the law or we'll have the A.C.L.U. all over us,' Sharpley said.

'But, can't you do something? You have a glaring clue.' Cory flushed.

'We've spent much time and manpower sifting through everyone connected with the place Grace lived. Nothing. And her place of employment has been a massive operation for us — from maintenance crew, delivery people, clients and employees, plus others who work in the building. So far, we've found nothing incriminating. Not a shred.'

'If only Superior could be infiltrated. If we could . . . '

'Right, Doc. In unusual circumstances the department could set something up. If we stretch our resources we can arrange to place an undercover officer on the Superior managed care plan. If we do this, you can help by sending an enticing treatment request to Superior,' Lewis said.

'A decoy! Progress. Wait a second. I don't

know if that'd work because the mental plan is purchased by employers, unless some woman in the department is a spouse of an employee on Superior's program,' Cory said.

'I'll check around. If we can't find anyone, it may be possible to arrange with a company already on the plan to hire our agent and make her a subscriber,' Lewis said.

'If she lived in a beach area, it'd be ideal, but that's asking too much,' Cory said.

'We'd never set up an operation in the neighborhood where the officer lives, Doc. However, there's an interesting situation that could work. One of our men wants to break his lease on a beach cottage in Cardiff. Maybe we can take it over. Set up video surveillance there and . . . who knows.' He smiled.

'Way to go!' Cory clapped her hands.

'Don't hang your hopes on it, because it's not something we usually do, you know. We don't want to endanger an undercover agent. All I can say is we'll try to work something out, Doc. There is someone who'd fit the part. She's thirty-five, but looks in her early twenties. Blonde pony tail. Tough gal. We'd have to pull her off patrol.'

Uh-oh, Cory thought. Not the rude, incompetent deputy who had responded to the mugging. On the other hand . . .

'You'll remember her, Doc. She almost got suspended for not collecting the knife when you told her about it, you know. Consenting to be a decoy may be her redemption.'

'In the meantime there's nothing to prevent me from gathering information, Sergeant. I'm not an agent of the police.' She rested her chin in her palm.

'That'd be called posse comitatus. I don't know what you've got in mind, Ma'am, and I don't want to know.' Detective Sharpley covered his ears with his hands and grinned.

Not too bad a guy after all. Detective Lewis turned and winked at Cory as the two men left.

With the San Diego Police and the San Diego Sheriff working the case, Cory felt encouraged. In preparation for the project, she asked Ann to phone Betty's office to get the names of therapists whose patients were victims of the caller. Ann called the therapists and requested faxed copies of their sanitized treatment requests, as soon as possible. She spent most of her time on the phone while Cory busied herself with patients.

At the close of the day, Ann brought Cory a list of the results. Of the ten patients contacted by their therapists, all complied. Cory expected the faxed authorizations in a day or so to help her entice the suspect.

★ ★ ★

Later that evening she sat in her dining room opposite Ron. 'Now how in the world could I find out if Harvey's patient works at Superior?'

'Listen. You're only going on a hunch, nothing concrete, so the cops can't do anything about it. We can't ask Harvey to compromise his ethics and we don't know anyone working in hospital records.' He heaped his plate with the brown rice and stir-fry chicken, Cory had whipped up earlier. 'Mmm. This is good.'

'I've an idea. I can call Superior. I'd say while I was in the hospital emergency room I'd sat next to a man from Superior who dropped a gold Mont Blanc pen . . . '

'That reminds me . . . ' Ron reached in his pocket and pulled out a tube of lipstick. 'Here. I found this in my bathroom.'

'This isn't mine.'

'It isn't? I wonder whose . . . Lupe cleaned the day after you were there, but I don't think she wears make-up.'

'Maybe your decorator?' Cory said. She thought Ron's face reddened.

'I'd have seen it earlier. I'll ask Lupe.'

Cory couldn't pinpoint her sensation. Somewhere between relief and threat. Sharing friends wasn't a problem for her, but a special man — whoa!

'So what about the pen, Cory?'

'Oh, yeah, the pen. I'd say it was dropped by a stocky guy, about six foot with jet black hair. Most important, he was treated for an eye ailment. Didn't Harvey tell us that guy had a bloody eye? Well, maybe he still does.'

'I'm not sure how fast the medicine clears the red away, but, anyway, what if you're asked for your phone number?'

'I'll take a chance that I won't be asked, and if I am . . . I'm an out of towner checking out of my hotel, and would leave the pen in an envelope at the front desk.'

His eyes widened. 'What are you talking about? What hotel?'

'Olie. Olie Baxter from karate. His dad's hotel. Maybe Olie would be on duty. He'd do it or ask the front desk clerk to. If someone shows up, we'd have a description and maybe a signature because we'd ask the guy to sign for the pen.'

Ron stared at her. 'Get real, woman. Why would someone who didn't lose a pen, show up for it? You worry me, Cory. You're not thinking straight.' A strand of sandy hair fell over one eye. His recent haircut made him less boyish, and Cory more comfortable.

'I'm not counting on anyone showing up. I hope when I make the call, the receptionist will say something like, 'Oh, that must be Mr. Russell's,' or maybe drop some kind of clue. No risk in calling for an off chance to hit the jackpot.'

He shook his head. 'But as the detective told you, it could be a coincidence. You're grasping at straws.'

Maybe Ron was right, she thought. Desperation warped her reasoning.

'Didn't Harvey say his patient was terrified of physical closeness to people, Cory? Would such a person rape? That's damn close!'

'When he rapes he's the one in control. It's different from someone else closing in on him. In that situation he'd see the other person having the power.'

'I see. You may know your stuff, Cory, but sometimes you're a little nutty.' He patted her head.

Ron took another helping of food. She hoped she had made enough. His appetite was as big as Noah's.

'This is great. What's the magic ingredient?'

'Aphrodisiac. Want some more?' she asked, surprising herself.

'Do you think I need it?'

'Do you?'

'Want to find out?'

Cory smiled and grew moist. If Betty knew

what she was about to do, she'd be pleased. Everyone would be pleased, except for Grandma. When you make love, it must be just the two of you. No trespassing. Your mind must be free of ghosts, she thought.

They moved away from the table. Gently, he pulled her towards him and caressed her neck, his warm breath arousing her. Then . . . sweet, tender kisses . . . lingering. Their mouths opened in search of each other. Craving. Lifting her blouse, he unhooked the bra. His fingers softly skimmed like a feather across her breast. Better than all she fantasized. She savored every second of his tender touch.

'Cory, Cory! Oh, what you do to me!' His words, his passion made her quiver.

They drifted into the bedroom and lay on the bed, their lips softly touching. He placed a condom on the night stand. Cory's body grew sultry as a Savanna summer. Yearning to feel his bare chest on hers, she unbuttoned his shirt. He slipped off his clothes. Her outstretched arms beckoned. Casting aside all doubts, she wrapped her limbs around him and clung to his firm body, excited by his smooth skin where a faint, clean scent of soap lingered.

Was sex intense because it was fresh, and she had waited so long? Or was Ron an incredible lover? Their chemistry, like their music, was pure synergy.

Sex with him was a symphony. Sweet sounds of passion . . . of harmony and rhythm . . . a slow rising. Passion growing deeper, more intense towards a crescendo. Sensations took the place of thoughts.

Cory had invited the symphony to play in her bedroom. The ghosts of her past had no tickets.

His eyes were closed. Caressing the outline of his face and body with her finger, she chased away the censors in her head. Enjoy the moment. Capture the memory. Store it like warm summer sunshine on a blustery winter day. Savor it like dessert.

Ron read her mind, 'Wow. What a fantastic dessert you served.'

'Hey, wait a minute, you brought dessert.' She giggled.

'For next time.'

The digital clock blinked 7:10 and they were due at Harvey's by 8:00. They had time for a quick, playful shower, but no passionate encore. Toweling off, she realized she had been distracted from her obsession. Ron was the best antidote.

★ ★ ★

Later, while waiting to jam, Cory asked Harvey if he remembered anything else about his strange patient with iritis.

'Why are you so interested, Cory? Don't you see enough odd patients?'

'Actually, not as odd as this character. He fits the description of the serial rapist. If you could provide anything more about him without compromising your ethics, it may help.'

Harvey paled, his complexion taking on the color of his hair. 'Like what?'

'Name, rank and serial number.'

'Well, he was evasive. Reluctantly gave me his name. Bet it was fictitious because when I called him by it, he looked puzzled. And we never did find his registration form. The hospital can't bill without it. What a sleaze! Let's have some fun with this and I'll drop a clue about his moniker when we play.'

They spent the evening jamming. The percussionist reminded Cory of someone who played with Stan Getz years ago. Carrying the rhythm with professional style, he nodded to her to take a solo. She made it short. He smiled at her. When Harvey took his bass solo, he thumped the melody of 'My Buddy.'

43

While waiting on the phone for Superior's response, Cory had to listen to a barrage of annoying radio commercials piped onto their line. She wished they played calming music instead. She also wished frustrated patients would abandon managed care and its false promises. First, they would have to feel empowered and without therapy it wasn't likely. Finally, a menu of choices came on, but none seemed appropriate. She pushed the number for Case Managers Southern California Division.

'Mr. Pope here.'

Cory hesitated, remembering his name from the last call, afraid he would recognize her voice as that of the trouble-maker. She hung up, redialed and pushed the number for Case Managers, Northern Division. A futile exercise, she reached voice mail.

On impulse, Cory called the karate studio and asked to speak with Olie or Jennifer.

'Yo, Cory. Olie here. Come on over. Jen and I are finishing a meeting.'

Cory hopped into the car and drove the short distance.

The door to the office was ajar and she entered.

Olie was behind the desk and Jennifer sat at his side. 'Have a seat, Cory,' he said. 'What brings you here this time of day?'

She plopped down on a futon facing them. 'There's something on my mind. Do you remember anything more about the guy who attacked you? Something you haven't told the police?'

'Christ! I don't want to go over this again.'

'I'm sorry, I don't want to tug at your scabs, but the sooner he's found, the sooner you'll heal.'

Jennifer glanced at Olie.

'Maybe something came back to you, Jen. Think. It could help the investigation,' Olie said, shrugging his shoulders.

She stared at the ceiling. 'Man, he was strong like he pumped iron. His hair looked like it was tinted with shoe polish. It was too black for his complexion. I'm not sure, but his beard and mustache might have been false. He had small evil looking dark brown eyes. He wore a black sweat suit.' She closed her eyes as though conjuring up a memory. 'Wait a minute,' she continued, 'Let me see. Actually he wore two sweat shirts, one on top of the other. The one on top was bulky with a hood and deep pockets. It must be where he kept the knife.' She opened her eyes and shuddered. Olie reached for her hand.

Cory wondered about the doctor who had attended Jennifer, but figured Jennifer had no interest in him. She had more in common with Olie.

'You spoke to him a few times. Was there anything distinctive about his speech?'

'For instance?'

'An accent or funny expression? Did he seem well educated, intelligent, average or dull?'

Jennifer rubbed her temples, as if trying to massage her memory. 'Yeah, I do remember. He spoke like he was showing off, trying to impress me with big words.'

'Did you tell that to the detective?'

'I don't remember.'

'Look. Something's come up to help us, Jennifer. One of the victims hired a private detective named Harry Hornsby to be her bodyguard and to help in the investigation. Is it okay if he gets in touch with you?'

'Yeah, sure.'

Jennifer's primary interest in the caller had been for sexual gratification, so she hadn't paid much attention to nuances. The intensity of her sexual drive was a subject for her and Betty to explore and not Cory's trail to track. She marveled at their sexual freedom, but did not envy it. She cautioned herself, afraid her newly liberated passion, could distort things, too.

Cory explained her plan.

Jennifer gawked at her, probably figuring she had turned into a real screwball.

Olie seemed pensive. 'Let me call there, Cory. They don't know who I am. I'll be working the hotel front desk tonight, anyway.'

Cory, surprised at his willing reaction, reached for a blank sheet of note paper from his desk. She scrawled Superior's number and handed it to him. 'Thanks, you two,' she said.

'I'll call you at home and tell you how I made out,' Olie said.

'I'd better get back to work,' Cory said.

Back at her office, she found a message from Mallory requesting an appointment.

Mallory answered on the first ring. 'Thanks for calling me back so soon, Cory.'

'Where are you, Mallory?'

'Staying with friends in Encinitas until I find a place for me and the dog. My cousin was a big pain in the butt, but she gave me her Rotweiller. She didn't want him anymore, anyway.'

'How's three, today?'

'Cool. I'll be there.'

★　★　★

When Mallory arrived, Cory noted the absence of her previous pained facial expression, but she appeared emaciated.

'How's your appetite?'

'Not great. Cousin Lou's a lousy cook and she wouldn't let me in the kitchen. I don't think I could have eaten, anyway.'

'No lectures. You know the importance of nutrition.'

'It's improving. My roomies and I take turns cooking.'

'How's your sleep?'

'Not great, but better. At least the AIDS test was negative and the pill they gave me at the hospital to stop me from getting pregnant worked, but I still get nightmares.'

'In time, it'll stop.'

'Yeah, when they string the bastard up by his balls.'

'I've got good news, Mallory. The parents of one of the victims hired a private detective to help find the rapist. Would you be willing to talk to him?'

'Of course. When?'

'Soon. Oh, there's something I want to ask you, Mallory. Did the rapist have a knife?'

'What? A knife? Oh, man!' She gazed at the

wall as though it was a movie screen of her past, horror written on her face. A few moments passed. She sighed and her facial muscles relaxed.

'If he had a knife, he didn't have time to use it on me. After he raped me, I hit him so hard, he just clutched his gut.' Her mouth formed a slight smile of satisfaction. She rubbed her forehead. 'Let's see. When he was on top of me . . . I think I felt something heavy in his sweatshirt pocket. Could've been a knife. I don't know.' She shook her head. 'Hell. I remember it like it happened today.' She shivered.

'Do you recall anything distinctive about him?'

'Huh?' She picked at her cuticles.

'Maybe he had a tic or a funny speech pattern. Or an accent.'

'No, but like I told you, he seemed awful smart. Sometimes he used big words like a college professor. Why are you asking me these questions now?'

'I'm playing detective. A friend of mine was raped and slashed and I think it may have been the same guy.'

Mallory covered her ears with her hands. 'Slashed? Is she dead?'

'She's okay, now.'

'A maniac! There's a maniac on the loose.'

She rose from her chair and paced, gripping her elbows.

'I didn't mean to make this worse for you, Mallory. I'm sorry.'

'It's okay. I know you're trying to help me. Believe me, I thought about your rape and was glad you told me. It made me feel close to you. Like we got something in common. It's super that you recovered from it. I think about that a lot and it helps. It shows it could happen to anyone. And now your friend! This is too, too much. And my cousin blamed me. Just what I needed, huh!'

'It's good you left. You don't need the added burden of a guilt trip. When she blamed you, what did you say?'

'Just like you showed me, Cory. I told her it hurt when she blamed me. I tried to be assertive but it didn't work with her. She never heard me, so I took off.'

'It's unhealthy to be with people who make you feel bad, Mallory.'

'When we'd stopped therapy, I was ready. I was feeling good about myself, but now, it doesn't take much for me to hate myself and get angry.'

'One day soon, no one will be able to shatter the good image you have of yourself. This is a set-back. What you've gained in therapy can't be taken from you. It'll be restored when you feel safe again.'

'Cousin Lou told me I take things the wrong way and like to feel bad.' Tears welled in her eyes.

'You *are* sensitive, but I don't believe you choose to feel bad. You have the choice to stay in a difficult situation or not. And leaving it shows you're taking care of yourself.'

'I know I did the right thing by leaving. My friend is letting me hang out at her place for a while. I'm sharing her room. It's crowded, but her roommate's cool. So far, anyway. I'm not afraid because there's four girls. They've got a two-bedroom house with a yard for the dog.'

'Maybe Cousin Lou isn't so bad after all, Mallory. Maybe she gave you her dog not because she didn't want him anymore, but because she cares about your safety.'

'Nah, not Cousin Lou. I don't think so.' Her head shook as fast as a mechanical toy.

'She laid a guilt trip on you.'

'Yeah, it sucks.'

'Consider that she gave you her dog. It's hard parting with a pet, a best friend. Also it's possible she didn't want you in the kitchen because you were a guest. Maybe she wanted to take care of you.'

Mallory rocked back and forth, tears streaming down her cheeks.

Cory handed her a tissue. 'Maybe you sensed that when you chose to stay with her.'

Mallory paused. 'Could be she really does love me, but shows it all wrong!' She smiled, dabbing her face with the tissue.

★　★　★

Cory arrived home to a phone call from Ron inviting her to meet him at the theatre for a six o'clock movie. Accepting, she checked her watch and raced to freshen up. As she toweled her face, the phone rang.

'Yo, Olie here. You put up with a lot, dealing with those managed care places, Cory. Computers run the phones. Frustrating. If I were a patient, I'd be so disgusted, I'd give up.'

'Maybe that's the design. And why suicide hot-lines are busy. Anyway, did you speak with anyone, Olie?'

'I finally got through to a live person, a woman, who said no one named Buddy works there and no one fits the description you gave me. One man uses eye drops, but she wouldn't give me his name. I got her to ask him if he lost something in the emergency room. A nice lady, she called me back at the hotel. I pretended to be a guest. Man, was she upset. She said the man denied being in any emergency room and was so mad at her that she was scared she'd lose her job. So that's it.' Olie sounded disappointed.

A chill of excitement rushed up Cory's spine. 'You did great, Olie. The guy sure overreacted. If he isn't the one, why would he be so angry at someone for asking such an innocent question, right?'

'I guess so. What next? I want to help.'

'You are. By the way, how's it going with you and Jen?'

'We've become closer since this happened to her. She trusts me.'

'Of course. Why wouldn't she?'

'Yeah. You and Ron are closer too. I got the vibes.'

'I wish I could play them.'

'Huh?'

'Nothing, just a play on words. Vibes as in vibraphone, one of my favorite musical instruments. Got to go. I'm meeting Ron at the movies.' She hung up and headed out.

★ ★ ★

Ron waved at her with tickets in his hand and a frown on his face. Pointing to the ticket line curled around the block, he said, 'I got here early to avoid this.'

'Must have had great reviews.'

'I don't go by them, Cory. I make up my own mind.'

'Me too. I prefer foreign films or the old black and white.'

'That's my woman.' He squeezed her hand.

Several times during the movie, they glanced at each other, giggling and agreed that it was the most hyped and worst pieces of idiocy.

Ron followed Cory home for veggie burgers.

They parked their cars side by side in her garage. She deactivated the security system and started dinner.

'We've been had with that dumb flick.' Ron pouted, setting the table.

His facial expression reminded her of a little boy. She stifled a laugh.

'Do you think the rapist realized my patient's phone had a trap and got cold feet?'

Ron groaned. 'I suggested a movie because I thought it would be get you off that kick for awhile.'

'Very thoughtful,' she said, zapping the veggie burgers. She sliced the knife into tomatoes and cucumbers and chopped vigorously.

'You have a hard time thinking of much else. It's getting to me. Cory,' he scowled.

'I'm sorry.'

'Well, in answer to your question, yes, he may be worried that the cops are on to him.'

After dinner they sat on the couch. Ron popped open a can of beer and took a few swigs. He peeled off his boots and stretched his long legs on the coffee table. 'Is it okay to put my feet up?'

'Sure. Starting tonight, I'll follow the Asian custom and have visitors leave their shoes at the door, like at the studio.'

'It'll be the only thing here that's Asian.' He waved his hand at Cory's collection of African masks and artifacts. 'You'll introduce a new continent.'

'What about the occupant? You wouldn't mistake me for anything else, would you?' Curling her legs on the couch, she snuggled next to him.

'No, but so what?' He put his arm around her and she rested her head on his shoulder.

'So I was uncomfortable growing up in a family and neighborhood where I was the only one with Asian features. Some people had certain expectations of me. Stereotyped me. I hated that.'

'I'm no shrink, Cory, but we see ourselves with our own eyes, not the image others have of us. Your appearance may not have seemed as unusual to others as it did, or maybe still does to you.' He caressed the outline of her face with his finger. 'I'm sorry you had such a hard time. Where I grew up in northern California, there were many Asian Americans. I had no thoughts of racial distinction. I just see you as a beautiful person. A beautiful woman. A woman I'm nuts about.'

'Thanks, Ron.' She kissed his soap scented cheek.

'Which one of your parents was Asian?'

'My mother. I never talk about her because I don't remember her. She took off to join the Tokyo Symphony when I was three years old. Left me with my father and his parents. Never returned. Made no contact.'

'Man, what a bummer!'

'My grandparents provided a good home life, but I felt socially alienated. My childhood was plagued with stupid questions and stares. You have no idea!'

Ron hugged her. 'It's hard for me to relate to that. I'm sorry for you.'

'I don't want your pity, Ron. Just your understanding. There's a gap in my heritage which I can't fill. My mother left me no legacy apart from her Asian genes. I've tried making Asian friends, but they reject me. They're proud. Reserved. My efforts put them off. Probably the same way my family's efforts did to my mother. She didn't understand their openness.'

'But you've got friends now. The Asians don't know what they're missing.' He ran his fingers through her thick hair. 'Maybe something happened that prevented your mother from reaching you.'

'No. My father runs into her on rare occasions at a concert abroad. She's a selfish woman. Wasn't willing to sacrifice for the sake of her child. He said she felt my chances for a good life were better with him since in those days, Eurasians were held in contempt in Japan, as would she, the mother of such a child. My dad tried to soften my hatred of her, but couldn't. Perhaps because of his own. I've always wanted to believe I was the only good thing salvaged from his brief marriage.'

'I bet you're a great mother.'

'I'd like to think so. My grandmother was the best role model.'

He buried his lips in Cory's hair. 'Your hair is as soft as feathers.'

'Feathers?' She pulled away to look at him. 'That reminds me about the canaries. What a pitch, making women feel sorry for him because birds were his only friends.'

Ron drew back, glaring at her. 'What? There you go again! I can't say anything to you without you jumping to that damn case.'

'I'm sorry, but it's on my mind all the time. I've got to . . . '

'You're obsessed, Cory. You must know it's unhealthy.'

'I can't stop until he's caught.'

'You'll drive yourself nuts. You're relentless. My patience is wearing thin,' he mumbled.

'I've got to deal with this my own way. Please indulge me, Ron.'

'Okay,' he sighed. 'What's on your mind?'

'I think he called from a phone booth because he was afraid his call would be traced. He wanted his target to think he was at home with his only friends. Canaries.'

'Very likely. The police are listening to you, now. Why not leave it to them?' He yawned. 'Sorry. I was on call last night.'

Cory noticed the red streaks in his eyes. 'Looks like you need rest.'

He tossed the can in the recycle bin and shoved his feet into his boots. 'I've got to be up early in the morning. The decorator is coming to go over my bedroom.'

Cory felt giddy, coughed a nervous laugh and wondered about the decorator's age, what she was like, and what they would do in his bedroom. Was it *her* lipstick in his bathroom? Was she a threat to Cory?

'I'll see you tomorrow at Harvey's,' he said.

Cory watched him jog to his car. He had

seemed too eager to leave. She started to fret over the possibility of his involvement with someone else, but caught herself. There was too little to go on.

She inserted a CD into the stereo and danced to the rhythm of Cal Tjader's 'Black Orchid' as she cleaned the kitchen. Cory replayed the disc, rolled out the Conga drum and accompained the music. Working up a sweat, she had a great practice session. A respite from thinking about who would be the next victim and when.

44

Erin had not made an appointment, nor returned Cory's call. No telling how she would handle 'Patrick.' It was her prerogative to quit therapy, but Cory's responsibility to terminate in a professional manner. Cory vowed not to be conciliatory, nor allow manipulation. She started to compose a letter and decided to phone again, half hoping for no response, but a weak voice answered, 'Hello.'

'This is Dr. Cohen. Are you okay?'

'No. I planned to ring you today. I'm crying a lot and haven't slept well. Seldyn took Megan for a few days. I simply couldn't cope with her.'

She gave Erin an appointment for that afternoon.

★　★　★

Cory was engrossed in charting, when Ann startled her.

'Erin's early. Looks like she needs your attention.'

Cory nodded and went to greet the young woman.

Erin had dark circles under her eyes. Her pallor matched her white jeans and sweater. The usual beautiful shiny red hair, was now lackluster and tied back. She looked ill.

'It's been a miserable time for me. I'm sorry I marched out of here in such a huff. Soon after, I realized you meant well, indeed. Patrick hasn't rung up since I told you about him. I sometimes wonder if I'd imagined him just to make myself think a lad cared about me.' She glanced away, tears streaming down her face.

Cory touched her shoulder. This time, Erin didn't shrug her off.

'You received those calls, Erin. You didn't imagine them. He called another woman who reported it to the police. They put a trap on her phone, but he'd used a public phone. He made a date with her, but didn't show up. We think he suspects he's in danger.'

'I suppose I ought to ring the police so they can trace my calls, too.'

'Splendid.' Cory scribbled Detective Sharpley's number on a slip of paper and handed it to her.

Erin agreed to learn coping methods for depression and loneliness. The session made a fine start.

45

rage, Hamilton felt all his
. How would anyone in the
m know he worked for
ı he had filled out the
n, had he automatically
__ ...s employer? Could he have
scribbled the name Buddy in place of his
own? Had the nurse noticed it before he
destroyed the form in the examining room?
Was someone else from Superior recently
treated in the emergency room for an eye
ailment? Finding the answer to that last
question was possible.

Hamilton sauntered into the personnel
office and examined forty files of his
co-workers, searching for medical problems.
No one questioned his activity. Why would
they? He was in charge. With mischievous
delight, for several hours he scrutinized the
files. Engrossed, he'd almost forgotten his
mission. There were no reports of eye disease
for any staff member. The records were
current, but did not include minor emergency
room situations.

Hamilton returned to his office, closed the

door and tidied his desk. How dare that woman ask him if he'd lost something in the emergency room and if his nickname was 'Buddy.' What impertinence! He wouldn't tolerate it. Hamilton was glad he had shouted at her and gleefully watched her tremble. For the moment, she had satisfied him with an apology.

'Don't you think Buddy is an incongruous name for me?' he had asked, laughing at her grim face.

Now, he steamed, worrying that Marge Abbott suspected he was the man at the hospital. She knew too much about him. Once he had overheard her speaking on the phone. She said she respected Mr. Pope's attention to details and his willingness to work late, but found him cold, calculating and uncomfortable to be around. What audacity! He would not let her get away with making him a subject of gossip. He summoned her to his office.

Hamilton heard a weak tap on his door. Marge Abbott, a plain looking middle-aged woman stood at the door bowing her head. He knew she was a widow with teenage children.

'Ms. Abbott. I'm sorry to interrupt your work, but I'm concerned about the question you asked me. Surely there must be someone else here who had an eye irritation requiring emergency treatment. I would like you to locate this employee so the valuable pen can be reclaimed.'

★　★　★

Marge wondered why he made such a big deal out of nothing. 'Mr. Pope, I've already asked the entire staff and you are the only one taking eye drops.' She nodded her head toward a tiny bottle on his desk. 'Carol over in our northern California section takes them for dry eyes when her contacts bother her, but she's not using them now and she hasn't been to emergency. Besides, the person was identified as a man.'

★　★　★

'Thank you, Ms. Abbott. You may go now.'

Puzzled, he counseled himself, a tiny tincture of logic entering his mind. He'd had a legitimate reason for his emergency care. Why should it matter if he had given his name and employer when he signed in?

Preservation of his privacy was crucial because he suspected one day a researcher would peruse medical records for some project and match his name with the

267

defaming psychological records of his youth. Someone could dig dirt about him for a nefarious purpose. Computers stored information available to anyone with technical skill. One day he would find a way to purge his record.

Hamilton was mystified as to why any one would try to find him at Superior when he hadn't lost a Mont Blanc pen.

A sense of urgency resurfaced near the close of the day. Hamilton could kill a few birds with one stone. Hah! The image made him laugh and he had a hard time composing himself. Fortunately, his door was closed and the noise from the air conditioner masked his laughter. He reached into his leather attache case and pulled out his Buddy. Buddy needed a history.

He scanned the newspapers for the movie calendar and located a convenient theater featuring a Richard Widmark film festival at five-thirty. An avid fan of the star, he had seen the four scheduled films many times.

Wearing a smile, so as not to frighten her, he summoned Marge Abbott, again. This time she stood at the door, poised, her face made up and her hair, usually drawn back into a bun, now draped loosely over her shoulders. He wondered if she was trying to seduce him. She must find him attractive.

What woman wouldn't? But why the hell would he want her? That hag wasn't even good for a fast fuck!

'Ms. Abbott, I would appreciate it if you can work a bit of overtime this evening. We're behind in sending out treatment authorizations. It'll probably take a few extra hours.'

'Yes, Mr. Pope. I'm happy to help. I'll just call my kids and have them send for a pizza for dinner. They'll like that.'

'That sounds like a good idea. Why don't you order one, too?' From his fine leather wallet he removed three crisp ten dollar bills and handed them to her. 'This should cover it.'

Marge Abbott looked surprised. 'Thank you, Mr. Pope. This is quite generous. When shall I tell my children to expect me?'

'You could complete this in about two hours,' he said handing her a stack of papers. 'Finish today's work first before you start on it. I'll be leaving early this evening, but the security guard will be around. Ask him to escort you to your car.'

At the end of the day, Hamilton left the office and rode down in the crowded elevator with his office workers. He nodded and said, 'Have a good evening.'

On his drive home he stopped at the box office and paid for the movie ticket with a hundred dollar bill. The young cashier summoned the manager to make change.

When Hamilton entered the theater, the usher tore the ticket and handed him the stub. Hamilton carefully slipped it into his pocket.

A few minutes later, making certain he wasn't seen, he exited from the rear entrance. Racing home, he rapidly changed into sweats, running shoes and a ski cap. He attached his beard and mustache and stuffed Buddy in his pocket.

Hamilton drove his black Eldorado to Superior. Parking one street from the building, he strung his keys on his shoelace and then jogged to the office. From observing the ritual of the security guard, he knew when it would be safe to enter the building and his office suite. Glancing at his Rolex, he dashed into the building and up the stairs.

He yanked out Buddy. The feel of the metal object in his hand thrilled him. Fondling it, his penis became erect. He sizzled. He went to the water cooler, drank two cups of water, then sneaked into Ms. Abbott's office.

★   ★   ★

At six-thirty the next morning, Hamilton arrived at his office building. Yellow crime

270

scene tape sealed off the entrance. A uniformed police officer posted outside, asked for Hamilton's identification.

Hamilton feigned a look of surprise as he withdrew his business card. The officer clicked his pen, flipped a page and scribbled on his clipboard.

'What's going on here, officer?' Hamilton asked.

'The building is tied up now. It's pretty messy in there. We've got a crew investigating a homicide. The sergeant will want to talk to you.'

'A homicide? Who?'

'In a minute, sir. Your home address and phone number, please.'

Hamilton had a cramp in his stomach that he identified as nervousness. He clutched his necktie as he gave the information. 'Now tell me who . . . '

'Marge Abbott, a member of your staff. Last evening.' The officer waved to another cop who marched toward them from the doorway.

The second cop skimmed the patrol officer's notations. 'Sorry, sir, I need a preliminary statement from you. When did you see Marge Abbott last?'

'Yesterday afternoon, around five just before I left. I'd asked her to finish some

271

work and stay a few hours longer than usual. I suggested she order a pizza. Oh, my! Could she have been killed by the pizza man?'

'How long was she employed here?'

'Personnel would tell you exactly.'

'Her marital status?'

'Widowed, I think. Personnel would know.'

'Homicide detectives will want additional information from you.'

'Where do we do this?' Hamilton expected an interview at the northern division sub-station. Several months ago, after work, he had watched women exit the community center gym adjacent to the station and had considered tailing one he had seen a few times. The way that bitch flaunted her body in a tight leotard, so haughty and over confident ... he'd longed to fix that. Stepping into her large, silver Mercedes, she acted as if she owned the world. Once, as he waited outside with his car windows down, he heard her speak to another woman. Both had snooty South African accents. Mrs. Prissy was too damn self-possessed. He wanted to show her who was the mighty one, but he had to be careful since a nosy detective could be working late.

'Since we can't use your office now, we could go to your home, or if you don't mind, we can transport you to police headquarters downtown now, if it's convenient. We'd appreciate your cooperation.'

'Of course. Whatever is necessary, but I'd prefer my own car.'

'Sure. Here's a card with the address and a daily report number. When you arrive, if you don't find parking, please use a meter and show this to the desk clerk. He'll direct you to the fourth floor. Do you know how to get there?'

Hamilton studied the address on the card and nodded. 'I'm on my way.'

He drove downtown in heavy traffic, but didn't mind. He was in no hurry. Hamilton pressed the button on his radio for local news. No mention of the homicide. He reviewed the events of last evening. When he went back to the office last night, he'd seen the empty pizza box which she had eaten before six. The cleaning crew usually arrived at eight. Someone must have discovered the body between eight and eight-thirty. Hamilton reasoned his alibi covered him from five-thirty to nine-thirty. The police would know Marge was murdered after the pizza arrived somewhere between six and eight-thirty, while he was at the movies. He had tried to make sure the cashier would remember him. Hamilton hadn't seen anyone when he sneaked out of the theatre. With no obvious motive, why would he be a suspect?

Within fifteen minutes Hamilton exited the freeway on Tenth Avenue. He rolled down the window and drove towards Broadway through a seedy neighborhood of dirty, disheveled street people. The stench of urine soaked streets made him gag. He closed the window and flicked on the air conditioner.

Reaching Broadway, he signaled left and soon arrived at the blue and gray eight-story building housing the San Diego Police Department on Broadway and Fourteenth. The parking area was full. Finding a space on the street next to a two hour meter, he fed it four quarters.

Hamilton strolled into the building. A line of people formed at the reception desk. He waited, reading a newspaper he had found on a chair. There was no mention of the murder. He figured it was probably reported after the paper went to press. With a handkerchief, he wiped the newsprint off his sweaty palms. Again, he rehearsed his statement to the investigators.

The long wait made him anxious. Feeling feverish, he strolled to the water cooler and drank several gulps. Certain that people stared at him, he wanted to leave, but knew it was not prudent. With time passing, his impatience grew. Hamilton tapped his foot rapidly and was about to object to the long detention when his turn came. He had to show his driver's license. Slipping it from his wallet, his hands shook. After making a notation, the clerk gave him a clip-on visitor's pass and directions to the fourth floor.

Homicide was located next to Sex Crimes. Hamilton's throbbing head felt warm to his touch. Was it from fever or nerves? Approaching the room where police slave to root out people like him, his heart quivered. He forced himself to suppress the excitement he felt from the thrill of being right there under their stupid noses without them having a clue. He grinned at the irony.

A plainclothesman escorted him to a back room where two men about his age, sat at a large table, tape recorders in front of them. One was a large man, the other small. Mutt and Jeff, Hamilton mused.

The men, neckties loosened and jackets slung on back of their chairs, rose and introduced themselves as homicide investigators. The tall man said, 'Thank you for coming. Sorry to inconvenience you. We need to get formal statements from everyone connected with Ms. Abbott.'

'No trouble. I am her supervisor and Vice President of Superior Managed Care Corporation.'

'What are your duties?' asked the tall detective.

Hamilton described his work and the organizational set-up.

The short detective asked, 'Did she usually work overtime?'

'No. But we're behind in our work now because of new contracts.'

'Did anyone else know she was working late?'

'She told me she would call her children. I really don't know if she had informed anyone else.'

'Who were her friends at work?'

'I'm not privy to personal matters of my staff.'

'Do you know anything about her family life? Ex husbands or boyfriends?'

'As I've said . . . wait. I do know she has, uh, had children, because she told me she'd have to phone them to tell them she'd be late. Oh-my-oh-my.' Hamilton put on his most concerned face and shook his head. 'Terrible. Absolutely awful. I feel responsible. I asked her to work late because we're overloaded with work. Oh, that poor woman. If she hadn't worked late — just dreadful. I'd never have asked her if I thought it wasn't safe. Security guards are on frequent patrol. She had a number to call for someone to escort her to her car. Wait a minute! Maybe. Oh, no!'

'What is it, Mr. Pope?'

'We've changed the security company. Perhaps one of them . . . ?'

'We're investigating everyone connected with the building and her.'

'I'll speak to the CEO, Mr. Russell, about improving security, and changing the company again. This is horrible.'

'Was anyone else aside from her in the office when you left?'

'I don't know. I can't recall if lights were on in other offices.'

'What did you do after you left the office last night?'

'I've been working very hard and needed recreation, so I went to the Richard Widmark film festival at the Guild.'

'When did you get there?'

'Let's see. It started at five-thirty, so close to five-fifteen.'

'How long were the movies?'

'About an hour and half each. There were four films, but I only saw three. I got tired and went home, had a snack, watched the news on TV, and went to bed.' Hamilton began to worry that they considered him a suspect. His knees shook under the table.

'What time did you get home?'

'A little before eleven.'

'Did anyone go with you?'

'No.'

'What were the films you saw?'

'*Kiss of Death, Street With No Name,* and *Road House.*'

'Who else was in them besides Richard Widmark?'

Hamilton paused. He began to sweat as he remembered vividly the scene in which Richard Widmark pushes an old woman in a wheel chair down the steps. Unforgettable. He loved it so much he replayed it in his head many times. 'Let's see. In *Kiss of Death,* Karl Malden, Victor Mature and Mildred Dunnock were featured. Cops and robbers, filmed in New York in the forties. Do you want to hear about the others?'

'No.' The detective smiled. 'Did you enjoy them?'

'Yes.'

'Do you know if they're still playing, maybe I'll catch them when I'm off duty.'

'I'm sorry, I don't know, but I think you'd enjoy them.'

'Do you happen to have the ticket stub?'

'What?' Hamilton's stomach churned. 'I can't believe I'm a suspect.'

'This is just routine.'

'Well, I'd have no reason to save the stub,

278

but I'll look for it. When may I return to work?'

'Our crime lab people should be finished later in the day. I'd say, tomorrow.'

'Are we done?' He pushed himself out of the sticky chair.

'No.' The detective motioned him to sit.

'Did Ms. Abbott have any problems at work?'

'Problems? She was a competent worker.'

'With co-workers. Did she have problems with them?'

'Not to my knowledge.'

'Did you have any relationship with her outside of work?'

Offended by the accusation, Hamilton's face flushed. 'Most certainly not. I'm an executive officer and don't believe in socializing with anyone from work, especially a subordinate. You'll probably find out more about her from the staff.' He heard his voice crack.

The short detective handed him a card and said, 'If you think of anything, please call. We appreciate your taking the time to come here.'

'Of course. I'll let you know if I find the stub.'

Hamilton drove home, confident he'd outwitted the police. They had thanked him for coming. Or was that to put him off? He dismissed that idea. If they'd noticed the sweat on his brow, they'd probably figure it was hot in that damn room. He yearned to shower and change his damp clothes.

Hamilton was happy he had chosen a condo in a complex housing several hundred people, most of them single who came and went with irregular frequency. Most of the units were rented temporarily by people in transition due to divorce, separation or a recent move to San Diego. Many parking spaces in the garage were filled by visitors. Anonymity was virtually assured.

He showered, dressed in jeans and blue T-shirt. Retrieving the stub from his coat pocket, he punched in the detective's number and was connected immediately.

'This is Mr. Pope. I found the movie ticket stub. What should I do with it?'

The detective replied, 'Just hold on to it. If we need it, we'll let you know. Thank you. Good Day.'

If the police suspected everyone connected with Marge Abbott, he could be followed on his escapades. It would be wise to buy an old car to use for his rendezvous.

Hamilton perused the ads until he found what he wanted. A Navy man due to leave the next day on a long cruise had a twelve-year old Honda in fair working condition.

Confident in his ability to repair cars, he phoned. The sailor was willing to drive the car to Hamilton's garage on condition Hamilton would drive him back to the naval base after the purchase.

While he waited outside his condo complex for the sailor, a young woman approached him. 'I'm looking for work as a housekeeper. Would you be interested? I do lots of apartments here.'

Hamilton felt his face flush. That woman could be an undercover agent. He'd never hire a housekeeper because he didn't want anyone snooping around his condo. Bristling at her intrusion, he replied, 'Sorry. Not interested.' She started to speak to him again, but he walked away. When he turned around, she'd vanished.

The young man in the old gray Honda rolled up. Hamilton inspected the car, drove him to the base and gave him two thousand dollars cash in exchange for the car and the pink slip. Hamilton told the sailor he was in the insurance business and would take care of all the paper work. The naïve nineteen-year-old looked as happy as if he had won the lottery.

46

Jennifer, back at work when Cory arrived at karate, looked unscathed from her ordeal. Swift and agile, she seemed to move with a vengeance, her power restored. Cory was delighted to see her in such good form. George Lewis, the detective, had become a regular at the studio and with all his experience, was no match for Jennifer. Olie, Lewis and Cory were warming up when Ron joined them.

At the end of the workout, Ron hurried off, responding to a page. Arm in arm, Jen and Olie scooted into the office. Lewis asked Cory to join him at the sushi bar next door.

Over green tea, she explained her scheme and Olie's experience with the woman on the phone who later was murdered.

George Lewis shook his head from side to side. 'You're not a cop, Doc. I wish you'd talked to me first.'

'If I did, what would you have done?'

'Tell you to forget it. Frankly, it sounds . . . I don't want to insult you, but . . . '

'Okay, so you think it was stupid. Now, I've got her murder on my conscience, too.'

'What are you talking about, Doc?'

'Before Grace was murdered, one of my patients was raped by someone pretending to be her phone pal. I suspected Grace was another intended victim and I'd left a message at her office, but it was too late. I should've called her home.'

'Listen, Doc. It's not your fault Grace was killed and you didn't put the knife in the hand of Marge Abbott's killer. Maybe I'm out of bounds here, but did you ever hear of individual responsibility?'

'Thanks. I know you're trying to make me feel better, but I keep thinking if I hadn't put Olie up to that dumb phone call, Marge Abbott might be alive.'

'That's unreasonable, you know.'

'Well, I wonder why he would kill her over something that dumb, unless it was the last straw and he was upset with her or something else.'

'He's a regular nut case. Listen, I've got news for you, Doc,' he said, stirring his miso soup. 'From our preliminary check of the security company, we don't think it was a guard. A few guys had minor scrapings with the law, but nothing violent.'

'Maybe Ms. Abbott had a phone buddy.'

'No evidence. We checked. She was open about her life so family and friends would've known. Rest easy, everyone at Superior is under investigation, you know.'

'I'm glad you joined the Karate Institute, Lewis.'

'Me, too.'

He walked Cory to her car and she waved to him as she drove away.

He had told her to rest easy, but it didn't help.

★ ★ ★

The next morning Betty phoned Cory to make a breakfast date.

When Cory arrived, her pal was seated at their favorite sidewalk café. The sky, a cloudless blue matched Betty's slacks and sweater. The sun shimmered on her long hair.

'It's terrifying, Cory. So many women. And this last one right at Superior. Incredible.' She stared at the menu and then looked up. 'It's scary that the cops haven't caught the creep yet. Just as Mr. Pope suggested when you first called him, it's possible the security guard is responsible. After all, someone struck right there at Superior.'

The server poured steaming dark roasted coffee into their cups. Betty raised four fingers, indicating her number choice on the menu.

It was about seventy degrees as they sat in the sun, but the conversation was chilling. Cory's heavy green sweater and long wool skirt weren't warm enough to ward off her shivers. She wrapped her hands around the cup.

'I've had patients who worked in security. Let me tell you, Cory. Many are disturbed. Pay minimum wage and put a gun in the hands of someone without doing a background check and what do you expect?'

'Betty, it isn't a security guard.'

'How do you know?' She turned her head and looked around the outdoor café.

'Detective Lewis said they've done a preliminary check. The security service employs a few guys with minor records, but none for violence.'

'They're probably investigating everyone at Superior. That's comforting,' Betty said.

'Listen. The perp called my patient from a hotel phone booth. Perhaps he realized she could have a trap on her phone. In the urgency of the moment, he'd made a date, but either had no intention of keeping it or got cold feet.'

'What more do you know?'

'His pattern is to make a date after a series of phone calls. Surprise! This last one occurred after one call.' Cory nodded to the server for a refill of coffee and gave her order. 'He'd rape and kill anyone, anywhere if he regarded his plan as foolproof. Even at Superior.'

'Good God!'

'Logic tells me Mr. Pope should be a prime suspect.'

'Wouldn't he expect to be investigated?'

'Pope's so cocksure, he's not worried. When I'd called him about our concerns, to divert suspicion he blamed it on a security guard. Now, I know for a fact the murdered woman was scared of him. She hadn't ever worked overtime. Why do you think he asked her to stay late that night?'

Betty raised her eyebrows. 'Why would he want to kill her?'

Cory hesitated, took a deep breath, revealed her scheme and Olie's call.

'This is incredible. Cory Cohen alias Miss Marple.'

'Detective Sharpley told me the evidence taken from the victims link these cases together. Semen, hair and fibers come from the same person.'

'What are they doing about it?' She scowled. 'They haven't notified the media.'

'If they do that, Betty, they'll blow a chance to apprehend him. My guess is Pope's covered his tracks well.'

'Can't they go to his house and look for clues?'

Cory noticed the host seating four people at the next table, and lowered her voice. 'Nope. They need probable cause. There's nothing to link him to the murders and rape.'

'But, Cory, he's an administrator of the mental health plan where *all* the victims were subscribers.'

'It's not sufficient. Lot's of people work there.'

'What about taking DNA samples?' She cut her french toast in tiny pieces and dipped each into a mound of orange marmalade.

'A violation of civil rights unless there's stronger evidence than what they have.'

Betty shook her head. 'Incredible. Samples would make it easier. Innocent people wouldn't object and those who do would look suspicious.'

'It's complicated, Betty. Not everyone is reasonable. There may be folks who'd refuse on principle. I'm going to do some investigating of my own.'

Betty's eyes widened. 'Don't do it. Look what happened when you called Superior. We were thrown off the panel.'

'So what? What can they do to me now? I wanted to quit.' Cory's voice rose. 'Magic 101 wasn't part of the graduate school curriculum. People can't change in a few sessions and I won't beg a clerk for more.'

'You're right. What good is all our training and experience? And the variety of forms we use for each company. Office staff can't do it, because it's supposed to be confidential.' Betty checked her watch and motioned the server for the check. 'Payments are denied arbitrarily. We argue. They pay and if we're lucky, three months later.' She tapped her glossy manicured fingernails on the table. 'We should all quit managed care and take them to court!'

At the mention of court, the people at the next table turned their heads in the women's direction. Cory figured they were probably lawyers.

Cory stared back and winked. 'Small Claims.'

The lawyer types looked away from her.

'Did the cops find out if Abbott had a phone bud?' Betty lowered her voice.

'They checked. It's unlikely.'

'I'm so anxious, haven't slept well. It could happen to anyone, Cory.'

'Yes, but you're cautious and have good common sense. True, you chose disappointing men, but none were psychopaths.'

'Maybe I've been lucky. I'm afraid it could happen, because I like having a man around.' Betty sighed.

'Don't you mean, a special man?'

'Sometimes I can't tell the difference.'

This was one of those times Cory wished she had an instruction sheet to give her friend, but she knew Betty had to figure it out for herself. 'That's what you need to learn.'

'I know. I know!'

'And I know you. Listen to me. You have a lot to offer. You deserve someone who shares your values and interests.'

'Cory, sometimes you miss the point. I have sexual needs.'

'So you settle.' Cory shook her head. 'Haven't you heard of sublimation? Mustn't let your gonads govern.'

Betty heaved a deep sigh. 'Thanks. I deserve the lecture, Mother Superior.'

The two women had covered this subject often, and each time Cory hoped her words had impact. Now, was no different. It was time to change the subject.

'If it weren't for that other cop who respects me, I think Detective Sharpley would've ignored me. It's funny. One of my patients has taken a shine to Sharpley.'

'Maybe that's making his blue eyes bluer.' Betty winked. 'By the way, how's it with you and the boy?'

'Give me a break, Betty, he's a real man.'

'So you found that out already?'

Cory grinned.

'Well, well. You've broken your vow of celibacy. Let's see. Do you look different?' Betty cocked her head. 'Buy any new clothes?'

Dr. Betty Pepper. Her name suited her. Hot as the spice. Refreshing as the drink, Cory thought.

'I'm not like you. I don't enjoy shopping. My wardrobe is sparse according to your standards, but there's enough to recycle.'

'Don't you ever treat yourself?'

'Are you kidding? Ron is a treat.'

'Glad you found that out.' She wiped the corners of her mouth with her napkin.

'I'm afraid it won't last, Betty. I'm afraid I'll get hooked on him and then . . . '

'As we tell patients, 'risk is part of living.' Just measure the risk-reward ratio.'

'Uh, sounds more like a stockbroker than a psychologist.' Cory smiled.

'You're right. I learned it from my last lover. Is Ron passionate?' she whispered.

'And how!' Cory felt her face grow warm. 'But wildfire turns it all to ashes.'

'Not ready for a permanent relationship, huh? Was he ever married?'

'No, but in med school he was involved with a woman who dumped him for another guy. First love. His hurt still shows.' She splashed the red salsa on the egg white omelet. It's resemblance to blood made her shiver.

'You've got yourself a soul-mate. Does he know about your kids?'

'It doesn't matter now, but if they were here instead of in Israel . . . '

Betty stirred her coffee. 'You've sacrificed a lot for them, huh?'

'What do you mean?'

'You're a tight-ass with yourself, but you spend freely on them.'

'I'm not a martyr. It's a pleasure. Like the fun you had as a kid buying clothes for your dolls.'

Betty smiled. 'Yeah. By your standards, I'm selfish.'

'Hey, wait a minute. I don't judge you.'

'Come on. You're always making judgments, Mother Superior.'

'I need to think about that.' She paused. 'You're probably right.'

'Cory, take advantage of your freedom. There's joy on your face when you speak about Ron. I envy it. Let yourself be close to him. Enjoy it while it lasts.'

'And if it doesn't, I'll have reruns for my sex fantasy. I like things the way they are.' She smiled. 'No commitment.'

Betty placed her elbows on the table and

cupped her flawless, fifty-year-old face in her hands. 'We're different, Cory. I want a re-la-tion-ship. I've dated a lot, but now, I'm skittish. I'm afraid of sexually transmitted diseases. I want to meet the right guy and settle down . . . share sweet moments and sorrows.'

'But you're afraid of involvement with the wrong guy,' Cory said.

'Cory, this latest murder . . . it really hit me hard . . . he made three teenagers orphans. The woman was a widow.' Betty trembled. 'Her husband was a motorcycle cop killed on duty ten years ago. I heard on the radio they're taking up a collection for the children. I'll send a check.'

'Good idea. I'll give you some money now. Include it with yours. I'd like to remain anonymous.' Cory wrote out a check from her personal account and handed it to Betty. She knew her donation would not assuage her guilt. She tried not to think of the bereaved survivors. It hurt too much. They would be offered grief therapy, courtesy of the state.

'This guy isn't done yet, Cory. He's on a spree. I wonder who'll be the next victim.' She rummaged in her oversize purse for her credit card.

They paid the bill, then stood at the corner watching traffic. Betty's face had developed tension lines. 'Please be careful. You're dealing with a very dangerous person. Karate didn't help Jennifer.'

'But she wasn't anticipating danger. I'm in good shape and have my wits about me. I'm going to get a good look at Mr. Pope.'

'God, *no!*' Betty shrieked.

47

To effect the plan, Cory told herself she needed a hefty dose of *chutzpah*. She taught patients to be assertive and was a good role model, but aggressiveness wasn't that easy for her. Necessity became the mother of courage. She steeled herself and entered her daughter's room to find supplies.

Rummaging through the closet, Cory caressed Rachel's clothes while searching for a clown costume that her daughter had worn a few Halloweens ago. Her favorite teddy bear with its worn fabric, a testimony of many hugs, stared at Cory from the shelf. Tenderly, she reached for it and sat on the floor, hugging the old stuffed animal. Her hands ran across the soft, furry fabric and caught on the rough seams she had sewn many years ago, to keep it from falling apart. She felt her sweet little girl's presence. The herbal scent of her lotion still present after all this time sent tears down her cheeks. Lord, how she missed her child! The softness of her light hair. The intensity of her blue eyes. Cory counted the months until Rachel would be home, matured from her experiences. She blotted her face with a tissue from the box on her daughter's dresser, but the constriction in her throat remained.

Was there anyone who loved and missed Grace? The love the young woman had received from her parents was too brief, and now the opportunity for anyone else to care for her was lost forever. An early session with her came back to Cory:

'I barely remember my parents. They'd given me a doll when I was little. I loved her. She was real to me. When she became shabby and soiled, my aunt tossed her in the trash. I was hurt, angry. I felt so alone.'

'How awful! That doll was important to you. It reminded you, that you were once loved.'

'Yes. My aunt's sensitivity was as big as a gnat. I cried a lot. No one tried to comfort me. They made me go to my room. That's when I started to draw. I made a picture of my doll and carried it with me everywhere. I used to speak to her and kiss her. She was my only comfort. Isn't it strange to have a cardboard doll?'

'Not at all. It showed your creativity. Lots of kids have imaginary playmates or a comfort object.'

Like Rachel's worn teddy-bear.

Cory's fists balled. Anger mounting, she

dug her nails into her palms.

What made that lousy sonofabitch kill her sweet patient? Malfunctioning chemistry in the brain can cause impulsive violent behavior, but this guy was not impulsive. He premeditated. Rehearsed. He was propelled by the thrill of power and control over women. How she wished he would run in front of a fast moving train instead.

Along his path of life, did horrible experiences shape him into a monster? Was he abused? Loved by anyone? Vicious fiends could be loved by their mothers. In courtrooms, Cory had heard women deny their sons were killers: 'He's a good boy. He couldn't have done it.'

She sat cross-legged on the floor, clutching Teddy who had as few answers as she did.

Rachel's school yearbooks and childhood photos stacked on a shelf beckoned her mother on a sentimental journey. Leafing through them, Cory's eyes moistened. The journals lined neatly in a row on the closet shelf were sacred and dared Cory to peek, but she prided herself on the trust she and her children had in each other.

A bright red cotton wig and red rubber nose in a plastic bag hung on the same hanger with the clown costume. Just like Rachel to keep her things in order. Cory donned the ensemble.

In her daughter's bathroom, she located the make-up Rachel had used to complete the transformation. Bright red rouge on her cheeks matched the nose and fluorescent pink lipstick exaggerated Cory's full lips. An eyebrow pencil made neat freckles and rounded her eyes and eyebrows. She stood in front of the mirrored closet door and admired the masquerade. The costume was a great disguise for her lean frame. The wig added a few inches to her height. Her race and gender were camouflaged. Cory replaced the shoe-laces of her running shoes with bright yellow and red ribbons and pocketed a small size pack of tissues from the cabinet along with her keys and wallet.

In Noah's messy closet, she found one of his cameras. He had discarded it because it was automatic and unchallenging to him. Cory inserted a fresh roll of film and slipped the camera strap over her head.

Slowly, she stroked his microscope and boxes of Monopoly, Scrabble and Trivial Pursuit, a fun part of family life. Most of the time Noah won. Recalling his childhood, Cory laughed at some of the practical jokes her son had played. Once, he placed a whoopee cushion on the dining chair of a guest. Another time, he hid a plastic black spider in his sister's bed. Cory dabbed her face with a tissue, and swallowed hard.

On her way to Superior she bought a bouquet of helium balloons in colors of red, blue and orange and attached a note on which she scribbled, 'Your secret admirer.'

Cory drove to Superior and parked a half block away. With heart flipping to fast mode and palms sweating, she entered the building. A few people gaped at her and chuckled. At the reception desk, in a voice two octaves lower than her usual, Cory asked for Mr. Pope. The giggling receptionist buzzed him. He came out immediately. Cory hoped he couldn't hear her heart slam against her chest.

Mr. Pope was much as she had pictured. Regal posture, neatly combed shiny black hair with silver streaks at the temples and peregrine eyes. A deep cleft in his chin resembled an antique key-hole. The pin-striped suit seemed expensive and his tie was similar to one she remembered from a shopping trip with Noah who had fingered the price tag and whistled. Pope's clothes looked incongruous on his weight lifter build. His neck disappeared into his shoulders. He resembled a well-paid Mafia body-guard.

'What is this?' he shouted.

Cory handed him the bouquet, quickly

snapped his photo and waltzed into the elevator. Her pulse quickened as she sprinted to her car, the keys jingling in her pocket.

Rapid footsteps came behind her. Cory's heart beat like a kettle-drum. She expected Hamilton Pope. She turned her head and saw a runner speed past her. What she hadn't seen was a black plastic trash bag. She slipped on it and somersaulted, red wig flying off her head, and keys clanging on the pavement. Landing upright, she peered around. No one in sight to view the spectacle. She grabbed the wig, stuck it on her head and jammed her hand in her pocket, relieved to feel her wallet. Keys in hand, she bolted to the car and drove away. Rounding the corner, she slowed down, checked the rear-view mirror and saw no cars behind her.

★ ★ ★

Arriving home, she activated the security system and phoned Detective Sharpley.

Before she could blurt out what she had done, he said, 'I've got news for you. Remember the knife you collected? The forensic identification specialist has determined the blood on the knife matches the DNA of the rape victims and Grace's.'

Her stomach took a roller-coaster ride.

'That means the man who attacked Ann must have thought she was me!' She plopped on a chair and gasped. 'He wanted to kill me before I told the police my suspicions. It wasn't a mugger. He's got to be the guy from Superior, Mr. Pope, because it happened right after I told him my suspicion. And now I've got him on film!'

'What?' Sharpley shouted. 'How did you do it? Never mind. I'll come right over and take the film to the lab. Hope it's better than the photo from the DMV. None of the victims were able to make a positive identification from it.'

And Cory thought she was smarter than the cops. 'Oh, so you've tried this already?'

'Yes, but the one we have is seven years old. Computer imaging showed what he'd look like now with a beard, mustache and jet black hair, but it didn't work. You have a recent photo. That's much better.'

She caught her breath and asked, 'What next?'

'After it's enhanced, we'll place it among photos of six other men and show them to the victims. If there's a positive identification, we can pick him up for questioning.'

'Then I've got something here?'

'Sure hope so,' Sharpley said.

48

Hamilton seethed. Who the devil played this joke? What did it mean? What to do about it?

He knew he must think logically and not act impulsively. After much deliberation he concluded someone at Superior must have a crush on him. After all, he was powerful, attractive, a well-spoken executive who wore fine clothes and drove an expensive car.

Allowing his focus to drift, Hamilton thought about arranging a fatal accident for his boss, Robert Russell, but dismissed the idea since he would benefit by it and thus become a likely suspect. With Marge, he had gained nothing by her death. Nothing that anyone else could figure out. With Russell's murder, the police would dig deeper into his past. He had to find a better way.

The photo trick gnawed at him. He must find out who played this silly game and make it clear that he found it unprofessional.

Hamilton called in his right hand man, Jim Corita.

When Jim arrived, Hamilton was seated at

his massive desk, his fingers forming a pyramid.

'Please take a seat, Jim. Something distasteful has happened here. A clown gained admittance to our offices and served me a balloon bouquet with this note attached.' He handed Jim the slip of paper. 'Do you know who sent this?'

Jim Corita, examining the note, stuttered, 'N-no, no. I've no idea.'

'Please find out and let me know. It does not amuse me in the slightest. I make it a policy to keep my personal and professional life separate. I value my privacy. Someone surprised me by taking my picture. This offends me. I demand that photo and its negative immediately.' He drummed his fingers on the desk.

'I'll ask around.' Jim frowned.

'I believe I can rely on your discretion. I expect a resolution to this before the end of the day.'

'I'll do my best, but the person who sent it may be too embarrassed to tell me.'

'You are clever and can find out through the office gossip network. This is your assignment today. Don't let me down.' The last four words reverberated in his ears.

★ ★ ★

The coffee room was awash with giggles and whispers when Jim entered.

'What's going on?' he asked.

The response was a chorus of laughter.

'Does this have anything to do with Mr. Pope's visit from the clown this morning?'

'Was it ever funny. You should have seen his face,' a clerk answered.

'I can't imagine,' Jim said.

'I nearly wet my pants,' said the receptionist, pouring coffee into a mug.

'Which one of you sent it to him?'

'I wouldn't bother. He's a dick-head,' the clerk said.

'Are you kidding? The guy looks scary to me. Why would I want to waste money on him? He had poor Marge work late and couldn't care less about her murder. Just business as usual for him. If you ask me, I think he's a creep!' said a case manager.

'Oh, I don't know. I think he's handsome. He looks so strong and smart. I can imagine some woman going for him. He dresses like he's super rich and drives a fancy car,' laughed Barry, a clerk, as he pranced around the room imitating Pope's demeanor.

'Contrary to what you believe, not all women want rich, smart, handsome men, Barry. Some prefer sensitive, gentle men. That's not Mr. Pope,' the case manager said.

'So who could have sent it?' Jim asked.

Another case manager tore off a piece of donut. Licking her sticky fingers, she said, 'I don't think anyone here would want to get close to him. Must be from someone outside work.'

'I'd give twenty bucks just to find out who played the trick on him,' Jim said.

'How much is Mr. Pope giving you to find out?' Barry teased.

'That's not fair, Barry. He's not paying me for information. I swear it!' Jim's face reddened.

'Has he threatened you?' the receptionist asked.

Jim sat at the table staring into his empty coffee mug and said, 'Mr. Pope sure gets off on power, big time.'

★   ★   ★

Hamilton continued his work, confident that the photo would be returned by the end of the day. He scanned his personal engagement calendar and saw the notation to call Erin that evening. Swiveling on his chair, he closed his eyes and fantasized their meeting. He visualized the expression on her face when he would pull out his knife. His penis hardened. He stroked it and opened his eyes, whispering, 'Later.' Breathing heavily, he reached into his attache case, removed the knife and fondled it. Cold and sharp. No longer a virgin.

Hamilton expected it would take less than the average number of calls to extract an invitation from Erin, especially when she would hear his canaries in the background. She had said her husband frequently took their daughter to the aviary. He had wanted to get at Erin when her daughter was not at home. Suddenly, the idea of killing the child quickened his pulse. A little girl! Much better. Imagining Erin's look of horror as he slashed her kid intensified his excitement. Hastening to the water cooler, he drank two cups of water.

Returning to his desk, he fingered the soft leather cover of his notebook as he perused it for a hotel with a private, quiet phone booth in the eastern part of town. It wouldn't be smart to phone from where he'd called Paige.

Erin, incredibly naïve, didn't deserve to live, nor her offspring who could grow up to spawn others of her ilk.

★   ★   ★

Jim Corita broke out in a cold sweat anticipating his meeting with his boss. After

305

all, it wasn't his fault that he couldn't find out who played the trick, but he knew Mr. Hamilton Pope had unrealistic expectations.

At the end of the day Jim ducked into the washroom to make himself presentable to his fastidious boss. Barry was looking into the mirror, combing his curly dark locks. 'Jim, you look awful. What's the matter?'

'You were right, Barry. Mr. Pope asked me to find out who played that trick on him. I've nothing to tell him and I'm scared he'll fire me.'

'What the hell is wrong with that guy? Can't he take a joke? Why does that pompous ass make such a big deal? Any normal person would just laugh it off. If you want, blame it on me. I don't care. I'm only a temp and I'll be leaving the end of the week anyway. He doesn't pay my salary.' Barry placed his hand on Jim's shoulder.

'Thanks Barry. But he wants the film.'

'Tell him there wasn't any. It was just a joke.'

'He'll want the camera.'

'It was a toy that I threw away.'

'What if he doesn't believe it?'

Barry heaved a sigh. 'Jim, that shouldn't be your problem. Don't be a wimp. Everyone thinks Pope is a dick-head.'

'He could fire me.' Jim bit his fingernails.

'Don't be a shmuck. He'd have to have grounds. The staff would vouch for you.'

Jim appreciated Barry's efforts at consoling him. It helped a little. 'Thanks, Barry.'

★ ★ ★

At five-fifteen, Jim combed his hair with his fingers and mopped his moist, wrinkled brow. He knocked on Mr. Pope's door.

'Well . . . what did you find out?'

'Barry admitted doing it as a joke. He said he meant no harm. He just wanted to see your expression.'

Hamilton's face darkened. 'Where's the film?'

Jim stood at the door, his hand on the knob. 'He said there wasn't any film, just a toy flash.'

'Who the hell is Barry?'

'The data entry temp. I told him you were very angry.'

'Did he say who put him up to it?'

'It was his own idea. He thought it was a funny thing to do. He's a comedian and only does temp jobs when he isn't working at his profession.'

'He's never to do anything to intrude on my privacy again. Be sure you tell him that. You may go now.'

Jim closed the door behind him.

Hamilton accepted Jim Corita's plausible tale. There was nothing more he could do about it. He decided to put it to rest.

Barry's antic triggered an idea about how Hamilton could push Russell aside: On a yellow legal pad, he scrawled with his left hand: *Mr. Russell, we know you are the rapist. The cops are on to you. Watch out.'* Examining his writing, he shook his head and shredded the paper. He'd need to perfect it. He tried three more times, each time shredding his graphic productions. The fourth effort satisfied him. When he was ready, he'd fax it to Superior from a public fax machine at night. It would be handed to his boss in the morning. He slipped it into his attache case. Hamilton knew Russell took blood pressure medication and hoped the man would get so upset he'd have a fatal heart attack. What a great scenario! Kill two ducks with one bullet. Pacing, he constructed his plan.

Hamilton required assurance that Russell wouldn't have alibis for the time of the meeting with Erin, and for the times of the other attacks. He also needed to leave something with Russell's fingerprints at the scene.

At the computer, he keyed in to Robert

Russell's schedule and compared the dates and times of the attacks with those of Russell's planned activities. Perfect. Nothing was scheduled on those evenings, but Russell had impressed upon executives the importance of a separate personal diary in which completed engagements were documented. Excited at the prospect of obtaining that information, he was bathed in sweat. His fingers worked rapidly on the computer keyboard. Damn! The information was hard to access. It must be in Russell's private file and required a password.

After a brief trip to the washroom where he emptied his full bladder and washed his face, Hamilton removed his shoes and padded into the personnel office. He located hard copies of files on all the employees. Hamilton reviewed his own sanitary record. No new entries since he had checked two months ago. He snatched Russell's file and placed it at the computer, hoping to find a detail that would provide the password. He typed in Russell's social security number and followed it with every name and number in the file, but the password eluded him. Tense, he breathed heavily. When his mouth became dry, he drank two cups of water, stretched and doggedly resumed his task.

Hamilton glanced at his Rolex. He had

spent three hours testing all probable passwords and now it was too late to call Erin. Usually, he would have a fit when things did not go as planned, but his priority had changed. Must be a sign of maturity or greater self-control, he thought. Perhaps he enjoyed the challenge of puncturing Russell's privacy more than another violent escapade. He rolled his shoulders, stretched, and continued his maddening search.

Hamilton's shirt drenched in sweat, clung to him like barnacles on a boat. It disgusted him, but he persevered, driven to find the elusive password. A burning sensation in his eyes told him to give up, but he made one last effort and typed 'bert,' a fragment of Robert Russell's name. Eureka! The file opened to Russell's private engagement calendar. Certain of the scrupulousness of the records, Hamilton was astonished to see few appointments, and none for the dates of the assaults. 'Yahoo,' he cheered like a schoolboy, elated at penetrating his boss' privacy.

Russell's routine included gym Monday, Wednesday and Friday from 5:00 to 6:30 P.M., massage on Tuesdays from 5:00 P.M.-6:00 P.M. and golf on Saturdays. Devoting evenings to TV. Russell had posted the programs he planned to view on his calendar. A barber and manicurist came to the office during regular office hours. The calendar included a weekly shopping list. Russell had no social life apart from his golf buddies whose names were listed in the calendar. It appeared Russell made regular lunch dates at the country club with them. Hamilton marveled at Russell's structured life, a prerequisite for success.

He shuffled to Russell's office, tugged a clean pale blue handkerchief from his breast pocket and used it to turn the door knob. He flipped on the lights. On top of the enormous mahogany desk sat an impressive briarwood box with an embossed silver 'Roses' emblem. Hamilton had seen an advertisement for such a box. It contained a sterling silver Menash fountain pen that cost eleven hundred dollars. To avoid leaving fingerprints, he resisted an urge to write with it. Holding the tip of the pen with his handkerchief, he noticed Robert Russell's name engraved. This would do, indeed. A companion pencil lay in the box too. No doubt the set was permanently housed in Russell's office. Hamilton planned to collect the pen later. He must act fast, before Russell had an alibi for the time of the projected attack on Erin and her daughter.

Unknown for sociability, Hamilton's plan necessitated something out of character for him, an invitation to Russell to dine with him for a business discussion. Thursday would be good, since Russell probably would be free. Immediately after dinner Hamilton would drive towards Erin's and change at a rest stop. With no time to tint his hair, he would wear the knit cap. He would send the fax from the all night convenience store near Erin's house, rush to her, do the job, leave Russell's pen, and speed home without getting caught. He reviewed the plan several times and realized he would have to wait until Russell left the office before he could snatch the pen. This meant Hamilton would arrive at the restaurant a few minutes after Russell.

The thought of dinner made him hungry. The burger he had eaten for lunch was not enough to sustain him. Tonight, he would order three more on his way home. Hamilton wondered if he should succumb to the propaganda of the food industry. Maybe vegetables were nutritious, but the sight of them, limp on his plate made him gag. No, he would not listen. Juicy burgers made his mouth water. First he would feast, then deal with the three biggies on his agenda: Do away with Erin and her daughter. Implicate Russell. Kill Dr. Cory Cohen. Another shrink. Another trophy.

49

After Detective Sharpley collected the film, Cory felt giddy, like a little girl with a new doll. Eager to celebrate, she called Ron. He accepted her invitation, but his voice sounded hesitant and unenthusiastic. Her excitement crumbled, leaving in its wake a premonition of approaching unpleasantness.

She glanced out the window at a sky darkening with a dense layer of shapeless nimbus clouds; a condition natives call, 'June gloom.' If the storm proved strong, parched San Diego's water conservation campaign should be lifted.

Cory gathered two dry logs from the garage and carried them into the den. She lit them in the fireplace. Soon the room warmed and glowed.

While she whipped up a salad, John Coltrane's 'Every Time We Say Goodbye' played on the stereo. She had just completed the vinaigrette dressing, when Ron arrived accompanied by howling wind, rain and a soaked pizza box.

He slipped off his wet parka and boots, and stretched out on the floor near the crackling fire, his arm over his face.

Cory kneeled beside him. 'What's wrong, Ron?'

Leaning on his elbow, he gazed into her eyes. A serious, far away expression replaced the usual erotic charge. 'Bad news.'

So here it comes. It couldn't last. He's going to end our relationship, Cory thought. She grew lightheaded and heavy hearted. 'What is it?'

'It's hard to talk about.'

'Please tell me.'

She was afraid of what he could say. She wasn't ready to end what they had.

'My dad's health is poor. I may move back to Davis.'

Cory gasped. 'I'm so sorry. What's wrong with him?'

'Parkinson's. None of the meds work. He's deteriorating, shakes so much, he can't treat patients. He wants me to take over his practice.'

'How soon?'

'I don't know.' He buried his head in his hands. 'It's not what I want, Cory, but my parents expect it. They're growing old. They have friends and aren't lonely, but I'm their only family.'

'I understand your conflict.'

'Who knows how long they'll be around,

but I'm settled here with a good practice, partners I respect, and a house almost done. Living near the ocean is neat. You may think it's superficial, but surfing is important to me.'

'Listen, Ron, you work hard. You're entitled to pleasure. It's not a crime.'

'If I lived up there, I could windsurf in Rio Vista once in awhile, but it's over an hour away.' The little creases on his brow deepened. 'Last, but not least, you're here, Cory. My life's right here.'

Cory's position on his list didn't escape her, nor was she mollified by his words, but she wasn't ready to confront him.

'You don't want to go, but feel obligated.'

'Precisely. If I go back, it wouldn't be hell. Except in summer. They get triple digit temperature.' He walked to the dining room table, motioning her to follow. 'The aroma of the pizza calls,' he said.

She handed Ron a frosty can of Fosters from the refrigerator and flipped open a can for herself. 'It hurts to see our parents grow old and sick,' she said, standing behind him, massaging his tight shoulders. 'When we were kids, they took care of us. We grow up and they need us.'

He turned and took her hand from his shoulder. 'Have the food, before it cools.'

She sat across from him at the table. 'Tell me about Davis.'

'It's a small agricultural town with a university. There's good med school with teaching and research opportunities.' Grimacing, he cut a small, stubborn slice of pizza and munched it. 'A great place for young families. Slow moving. More bikes than cars. Big on community events. Lots of spirit.'

'Why did you leave?'

'I like the pulse of a larger city.'

'It'd be a sacrifice for you to move back.'

'They've sacrificed for me.' He took a swig of beer.

'It's not a sacrifice when you do for your kids. It's a privilege.'

'I guess you'd know about that.'

The difference in their experience was clear to her. Sadness nudged at Cory, but she refused to absorb it.

'Would they consider relocating here?'

'I've suggested it many times, but they're involved with all kinds of civic projects. They have a history there, and love their house. Dad's done the carpentry himself.' He reached for his drink. 'It's hard for older people to make changes.'

'If they had a vacation home here, no one would have to give up anything.'

'That's an idea. But it's hard for them to go

back and forth, especially now with Dad's failing health.'

'It's about a two hour flight from here. Maybe it'd help if you visited more often.' She gulped the cold beer.

'It's a partial solution.'

'Time would tell if it's enough to assuage your guilt.'

'I'm just caught up with my own life, Cory.' He buried his head in his hands. 'Selfish, huh?'

'What's selfish? Being caught up in your own life, or your parents wanting you back?'

'Good question.' Ron seemed to mull it over, remaining quiet for awhile.

Cory waited for him to continue.

'My parents have given me a lot,' he said, slowly. 'It's payback time, but the idea of moving back to my stale hometown is repugnant.'

'I understand.'

'Dad could find someone to take over his practice, but it'd be a blow to him if I didn't inherit it, as he did from his father.'

'The Miller medical dynasty,' Cory said, noticing the muscles in Ron's jaw twitching. 'It's important to your father. He was raised that way and passed it on to you. You'd feel guilty dropping the legacy, right?'

'Stop being my shrink!'

His contorted face surprised her. 'Sorry. I'm used to talking that way. Most of my friends are psychologists.'

'It doesn't work with me,' he snapped.

'I'll remember that.'

They sat in silence for a few moments. Cory felt shut out by his anger. His over-reactive style would be hard to tolerate, long-term.

Suddenly, his mood seemed to lift and he beckoned her to curl up on the couch with him.

'You're delicious,' he whispered after their garlicky kiss. 'And a problem solver.'

'You thought of a solution, Ron.'

'Yeah, because you're a catalyst. That's what psychologists do, huh? When it comes to myself, I don't see the whole picture.'

Cory figured that applied to the downside of a long term relationship with her. Was it her duty to tell him? Her mind clicked double speed. If she let herself, she'd be addicted to him in a New York minute. She wondered if he was aware that his moodiness turned people off. But who's perfect? Their intimacy offered comfort and joy, but Cory felt it was destined for disappointment.

'What's going on? When you called, you said you wanted to celebrate. Did I steal your thunder?' Ron asked.

She gave him the scoop on her adventure at Pope's office.

He scowled and kept quiet.

Cory didn't know if he was shocked, angry or confused.

'Ron, I don't dig this silence. Let me in, please.'

'Frankly, I'm shocked that you'd go to such lengths when there are real professionals handling it.'

'I thought you'd be pleased that I accomplished something.'

'Pleased? Your ridiculous obsession turns me off.' Shaking his head, he drifted to the corner of the couch and paused for what seemed forever.

'Uh, I don't know, Cory . . . I've given this some thought. We won't be seeing too much of each other. I'll be spending a lot of time in Davis.'

'Are you still angry with me?'

'More like disappointed. I care about you, but I can't be part of a crazy scene. You don't see the unnecessary risks you take. You need a therapist. You're flipping out.'

So he thought she needed therapy. Well, she thought he needed it, too. His moods were like the waves he surfed. If she suggested it, he'd probably think it was tit for tat.

'You don't understand. I had to do it,

319

because the police can't.'

'That does it! Do you realize what you said, Cory?'

'Let me explain. The law prevents the police from doing certain things that ordinary citizens can do. This guy is on a spree of escalating violence. He must be caught.'

'Sorry, Cory, but I don't see a role in it for you.'

Perhaps he didn't see a role for her in his life, either. Saddened, she didn't want to end the good things they had. 'I'm sorry, it's just that I . . . '

'You're involved with something that's not your damn business.'

'You don't understand.'

She wanted to tell him about her rape, but his icey stare put her off and she figured it would be better to change the subject. 'Perhaps I can join you in Davis once in awhile? I promise to keep you from being bored.'

Ron leaned his chin in his fist. Cory waited, afraid of his response.

'Sure,' he said.

Unconvinced, she persisted. 'How would you explain me to your parents?'

He hesitated. 'What do you mean?'

'Our relationship?'

Another long pause. 'Best friends.'

Like a lullaby, she hummed a refrain from 'All Too Soon.' Ron rocked her in his arms, but she felt empty. Her kids on another continent and her romance unraveling.

Cory's feelings shifted. Although sad for his situation, she recognized a tincture of relief. If he left, it would stop her from fretting about the consequence of falling for a younger man. The longer the relationship, the more painful its end. They were at different junctures in their lives and friendship was all she could expect. Would it be enough? He pulled her toward him, but the phone rang and she ran to answer it.

Her service had Erin on the line.

'Sorry to disturb you, Dr. Cohen, but the chap who calls himself Patrick rang recently. He promised to call again, but he did not. The phone company put a trap on my line so the police can trace my calls. I wanted you to know, straight away, I am cooperating.' She sounded sensible and mature. Like a toddler's first step, Erin's growth highlighted a gloomy time.

'I'm glad you called and are helping the police. He didn't show up for a meeting with another woman he'd phoned. Maybe he suspects the cops are getting close, Erin. Would you be willing to talk to a private detective hired by a victim?'

'Oh, yes, quite.'

Ron's pager went off. He needed to make a call, so Cory signed off.

When he finished, he said he had an emergency at the hospital and would spend the weekend with his parents. They kissed as if it was their last goodbye.

50

Incessant rain pelted the windows after Ron had left. The storm provoked her yearning to be cuddled and she fantasized intimate times with him. Their brief relationship wasn't officially over, but she felt it was doomed. He was ambivalent. She despaired over her dependence on his decision for their destiny. She wanted to grab the remnants of an imperfect union.

At six, the clock-radio awakened her, reporting the results of the storm. Uprooted trees blocked streets making parts of the county inaccessible. Numerous freeway accidents occurred because cavalier motorists refused to accomodate to weather conditions. Several homes in Laguna Beach and Malibu slid down cliffs towards the sea, but precariously perched hilltop San Diego houses had remained intact.

The weather, the absence of her children, Ron's distancing, and 'The Case' justified her foul mood. A notice of a long-awaited opening in a percussion class lay on the bedroom desk, but she tossed it aside.

Cory turned on an aerobics video and

worked out. The phone rang just as she popped a sesame-seed bagel in the toaster.

'Hi. Sharpley here. The photograph came out fine.'

'You sure acted fast.'

'Well, sorry to tell you, but it didn't work. We contacted the four victims. Very cooperative girls-uh-I mean women. They were shown photographs of six men with similar facial features. Among the photos was Hamilton Pope's. Only Mallory saw a resemblance, but not enough to give a positive identification. Another woman picked out a photo of one of our officers. The others were uncertain. Insufficient to pick up your Mr. Pope.'

'Damn!' She banged her fist on the table. 'Thanks for trying and letting me know. May I have a copy of the photo?'

'Stop playing detective, Dr. Cohen. You've done enough already.'

'I just want to check it out with my friend . . . see if he recognizes it.' Cory noticed that Sharpley's attitude toward her had changed for the better. He no longer called her 'Ma'am and identified her by name. 'Doctor,' suggested he held her in esteem.

'You mean the ophthalmologist who treated a guy you think was Pope? So what if it was Pope? It won't matter.'

'It would validate my hunch.'

'Okay. I'll send it over today.'

'Thanks.'

'Listen, I'm just as disappointed as you are. Maybe we'll get lucky and the phone trap will work.'

'Sure. If it's Pope, I gave him a head start, so he'd be wary. I shouldn't have called him in the first place. I can kick myself for it.'

'How would you know you were talking to a potential suspect? You're not trained in these matters. Exercise caution.'

His warning frightened her, but she was pleased to hear he cared. Must be Paige's influence, she figured.

'Any progress with the phony patient set-up?' she asked.

'Just about to give you the good news. It's been much harder than expected finding the right company. This is a sensitive operation. Too bad our limited resources have to be spent on Superior.'

'What?'

'We had to ask the President of Express Electronics to buy the plan for his employees, since they didn't have mental health benefits. I felt like a first class . . . salesman. We've gone overboard in helping him with his security, so he was willing to cooperate.'

'It's worth a lot to trap that fiend. Just

sorry that they're getting a bad deal, detective.'

'Not according to the contract. It looks sweet for the subscriber. Let's hope this pays off. The undercover officer is listed as a clerk at Express Electronics and qualifies for benefits. We're paying the insurance.'

'So who's my new patient?'

'Your favorite deputy.'

'Wonderful,' Cory said, smirking. 'I wish the photo had worked.'

'It was creative. Actually, I've heard Deputy Kelly can use your help.'

'How so?'

'Well, she's harsh, doesn't know how to handle the public.'

'Should I teach her good manners?'

'Wouldn't hurt.'

'Sensitivity training revisited in three sessions. Will she go for it?'

'To tell the truth, therapy was recommended in her review. Maybe our investment in this scheme will pay off in more than one way.'

'I sure hope so.'

'Here's the operation: A new phone line is installed in the beach cottage, her headquarters in our Cardiff rental. All calls are monitored from an extension at the nearby sheriff's station. You'll list that number in your bogus treatment request. Except for her appointments with you and a weekly trip to the market, she shouldn't leave the house.'

★ ★ ★

Deputy Franklynne A. Kelly, a.k.a. Frankie, arrived at Cory's office wearing tight jeans, a red sweat shirt and an abrasive attitude. She appeared ten years younger than her age of thirty-five and had the demeanor of a gang member. Frankie didn't mention nor apologize for her earlier confrontation with the psychologist. Cory had serious doubts about Frankie's ability to carry off the operation. For the deputy to pretend she was docile and lonely would be a stretch. To improve her public relations, she would have to start from square one and learn basic civility. The most Cory could expect from her was to act pleased to hear from the caller.

Cory's first step was to counsel Frankie on the best response.

A study of the culprit's mode of operation showed it was necessary to allow him a few weeks in which to woo her. No immediate date was to be made. Specific instructions were given to make it appear she was a loner. No visitors for the next month, in case he watched her house. At first Frankie balked about social deprivation, but when she realized her career depended on it, she agreed.

Only a few weeks remained in Cory's contract with Superior. Frankie had three allowable appointments scheduled for successive Tuesdays at ten. Penetrating her armor called for a massive effort. Frankie wouldn't learn sensitivity in the limited time. Continued therapy with her was not on Cory's agenda. The primary goal was to establish a decoy.

Frankie's first session was replete with resistance at every juncture. When finished, she sauntered out of the office, hands jammed in her jeans pockets, ignoring Cory's polite goodbye.

Cory faxed the invitation; the treatment request on Franklynne A. Kelly, a clerk at Express Electronics. Just as in Grace's report, she stated Franklynne, a shy, lonely woman unable to function adequately due to depression, was on sick leave and housebound. To further whet his appetite, Cory stated the patient appeared ten years younger than thirty-five and lived alone in a beach cottage. She provided a tempting, mouth watering dish with his favorite ingredients and hoped he would soon swallow the bait.

Cory welcomed her next session with

Mallory, a tough, but sweet cookie.

'I still can't sleep well. I'm scared he'll come back and slash me like he did the others. How come he didn't do that to me?' she whined.

'He didn't get a chance because you knocked the wind out of him.' Cory pointed an index finger at her.

'I wish I'd fried his balls and served them to him on a red-hot skewer!'

Sickened by the imagery, Cory winced.

'Just look at how ugly I am.' Mallory pivoted sidewards. 'I better get my appetite back.'

'I don't think you're ugly. You're a bit too thin, but that's temporary.'

'I'd like to be normal again. My roommates fix me up with guys, but who'd look at this bundle of skin and bones?' She stared down at herself and sank into a chair that had enough room for two of her.

'Mallory, you're more than a body. People like you because of your personality, your interests, and besides, you are attractive.'

'You just say that to make me feel better.'

'Of course. But it's the truth nevertheless.'

'Huh? What did you say?' she laughed. 'I've never thought of myself as pretty. I'm jealous of girls who are.'

'Jealousy comes from insecurity, Mallory.

We make a fuss over the so-called, beautiful people whose faces lack character. They look as if they came from the same plastic surgery mold. That's not you.' Nor me either, Cory mused to herself. 'So what? You have other attributes. You're athletic and healthy. That enhances your appearance, and in my book, preferable to pretty.'

'I guess you're right, but lately, no guy is interested in me.'

'Probably because you've sent them a keep-away message. I'm glad you want guys to be interested. It means you aren't set against men now.'

'That makes sense, but I don't know how I'll do in the sex department after what's happened.' She pulled a tissue from the box and covered her nose. 'I was practically a virgin until that scum bag messed with me.'

'That wasn't sex. That was assault.'

She nodded. 'I'd like you to know Cousin Lou and I patched things up,' Mallory said, tossing the tissue into the trash. 'I told her we misunderstood each other and I wanted a chance to explain. Guess what? She let me. She was upset I'd raise her water bill from all my showers. Now she understands I was trying to wash the disgusting rape away. She's glad I realize it was a big deal for her to give me her dog. You were right. She did it because she loves me. Imagine that! She really loves me!'

Mallory and her therapist exchanged smiles. A fine way to end the work day.

★ ★ ★

When Ann and Cory left the office, few cars remained in the parking structure. Bright lights had been installed after the complaint to the building manager. Following the attempted assault, the security guard patrolled the area with greater frequency on an erratic schedule.

Upon exiting the garage, sheets of rain pounded her car. Visibility vanished as in a drive-through car wash. Cory switched on the defroster, but it was on the fritz. She gripped the steering wheel tightly navigating by rote while windshield wipers played a fast Caribbean rhythm. The usual ten minute drive took the longest thirty minutes she could recall.

Arriving home, she played a tape of Mozart's 'Jupiter Symphony' and foraged through the refrigerator for dinner. She snipped herbs from the window-garden, sliced juicy tomatoes, and calmed down.

The kitchen, warm and comforting was where Cory would run to her grandmother when hurt. Grandma would kiss the bruise and say, *'Bubbie will make your boo-boo better.'* Cory kept her alive by remembering many of her sayings. Grandma had given her love in many ways. Understood what it meant to Cory to look different from schoolmates and raised by grandparents instead of parents. She knew Cory's deepest secrets. Secrets she hadn't shared with her father or grandfather. From her family, Cory incorporated the work ethic and a love of learning and music. And big time Jewish guilt. 'Guilt is justified *only* when a person is *truly* responsible. Guilt can be assuaged by restitution,' she had said to patients, but in her own case, she felt guilty for stuff she *assumed* was her responsibility.

After a hodgepodge dinner of left over vegetables and a quesidilla, Cory luxuriated in a warm tub of lavender scented bubbles with sweet memories of her grandparents. She listened to the rhythm of the rain strike the windowpane. Suddenly, she remembered she had been so intent on finding the way home accident-free, she had neglected to activate the security system.

51

A bad omen. The Honda wouldn't start. Hamilton lifted the hood, poked around and realized he had to order a part. Now he'd have to use the Eldorado instead. He unscrewed his license plate and replaced it with an old one he had found in a junk yard.

Hamilton followed the shrink from her office to her home. Stupid woman didn't have enough sense to see him in the rear view mirror. He slunk in his seat in the Eldorado and watched her enter through the garage. In a brief moment when the rain let up, he recognized the security system warning sign posted outside the house. He drummed his fingers on the steering wheel, contemplating his next move as the rain poured hard and the wind whipped up the street.

If he lifted a window, he'd set off the alarm. By the time the cops came, he would have killed her and made his escape, but he wasn't sure she was alone. He had noticed a light turned on upstairs before she'd pulled into the driveway. He hated knowing so little about his victim. Much of the pleasure came from his secret intimate knowledge of them. It gave him power. The contract Dr. Cohen had signed with Superior listed no personal facts apart from her birth date, psychology license and social security number. Because the bitch gave a post office box for her home address, he had to follow her.

Suddenly, through the rain, he noticed the headlights of a dark car approach his rear. Damn it to hell! The driver parked a few feet behind him and stayed in the car. Hamilton's pulse throbbed. He reassured himself. Perhaps the person waited for the rain to stop. He would wait too.

The rain increased in intensity, accompanied by strong wind. Trees swayed and a palm swooned as the two men played a waiting game. Hamilton's hands gripped the steering wheel. The key in the ignition, his foot was ready to hit the gas pedal.

★   ★   ★

Sergeant Sharpley had asked Detective Lewis to send a patrol car to check Dr. Cory Cohen's neighborhood. Lewis knew that on a night like this it would be hard to find someone available, so he did it himself.

The detective saw the black car parked in front of him with what appeared to be a heavy-set figure slumped in the driver's seat. Though the rain fell heavily, from his headlights he made out a late model black Cadillac Eldorado with a battered license plate. Incongruity aroused his suspicion.

He called in the license number and learned that it did not belong to a registered vehicle.

★ ★ ★

The bath water was getting uncomfortably cool when the portable phone rang and Cory picked it up.

'Hi. Lewis here. I'm in my car outside your house. There's someone sitting in a late model black Cadillac Eldorado in front of me, Doc. Any idea who he could be?'

'N-no. What are you doing here?' Chilled, she stepped out of the tub and wriggled into a warm terry robe.

'Checking to see if all's well.'

'That's a relief. Thank you. You're outside in this storm?'

'It's my job, you know. I don't mind.'

'I don't know anyone who'd sit in a car on this street. My neighbors usually garage their cars. I'll check and call you back.' She scribbled his cell number and phoned the three neighbors on her street. All were home with cars garaged and none expected company.

Cory reported this to Lewis. She peeked out the window and watched him step out of his car and head towards the black car. When he approached, the driver sped away. With fear for her new friend, she saw him jump into his car and race off.

★   ★   ★

Hamilton knew his predicament was serious when the car behind him flashed a light and a siren screeched. He started to panic. He was furious at himself for not finding out more about Dr. Cohen and her neighborhood before he set out to do damage control. Was the area patrolled by an unmarked car? Why was he pursued? Obviously, his car did not belong in her enclave. He should have investigated, before he made the trip. He berated himself for acting precipitously, but realized he hadn't had time to check.

Sweat chilled him. His heart thumped so hard, it felt as though his chest would explode. The throbbing in his head increased. A sharp pain in his left eye alarmed him. A revival of iritis. He had no time to stop and insert eye drops. First, he must escape.

Hamilton drove through a deep trench-like

puddle, his panic increasing. His mouth was incredibly dry. He felt his blood pressure rise and heard himself pant. Afraid he would collapse, he steeled himself, applying light pressure to his brakes, relieved to find they weren't damaged. A succession of deep breaths reduced his panic. Craving water, he felt he'd soon die without it. He thought of opening the door and let the rain pour into his mouth, but it would be insufficient and waste precious time. He steeled himself against the compulsion to do so.

The street seemed wide and easy to drive, but as he headed uphill, falling rocks obstructed his path. With difficulty, he skirted over them. His Eldorado bumped and swerved along curves. Soon Hamilton reached a rural area of ranches. His headlights shone on white fences that formed corrals for horses. Orange groves and eucalyptus trees were in abundance. He had arrived in Rancho Santa Fe. Not as he wished to arrive. Not like the big shot affluent executives who lived there, for whom he had contempt, but emulated.

From his rear-view mirror he saw the car pursuing him spin out of control. Hamilton pushed hard on his gas pedal. Coming to the crossroads, he could no longer see the car behind him. He turned left and drove into the driveway of a mansion. The main house was barely visible from the distance, and he saw no lights coming from it. Hamilton drove behind a bank of orange groves and shut off the engine. He sat hidden in the dark with rain splashing against his windows. A chorus of coyotes howled from a nearby canyon and a dog barked hoarsely in response.

Hamilton heard sirens. Surely, his suspicious car wasn't enough to send a team of cops out to chase him in such a rainstorm. The sirens were probably responding to an accident.

His thirst demanded quenching. Slowly, he opened the car door and shut the interior lights. He raised his head and opened his mouth. Raindrops trickled on his tongue. Hamilton gulped several times. Careful not to make noise, he left the door ajar, slid back the seat and allowed himself to get drenched. He pulled the precious bottle of eye drops from his pocket and inserted the liquid. Relief replaced his panic.

When Hamilton arrived home he had a fever. The thermometer read 102. He was burning up.

Not since he was twelve-years old, had his temperature risen so high. He remembered that time well. His foster parents at work, he was home alone. Although sick, he slid out of bed to snoop in the master bedroom where he found several magazines with color photos of women in bondage and other sado-masochistic poses. Studying the pictures, he had become sexually aroused and mastur-bated. He pilfered one of the magazines and stored it in his notebook, treasuring it. When the pictures became frayed, he photo-copied them and discarded the originals in the mailbox of a rectory, delighting in his mischief. Through the years, he had relied on graphic images of women with bloody gashes to give him an instant erection. A collection of print pornography served as a springboard for his erotic pleasure. Not tonight. His energy was spent.

Hamilton swallowed two aspirin tablets and three cups of water and fell asleep. In the middle of the night he awakened, his silk pajamas plastered to his skin. For a moment he panicked, thinking he had peed in bed, but realized the fever had broken. He showered, changed his bed linens and drank water. Naked, he slithered back into his fresh satin sheets, prepared to sleep. Chuckling to himself, he remembered reading that most wrong-doers stricken with guilt, have insom-nia. Hamilton felt superior since guilt didn't exist in his repertoire.

52

After Detective Lewis left in pursuit, Cory set the alarm, brewed double strength chamomile tea, and flicked on all the house lights. She slid between the bed sheets, flipped the TV remote and set the phone and a flashlight on top of her blanket. Hoping the good detective was not in danger, she waited to hear from him.

Two hours later, he rang.

'Here's an update, Doc. I chased the Eldorado with my siren and flashing light on, but he didn't stop. His license was bogus. Unfortunately, I got stuck in a gully and the no good creep got away.'

'Wow! Are you okay?'

'Sure, Doc.'

'What a job! I appreciate all you've done.'

'I rarely get thanks, Doc. It feels good.'

'I bet I know whose car it was,' Cory said.

'You might win, but we've got no evidence. You know something? If I'd apprehended him tonight, I sure as hell would have hauled his ass in. What a grilling he'd get for using a phony plate and resisting arrest. He'd be in a cell full of piss and vomit. Guys like him think they're pretty smart, but they mess up, and when they do, we're ready for them, you know.'

'This is so damn infuriating.'

'Tell me about it. Listen, you better lay low for awhile. I'm certain he won't return to your house, but I think you may need some protection at the office. I'll get someone to check both places periodically, okay?'

'Maybe I should go away for the weekend?'

'Not a bad idea. Give me a call if you do. Take care now, Doc.'

Cory examined her options. Get out of town alone for the weekend or ask Ron to join her. She punched in the first four digits of his phone, and hung up. Taking a deep breath, she picked up the phone again, this time completing the call.

'Ron, I need to get away. Would you like to fly to San Francisco with me this weekend?'

'Sorry, Cory, but I'm going up to see my folks.'

'Would you like me to — '

'I'd better go alone.' His words were quick, terse.

'Oh, last night — '

'Look, I've got to go now, Cory. I'll call you when I get back.'

Disappointed and hurt, Cory wanted to tell him about the recent event and the detectives warning, but he had interrupted. After hanging up, she berated herself for not confronting him with his coldness, but realized she was not ready. His ambivalence mirrored her own. Hers born of his moodiness, his, of her obsession. It hurt to think about him, because there were things she would miss. Sharing music, physical pleasure, and he had the capacity to be compassionate, like the night of the attack on Ann. But he was like an erratic faucet pouring steamy water one moment, icey, the next.

With danger close, she could not afford pondering the destiny of her relationship. She had to act fast to protect herself. Pope was devious. Not knowing what to expect or when to expect it was intolerable.

Cory examined her options. She could stay with Betty, but was afraid to put her friend in jeopardy. Better to leave town.

She stuffed a small carry-on with essentials, shoved a paperback novel into a large handbag, and stashed it all in the car trunk. She figured she would be safer in another vehicle.

Since the defroster was not working and the car needed repairs, the next morning Cory scheduled an early appointment with Jerry, her mechanic. When you have an old

BMW, you have a long term relationship with your mechanic, she remarked to herself.

The storm had stopped, leaving the streets wet and shiny and the air cool and fresh. Fallen eucalyptus leaves made travel slippery. A giant palm lay across a main street, causing a traffic jam.

Cory's cautious drive up the Coast Highway to Jerry's took fifteen minutes.

It was not surprising, what with all the foreign cars in the area, to find his shop full of BMW's Mercedes and Porsches. Although Jerry catered to all German species, BMW was his specialty.

'Are you having trouble with Eva?' Cory would not let him forget Eva Braun was her nickname for the misbehaving car.

'Right now, it's the defroster and it's time for a tune-up and oil change, Jerry.'

'Well, you see how busy we are . . . '

'That's okay. I'm in no hurry. Do you have a loaner to spare for awhile?' she asked.

'Uh . . . '

'I need to drive a different car for awhile.'

Catching her drift, he cocked his head and smiled. 'Listen, I've got so much work and everyone's in such a hurry that I can lend you something for a few days or longer.' With his wrench he pointed to a twelve-year-old gleaming emerald green BMW 725. He took the key off a hook and handed it to Cory. 'Don't hold your breath waiting for me to call when Eva's ready, okay?'

'Good deal, Jerry. She's in great company. Thanks.' Cory wanted to kiss his grease smeared face, but settled for a thumbs up gesture.

Grinning, he waved her away and turned his attention to the engine of a late model shiny silver 925. Cory wondered whether Jerry felt as much passion for women as he did for Beemers.

After filling out a work order, she grabbed the stuff from her car and stashed it on the passenger's seat of the luxurious loaner. She sank into the soft leather seat and felt like a million well used bucks. Cory stopped to fill the gas tank, then drove to the airport where she grabbed the next flight out to San Francisco, her escape to anonymity and safety.

Before take-off, she phoned Detective Lewis and told him her plans.

'Have fun,' he said.

'Thanks. I intend to.'

The plane climbed towards cruise altitude. Feeling safe, she closed her eyes and imagined the tastes and architecture of her favorite city and thought she heard a distant fog-horn. When she opened her eyes, the man next to her was snoring.

After landing, she phoned the Tuscan Inn. A room awaited her, as did the airporter bus to Fisherman's Wharf. Cory arrived at the hotel in under an hour. Greeted by the doorman, she felt secure. Apart from a pushy street person's approaching her for a handout, she expected no other encounter.

Tired and hungry, she had a glass of wine and stuffed herself with focaccio bread in the hotel dining room. By the time her dinner arrived, she was satiated. She tucked herself in bed early, the paperback a satisfactory companion.

Saturday, after a continental breakfast in the hotel lobby, she trotted towards Washington Square and joined elderly Asians for an hour of TaiChi. She traipsed through North Beach and stopped at City Lights Bookstore to breathe the intellectual atmosphere. Cory bought green tea in Japantown and lunched in Chinatown. In the evening, she rode the cable-car to Union Square and window-shopped the art galleries. Sunday, she ferried to Sausilito and dined in a Victorian house. When it was time to head home, she didn't want to budge.

Cory realized she had not given much thought to what she had left behind. She had successfully dropped out for the weekend.

Reluctantly, she surrendered to her responsibilities and flew back to San Diego. At the airport parking lot, she searched for her white car and was about to panic until she noticed the loaner and realized she had switched cars.

Cory's home alarm was dependable and she had set three house lights on timers. Detective Lewis said the place would be patrolled, but this did not remove her fear. Pope had evaded police for God-only-knows-how-long.

By the time she headed up her street, night had fallen. The house was dark. Positive she had set those reliable timers, she felt her stomach flutter.

She parked a few houses away from hers and made several calls from a cell phone. Lewis was off-duty. Her home security company said the alarm had not gone off. San Diego Gas and Electric had no reports of power outages on her street. Finally, she pressed the emergency button, connecting her to the sheriff dispatcher.

Within ten minutes, a black and white pulled up and two officers approached. Cory stepped out of the car and they accompanied her to her front door. Unlocking it, she disarmed the security. One of the officers held a large flashlight and told Cory to wait in her car. The other had his gun drawn as they entered.

Watching from across the street, she was about to start a nail-biting habit, but soon the house was ablaze with lights. About fifteen minutes later, the officers came out and said the house was secure. There was no evidence of a break-in or any tampering. They had no explanation for the disconnected timers, other than she had not set them. Cory thanked the men for their help, kicked the door shut behind them and secured the alarm.

Puzzled about the mysterious timers, she fiddled with them and they worked fine. She could not understand why she was so sure she had set them. She distinctly remembered doing it. Unless she was losing her mind. Or Pope had been there. No. That made no sense. She expected much worse than mischief from him. It was bad enough that he slashed, raped, murdered, but to be so damn devious — for what purpose?

Karate did not help Jennifer, who was more expert than Cory. It did not help because her guard was down. Cory was vigilant. She double checked the security system, flipped on lights in half the house and tuned the radio to KLON. Blues night.

Visions of a terrifying shower scene in

Alfred Hichcock's *Psycho* have made many women afraid to take a shower when alone or in a strange place, but it never bothered Cory before. Tonight she showered in record time and crawled into bed with The New Yorker. Rattled, she could not concentrate. She switched off the bedroom light and reviewed her comfortable solo weekend. The satisfying bed-time story put her to sleep.

★ ★ ★

The next morning, Cory awoke alert and eager to start the day. At seven, she drove to the parking garage of Superior. It didn't take her long to spot the only black Cadillac Eldorado. She jotted down the license tag number and would check again for a possible late arrival.

With ample time before her first patient, she parked the loaner and surveyed the area.

Superior occupied two stories of a three-story modern glass and steel office structure. The center of the lobby floor contained an atrium, waterfall and café. Four tables stood on the periphery sheltered by dark blue umbrellas. The scent of fresh made coffee announced the café was open for breakfast. Cory ordered a well-done scrambled egg, wheat toast and coffee. She

348

hoped to be fortunate enough to eavesdrop on staff from Superior. She sat at a table and read the newspaper while waiting for breakfast and the arrival of patrons.

In a few minutes two women sat down at a table within earshot. Cory judged one to be in her forties, the other mid-twenties.

'Superior isn't the worst place to work,' the younger woman said.

Cory concealed her excitement and pretended to be engrossed in the newspaper.

'Except for that Mr. Pope. What a dick-head! He gives me the creeps.' The younger women frowned. 'Works all hours. No one knows anything about him. He keeps to himself. What's he afraid of, anyway?' she asked.

Cory continued to gaze at the newspaper.

'Please pass the marmalade, Sue. Yeah, I think there's something weird about him. He's too, too private. So cold. Never even cracks a smile. Such a snob. And what a fuss-pot,' the older woman said, digging her knife into the jelly jar. 'Everything in his department has to be absolutely perfect.'

'That business with the clown really spooked him. Can you imagine, he made poor Jim Corita ask around to see who did it?' She poured cold milk on her cereal and it snapped, crackled and popped. She peeled a ripe banana and bit into it. One bite of banana followed by one spoon of cereal. The pattern repeated until the woman finished eating.

So orderly. Pope was orderly too. His crimes were well calculated. Cory wished the cops could demand his semen, hair and blood samples, but it would violate *his* civil rights. The authorities would have to establish probable cause and they had no *substantial* evidence linking him to the crimes.

'Did he ever find out who put the clown up to it?' the older woman asked.

'I heard it was Barry. He's such a comedian. By the way, I have a date with him next week.'

'Really?' The older woman smiled and sipped her coffee.

Cory wished they hadn't changed the subject. Soon the server presented the checks.

After Cory paid, she rushed into the elevator with the women, stepping behind them. She hoped to hear more about Hamilton Pope, but they rode in silence. When they reached the second floor, the women got out and a man rushed to enter. The man was Hamilton Pope. Cory's stomach did cartwheels. She adjusted her wide-brimmed hat and leaned on the 'door close' button. The elevator closed in his face.

Cory heaved a heavy sigh. What would have happened had she been in the elevator alone with him? She knew him, but would he recognize her in sunglasses and hat?

On the next floor, she stepped from the elevator and pretended to study a suite directory. She scanned the vacant hallway and ducked into the stairwell leading to the garage. Jittery, she peered around to see if Hamilton Pope had followed, but he was nowhere in sight. She searched the garage for black Eldorados and jotted down three license plate numbers. One she had spied earlier and two more.

Cory planned to return later to wait outside the garage for Pope. She would follow 'the cold, dick-head, weirdo' to his house. Maybe learn more about him and catch him off guard before he would attack another victim, or her.

When she arrived at her office, she phoned Detective Lewis and left a message for him to check the license numbers she gave. She said she'd be at karate in the evening.

Deputy Frankie Kelly was the first session of the day. No miraculous surprises. She had not shed her porcupine quills. Frankie had not received any calls, but seemed willing to talk to Cory.

'Never like being alone. Always have some

351

dude around me. Makes me feel wanted.'

'What was it like when you were alone this week?'

'I wasn't completely alone. Hernandez was nearby at all times staking out the place, but he may as well have been invisible. I don't like being alone and having to get into my own head. Gives me the creeps.' She shrugged her shoulders.

'What do you think about that triggers the creeps?'

'Me. I have to make conversation with myself. It feels weird — scary.'

'So you like others around to keep you from feeling scared?'

'Uh-huh.' She wiggled her foot.

'Why did you choose a career in law enforcement, Frankie?'

She rubbed her chin with her palm. 'You think there's a connection?'

'Do you?'

'Just like a shrink to answer a question with a question.' Her face flushed. 'You answer. That's what you're paid to do.'

'Seems like you're angry at me for making you work.'

'Is that what you're doing? Aren't you supposed to do the work?'

'We do it together. If I spoon feed you, you won't learn to do it yourself.'

'Oh. Sorry.'

'We're making progress. You apologized.' Cory smiled.

'Getting back to your question. I like the uniform and I like the gun.'

'Maybe the props help you compensate for that scared feeling.'

Frankie wiggled her foot faster. 'Don't like to admit it, but you're probably right. Although when we're in pursuit, I'm scared too. But it's different. Have to act tough. Besides, I have a hot partner, so I'm never alone. Got my piece, too.' She slapped her side as if the gun were sitting there in a holster.

'You could get somewhere exploring what's behind the feeling, but our sessions are limited. Would you consider continuing therapy on your own with another therapist?'

'Oh, you really think I should, do you? You're so smart, you've got to be right, huh?' she sneered. After a long pause, she said, 'Well, maybe there's something to what you say. I got a lot more issues to look at.'

'Like?'

'Thinking about quitting the department.'

'A word of caution, Frankie. When you start therapy, it's unwise to make impulsive decisions. Give yourself time to figure things out.'

'Oh, is that right? Thought you weren't supposed to give me advice.'

'I give suggestions. It's your decision to follow them or not. I think you'd learn a lot about yourself if you figure out why you want to turn me off with your criticism. Let's make that a homework assignment.'

'You're the Doc.' She snarled.

* * *

Pleased that Frankie was a rarity in her patient load, Cory concentrated on those who were eager to learn and change. Those who chose therapy on their own.

The last session of the day was at four o'clock, but the patient had canceled.

At three forty-five, Cory hurried to Superior. Spotting the sole black Eldorado in the garage, she parked the car on the street outside the sole exit. From what little she had gathered about Pope, his was probably the first car in the garage and the last one out.

Having read that Mozart's music calms, she brought cassettes of his last five symphonies. Slouching in the seat of the car, she listened to her Walkman. She soon learned detective work requires patience and a giant size bladder.

Cory sat in the car for two hours until she

nearly burst. She wondered how cops managed after drinking copious amounts of coffee during surveillance. Maybe they carried containers for voiding. This could work for men, but how did women officers relieve themselves? She imagined Deputy Kelly in that uncomfortable position, and chuckled.

Cory's anxiety grew with the pressure from her full bladder. Hamilton Pope could be examining treatment requests right now, planning his next attack, while she just sat there in misery. *Were I my own patient, I would counsel myself to focus my energy elsewhere and leave the cops and robbers stuff to professionals,* she told herself. The message from her body, clear and urgent, required a rapid response.

At the fancy restaurant next door, she asked directions to the restroom, but the pretentious, tuxedoed maitre d' screwed up his face and replied, 'It's for patrons only.'

'I'll order something.'

'We have no tables.'

'I'll wait.' Cory started for the restroom when the man blocked her and said, 'This isn't a public facility.'

'And you aren't a penguin, but you could have fooled me,' she snapped, ready to burst. 'If I wasn't a lady, I'd whip it out and pee on you,' she muttered, surprised at her outburst.

By the time she had used a gas station restroom and drove back to Superior, the Eldorado had left. Some detective I am, she thought.

★ ★ ★

That evening Cory met Detective Lewis at the karate studio, returning his wink with a smile. After they worked out, he walked her to the green BMW. 'Classy car, Doc,' he said and whistled his approval.

'It's a loaner while my old 325 is getting repaired.' Cory always apologized for having a BMW, unless she was speaking to the owner of a more luxurious automobile.

'You're smart to drive a different car since you've been followed. It could happen again, you know. How was your weekend in Frisco?'

'So good, I didn't want to come back. Thanks for having my place checked. It's a comfort. Was there anything suspicious?'

'Nope, but your house was dark. I expected the lights on timers.'

'I thought I connected them, but when I got home, they were off. I called nine-one-one. The officers investigated my place and found nothing wrong.' She shrugged her shoulders.

'Sometimes we think about doing something, get distracted and think we've already done it.' He scratched his chin. 'But you're the shrink.'

'Doctor Lewis, I think we've changed roles.' Cory related her adventures at Superior. The detective rolled his eyes.

'What about the license numbers I called in?'

'One is registered to Hamilton Pope with a post office address. But we've got his home address anyway, you know. We've already run a check on him and he came up clean. DMV didn't give us the info on the Eldorado. Either he bought it recently, or DMV slipped up.

'The other two belong to men who don't fit the description of the man I'd followed. One is a huge African American and the other is a slight, blonde man. They work at Superior, too. Maybe they all got Cadillacs as bonuses. Getting back to Pope . . . he's got no criminal record, Doc. Not even an unpaid parking ticket. No military record. Doesn't even own a credit card.'

'No credit card? That's odd. Most people charge expenses for business records. Unless he's bankrupt and can't get credit.'

'No record of bankruptcy. No debts.'

'Like he wants to make sure there's no

record of his activities or purchases.'

'Yeah. No paper trail. He's a strange guy. Super-cautious. Probably paranoid. Wouldn't you say, Doc?'

'Sounds that way. What about past employment?'

'Neat freaks usually have job problems, and a study of the crime scene shows our nut-case is well organized. But there were no problems on his last job. At least none they'd tell us. Nowadays, you know, everybody's afraid of getting sued for giving out too much information.'

'What've you found out about the murder at Superior?'

'No apparent motive. No known enemies. So far we're not able to pin it on anyone at Superior or anyone else in the building. Security looks clean too. No suspects yet. Seems baffling right now. Nothing more I can do about your suspicion, but I do agree with it, you know.'

'Detective, Pope was Marge Abbott's supervisor. She was killed after she asked him about eye medicine. A perfectly innocuous question infuriated him. Don't you consider that odd?'

'Your friend Olie Baxter said Ms. Abbott's boss flipped. It's hearsay and wouldn't hold up in court. Maybe Pope was just annoyed and it had nothing to do with what Abbott asked him, you know. Look, his alibi checked out. He was at the movies the time she was murdered. The cashier remembered him because Pope paid with a hundred dollar bill and the manager had to make the change.'

Cory sighed. 'A sure way to call attention to himself.'

'Yeah, but we can't prove it.'

'Damn. If we knew more about him, we could predict his next move.'

'Oh yeah, you and the FBI.' He nodded.

'I've read their profiles of serial rapists and murderers. The FBI guys are sharp. From what you know, does Pope meet the criteria?'

'So far, we haven't been able to find out much about him. He keeps a low profile.'

'Has he recently surfaced here?' Cory asked, leaning against the car.

'He worked for Behavioral Health before the merger with Superior, you know. The company moved him down here when they relocated. Nothing negative on his personnel record.'

'Have you checked other locations for similar attacks?'

'Of course, Doc. It's routine. We get hot sheets and a daily briefing with other law enforcement agencies. Currently, there are no reports of rapists fitting the description obtained from our victims.'

'No slashers on the loose that also rape?' Cory asked.

'One still on the loose is a biter. Another is short and thin.'

'I wonder how many rapes go unreported.' She turned the key in the car door lock.

'We estimate about eighty percent. Most women are afraid to report it. Scared he'll go after them.' The detective held the door open for her.

'Or, they're ashamed. I wonder how long he's been out there doing his number. He couldn't have just started. There's usually an early history of sociopathic behavior. Killing or torturing animals, fire-setting, stealing, fighting. Something.' Cory slid into the car.

'This guy is a well organized offender. He premeditates. Plans. He's logical. Cautious. A nut case like this can get away with his crimes for a long time. And because he doesn't get caught right away, he thinks he's . . . what's the word?'

'Invincible?'

'Yeah, but he's so confident, he gets sloppy. Starts making mistakes. Then — bam!' Lewis struck his fist into his palm. 'That's when he gets apprehended. Most of the time it's by accident, like when they run a red light.'

'Detective Lewis, please don't tell me we

360

have to wait for him to screw up. It can take years.'

'A murder case takes priority. We put a lot of resources into it. As for you, Doc, you ought not take it upon yourself to do any more surveillance. First off, it can be dangerous. What would you have done had you tailed him? If he is the one, you'd be up shit creek. Oh, excuse me, Doc.' Lewis blushed.

'Second, it ain't easy. Surveillance can be boring and a waste of time, you know. Leave it to us. You've got other things to do in your rightful profession for which you *are* trained. Detectives working the case have staked him out. They did that with all the employees after the murder at Superior.'

'And?'

'Zilch. The guy works late and seems to have no other life. He's clever, but we're no fools either, you know.'

'Detective Lewis, I know you're a smart guy. Bronx High of Science accepts only the cream. And police work requires technical skills and good judgment. I have to say, I respect your heroism.'

'Don't make me blush, huh? Well, maybe I'm too sensitive. Not a good attribute for a cop, huh, Doc?'

'Actually, I think sensitivity is a good trait

for everybody. I bet you've had your share of undeserved abuse.'

'Everyone does, you know. Used to be we got no respect. Dumb cops. That's what people thought. If TV is good for something, it educates the public about our work. Shows us doing smart stuff like examining crime scenes — collecting forensic evidence, using computer technology, you know. And in the line of fire, too.'

'And when you're shown as real people, the public can be sympathetic.'

'Yeah, Doc. Not all cops are racist, you know. Some of us are real social workers, you know.'

'With personal lives.'

He grinned. 'Not much time for that, you know.'

Cory really liked Detective George Lewis and sensed the seeds of friendship taking root. He didn't talk down to her, was open about his work, and himself. Conscientious, he wanted to catch the bad guy as much as she did. Lewis, punctuating his sentences with 'you know,' typical of some New Yorkers made Cory feel at home.

He shut her car door and tapped on her window. When she cracked it open, he said, 'Be careful, Doc.'

Cory considered inviting the detective for

coffee, but thought he'd get the wrong impression and she was determined to maintain a professional relationship. 'Thanks. I wish he were as easy a target for you as his victims are for him.' Driving away, she waved.

Although Cory enjoyed solitude, she didn't feel like going home. She shuddered thinking that if Detective Lewis had not been around the night before, she might have been murdered. For several years after her rape, she had felt vulnerable, but after she had studied karate, completed grad school, and raised a family, the feeling gradually went away. Until now. Now, the fear of being alone bordered on terror.

She punched in Betty's number on the cell phone.

'Sorry, Cory, I'm plumb tired. I'd like to see you, but I'm going to bed now. Alone. It's going to be that way for quite awhile. I may not like it, but . . . '

'Being alone isn't so bad. I should know. We'll get together another time and I'll list the merits of celibacy. Sleep well.'

In the misty evening Cory cruised around with apprehension that grew to anxiety when she contemplated being home. What had been her sanctuary, became a place of dread. She should have invited herself to Betty's. Pope wouldn't know she had changed cars, but hypervigilant, she scanned the rear view mirror with great frequency.

Cory had no experience in discerning a professional tail. Pope, good as a pro, could have followed her. Too worked up to go to sleep, Cory wrestled with the possibility of staying in a hotel again, but figured it was less secure than her house.

Tonight she felt safer staying out late in the borrowed BMW than alone at home. Needing a distraction, she checked out a new coffee house that promised jazz. A cheery display of abstract paintings in primary colors reminiscent of Miro perked up the otherwise gloomy café. A trio on keyboard, trumpet, and drums, who from their physical appearance, represented three generations had taken their positions in the small space allotted them. They seemed stricken with stage fright. Maybe this was their first gig together, or at all. The uncrowded café offered a choice of seats. Cory chose a table fourth row center from the make-shift stage and gave the musicians an encouraging smile. She ordered a cappuccino, settled in the comfortable chair and prepared to relax.

In the first set, the trio approached each other tentatively, like shy suitors speaking different languages, ignoring each other's musical ventures. A wandering horn intruded upon a technically flawless keyboard. The monotonous hammering drum suggested the drummer invested heavily in headache remedy stock. Cory understood that musicians needed time to warm up. She would give them a chance to get acquainted. She did not want to face the music at home.

After a short break during which she munched on a biscotti and politely warded off the attentions of a fellow sitting nearby, the trio returned. This time, sheet music helped their timing with fine arrangements of Cole Porter tunes. Laid back mellow music lightened the mood and from the sound of it, their confidence increased.

The set over, Cory left the café, enveloped by fog. She realized she should have expected it from the mist she had seen after karate class. She was angry at herself for not thinking ahead.

Cory had parked the borrowed BMW next to a lamp post a few yards away. On a murky night, she would have preferred her more visible old white car.

With caution, she surveyed the area as she trotted towards the car. From the corner of her eye, she glimpsed a huge shadowy figure in the gray mist behind her. Gripped with fear that she had been shadowed, her muscles tensed in readiness. The jagged edges of her keys stuck out from between her fingers prepared to plunge at an assailant. She took a deep breath ready to scream as the figure came closer. Another bulky figure joined the first and suddenly there was laughter. Turning, she faced two of the musicians lugging their cumbersome instruments. She heaved a sigh of relief, climbed into the car and slowly pulled away.

Through the years she had studied karate and learned to be aware of her environment, fear had not touched her. During the assault on Ann, she had reacted fearlessly, but now she was scared. Cory knew he was after her, but did not know when he would attack. Frequent glances at the rear view mirror were futile. Vapors obscured the car behind her except for the blur of headlights.

Cory concentrated on the yellow line in the middle of the street to guide her home. Her hands clutching the steering wheel, gave off a shiny hue. The rumbling in her stomach was a counterpoint to the noise from the defroster. Her heart beat in rhythm to the windshield wipers.

No cars were ahead to lead the way. The one behind was the only one she had seen on the road. Silhouettes of houses and trees were indistinguishable. Afraid of getting lost, she considered parking on the street and spending the night in the car, but it was cold and the dense fog made street parking unsafe. Pope could be behind her.

Uncertain of danger from front and rear, terror gnawed. Cory inched the car forward. The driver behind did likewise. All she wanted now was to arrive home safely, activate the security system, and adopt a German Shepherd. When she would want his protection, she would give him German commands and tow him around in her car named, Eva. He would have two personas: Adolf the Vicious, and Hans the Gentle.

The signal light turned green. Cory proceeded straight ahead, and noticing the headlights at her rear had disappeared, she exhaled a whistle. The rhythm in her chest slowed. The fog evaporated as she passed a familiar street. Rounding the corner, she ran into a bank of heavy fog obscuring visibility as she approached her house, but the lights she had left on were a beacon, guiding her to safety.

Once inside, Cory armed the security system. The answering machine blinked and she retrieved the message: 'George Lewis here. Just a reminder. Take care, Doc. Remember you're not a police officer.'

53

Hamilton's plans were in motion. He phoned Erin from a phone booth, played his cassette of the canaries and told her he would call again Thursday evening. He expected her to be primed for a visit from him. Russell had accepted his dinner invitation for Thursday evening.

Now he had to figure out a plan to kill the psychologist. He did not want another misadventure at her house. Hamilton checked her well-lit office garage and noticed frequent security patrols. Doing it there would be risky. Many of the tenants in her building were psychotherapists who contracted with Superior and Behavioral Health. That gave him an idea.

Mid-day, Pope left the building and strolled on the shady side of the street to a phone booth six streets away and telephoned Dr. Cohen's office.

'This is Robert Russell. I need an appointment with the doctor right away. I'm immensely depressed since losing my wife. I can't function. I can't live like this.'

'If it's that bad sir, you could call the

Suicide Prevention Hot Line. I can give you the number,' Ann replied.

'No. I'm not about to kill myself today, but I want to impress you with the fact that I *am* quite depressed.'

'Who referred you, sir?'

Hamilton was ready with a name on his list. 'Dr. Jolson. He told me she's a good psychologist. I want someone experienced.'

'If you're on a managed care program, you'll have to call there first to get a treatment authorization.'

'No. No. No. I'm a private patient. I'll pay in cash on the spot. I need an appointment today.'

'I'm sorry, sir. Dr. Cohen is booked, but she has an opening tomorrow at three.'

'Yes. That will have to do.'

'May I have your phone number, please?'

He hesitated. 'Why do you need my number? I'm not home and I'll be at your office tomorrow at three.'

'I'm sorry, Mr. Russell, we don't make appointments with people who won't give us a phone number. You can call the Suicide Prevention Hot Line. The number is . . . '

'Oh, all right. My number is six-three-two-thousand,' he mumbled and hung up.

Hamilton hurried back to his office and slammed the door behind him. He hated delays. Even though he had offered to pay in cash on the spot, he could not get in to see her until tomorrow. Who the hell did that haughty bitch think she was anyway, making him wait.

Spotting the stack of faxed treatment requests on his desk, he calmed down. He knew they were a good antidote for his anger.

Thumbing through the batch, he fixed his eyes on Franklynne's. The hair on back of his neck rose. A dream come true. At a beach cottage, no less. Never had he expected it to be this easy. Lucky devil. He could hardly wait. The rush of excitement was so great, he thought he would pass out.

He had to work fast and repair the Honda. Hamilton phoned an auto supply shop. What luck! They stocked the part.

Hamilton headed out for the materials. He rode the speed limit and parked one street from the auto parts shop. He jogged the rest of the way. The clerk had the part ready. Hamilton, the sole customer paid cash and rushed home.

After Marge's murder, he was more cautious than ever. Concerned that the cops could be watching him, he maintained a low profile. To assure he would be unrecognizable, he changed into jeans, baseball cap and the Navy T-shirt he'd bought at a surplus store. Hamilton slipped a Band-Aid over the cleft in his chin. The cap covering his head made a difference. He grinned at his reflection in the mirror. He took the stairway to the garage.

Within two hours, he completed the repair. The Honda hummed like new.

In the middle of the night he drove it to Frankie's neighborhood where he noticed several parked cars, one in her driveway and several on the street. He spotted a dumpster in front of a house under construction a few doors from hers. From the state of the structure he knew the dumpster would be there the next day.

The following morning he drove the Eldorado to work. At lunch time he surveyed the corridor for personnel. The place was deserted. He locked his door and bolted downstairs. Hamilton stopped at a Mexican fast food place and bought four beef burritos with extra salsa and a large coke which he consumed on the bus ride home. He changed into his rendezvous disguise and drove the Honda towards the beach cottage, humming all the way.

Scanning the area for parked cars, he glimpsed one in the driveway and another a half block away. The street was empty of pedestrians. Hamilton figured people were at work or school. Except Franklynne.

He lit a cigar stub and placed it in the fold of a book of matches. The burning end of the butt stuck out one-half inch. Quickly, he dropped it in the dumpster and jumped in his Honda. Hamilton pulled away and parked around the corner. The alley behind her house provided a good hiding place. Soon the dumpster was aflame.

An easy mark, that Franklynne. House bound and lonely.

Astonished, Hamilton saw a man run out of her house. Had things changed over night for her? Well, he would make damn sure they did again. And how! It was good luck for him that she did not run out, too.

Hamilton climbed into the window expecting to shock and overpower her, but was disappointed to find her appearing comatose. He remembered scrawling his recommendation for anti-depressants and sleep medication on her treatment authorization. She had probably overdosed. He shook her and she stirred. He slapped her face. She murmured, but failed to awaken. His luck turned lousy. He would miss the pleasure of witnessing her expression as he ripped through her. It was for the best. Someone might hear her scream.

Hamilton whipped out his knife and pulled

down his sweat pants. He slashed and raped her as she moaned, eyes shut. Spittle fell from his mouth as he watched the blood gush out from her neck and chest. He thought for a moment her eyes opened, so he smashed his fist at her head and heard her skull crack. He looked at her eyes again. They were closed.

Blood splattered her bedding. Blood ran on her clothing. Blood saturated his gloves. He had to get out of there fast.

Hamilton dangled his feet from the window sill and surveyed the area outside. When he was certain no one saw him, he leaped out.

The dumpster-diversion tactic had been effective. A throng of elderly people, a fire engine and equipment littered the street.

In the Honda, he peeled off his soiled gloves, shirt and shoes and tossed them in a plastic sack next to him, paying attention to the speed limit as he took off, gloating over an adventure that had worked out just like those of years ago when he had stalked women, but better because this mission was special.

At home, Hamilton threw his blood stained clothing into his washing machine with bleach and detergent on the extra heavy cycle. He planned to run it through twice. Noticing a pile of crumpled clothing, he flew into a rage and hurled it across the room. His hands shook. What the hell was wrong with him? This wasn't like him — a man who prided himself on neatness and efficiency.

With a hard bristle brush, he scrubbed Buddy. He dried and kissed the knife and his penis hardened. Aroused, he stroked himself and fantasized his recent exploit, moaning with pleasure as he climaxed.

Hamilton took a long shower and whistled a jingle he had heard on a radio commercial. He grabbed the terry cloth robe from behind the door, but it was damp. He had used it early in the morning, and by this time it should have dried. Alarmed, he yelled, 'Who the devil was here and wore my robe?'

Shivering, he snatched the only dry towel in the bathroom. He stepped into the last fresh pair of gray sweats. Sniffing the damp robe, he detected no foreign odors, only the scent of Dial. Cursing, he threw the robe near the washing machine.

Was someone trying to drive him crazy?

Hamilton darted through his apartment to see if anything else was amiss. Everything appeared as he had left it.

During his perusal, he noticed he had not shined his shoes. I'm really slipping up — going off the deep end. Better take it easy, he counseled himself. The thickness of the velour robe could make it take longer to dry, he reasoned. It was new and he had used it only once. The long shower he had taken in the morning had dampened the bathroom. He remembered having neglected to turn on the ceiling heat light. Hamilton wondered about what else he may have forgotten.

He slid his tongue along the inside of his mouth and ran to the kitchen for bottled water, but the bottle was empty. He had neglected to replenish it. Tap water was unpleasant and unhealthy, so how could he have forgotten? Too many other details on his mind had interfered with day to day stuff, he figured.

He paced every room. Upon entering the kitchen again, he saw on the counter remnants of the bomb he had made for the shrink's old car. Damn! He'd forgotten to stash the stuff in a safe place. Carefully, he collected accelerometers, triggers, casings and plastic explosives placing them in their respective shoe boxes. Lifting the wood veneer panel of a cabinet, he opened the bomb-proof safe and stored the materials. In a furor over his forgetfulness, and thirsty, he cursed, hurling the empty water bottle across the room with force. It made a loud blast as it shattered against the wall, particles flying everywhere. He hoped his neighbor regarded the noise as a sonic boom.

Weekly water deliveries were made to his building, but he had refused the service. Now, he didn't want to leave the condo to buy water. His mouth felt parched from those damn burritos and hot salsa. Lousy Mexicans.

Hamilton emptied three trays of ice cubes into a large plastic bowl and microwaved it. He filled the tea kettle with tap water and heated it on the stove. He paced until the ice cubes melted. Gulping the water rapidly, he burped. Now that's better, isn't it?

He made himself three peanut butter and jelly sandwiches on spongy white bread and wolfed it down. Sniffing the sour milk container, he nearly threw up. He had not shopped at the market for ... he couldn't remember. A warm can of coke was in the pantry, but he had used up the ice. 'Damn, damn, damn,' he wailed.

It was time to tidy up. He sorted the soiled laundry for another machine load. Hamilton swept up the glass and placed it in the trash bin. After completing his household chores, he shined his shoes until they glistened. Creating order restored his sense of control. He hummed a tune he did not recognize.

His thoughts returned to the bitch-shrink. The car bomb might work, if he lessened the risk. He could stop in her garage on the way up to the appointment and drop pocket change near her BMW. Crouching to retrieve the coins, he would have a chance to install the magnetic bomb under the car on the driver side. When the bitch accelerated, she would be blown to bits, much like what happened to those two shrinks who examined him when he was a kid. This time, he would watch it. Better than fireworks. If installation seemed chancy, he would keep his appointment and kill the receptionist, too.

The tea kettle whistled, startling him. With shaky hands he poured boiling water into an insulated jug, placing it in the freezer.

He lit a cigar, closed his eyes and visualizing the step-by-step killing of both bitches: A few minutes after three o'clock when people were ensconced in soundproof sessions, he would enter her office, introduce himself as Robert Russell and request coffee from the receptionist. When she approached him, he would cover her mouth and slash her neck in the place from where blood gushed like a raging river. When Dr. Cohen came out, he would repeat the process.

The cigar made him more thirsty. He stubbed it out and ran to the kitchen. Grabbing the jug of water from the freezer, he put it to his mouth, but it scalded him. The jug fell, flooding his kitchen floor. Hamilton ran to the bathroom sink, rinsed his mouth with cool tap water and splashed his face. Get a grip, man. What the hell is wrong with you?

Panting, he returned to the kitchen and mopped the floor.

Tired, he rested in an easy chair, closed his eyes and returned to his imagery. Hamilton saw himself muffling the bitches' screams, Buddy in his hand, piercing pale skin, blood everywhere. He watched himself race away and felt his heart pound. The fantasy was so vivid, he wondered if it had already happened. He opened his eyes, checked his calendar watch and realized he had been day dreaming.

Now, everything was in order and on schedule, just as he liked.

54

Convinced Pope had killed at least twice before, Cory knew the danger was real and his attempt on her life, imminent. Not knowing where or when he would strike had compounded her ordeal in the fog. Arriving home exhausted, she slipped into a dreamless sleep.

When she awoke, the bedroom clock-radio blinked 7:00. She had planned a busy day.

She opened the front door to collect the newspaper, and was greeted by a cardboard gray sky and slick streets — not good for running. Hopping on her exercise bike, she flipped the TV remote to CNN, but thoughts of Pope intruded. She wanted to worm herself into his head to figure out his reasoning.

The first time he had tried to kill her was after she had called Superior. His goal was to shut her up before she had a chance to notify the police, but he had mistaken Ann for her, and Cory had foiled his attempt. Pope had tailed her from the office to her house without arousing her suspicion. Cory wondered what he knew about her and if her friends were in danger too. She thanked God her kids were in Israel.

Pope raped young women for the fun of it. A power trip. It thrilled him to terrify them. When threatened, he killed, or accidentally, going too far with his slashings.

Lewis said Pope left no paper-trails. A sure sign he valued secrecy. And when Harvey had examined him, Pope said, 'Stop violating me.'

Paranoid, he had killed Marge Abbott because she knew too much about him — knew insignificant things, like his eye ailment. To Pope, it was significant for she had invaded his privacy.

It was hard to imagine mild mannered Grace as a threat to Pope, despite his disturbed mind. Slashing was part of his repertoire. Was it indiscriminate, or was he motivated to kill passive, docile women? The three other victims Cory knew, were assertive.

He had slashed Jennifer, but did not kill her. Perhaps he thought he had.

According to Steve, his patient was not a push-over.

And Mallory knocked the wind out of him before he had a chance to pull a knife. Good for you, Mallory!

What did all this mean? A sneaky, paranoid psychopath was on Cory's tail, ready to pounce on her any time, any place. His preference for killing was by knife, but he could choose another way. Until he was caught, she would need protection. Karate was not enough. Cory needed another pair of eyes.

She jumped off the bike and phoned Harry Hornsby, the private investigator. They wasted no words. He promised to be at her office at noon.

★   ★   ★

At ten minutes before noon, on her way to pick up phone messages, Cory spied Harry Hornsby in the reception room. With briefcase, conservative dark suit and striped tie, he could be pegged for one of the pharmaceutical sales reps who frequented the office complex. Hornsby, in his forties was medium height, wiry and attractive enough — if you like pale men with vacant blue eyes — to catch Ann's attention. At noon she rapped on the door and handed Cory his card.

'He's not a patient?' she asked in a way that made Cory think she wanted a go-ahead signal.

'No. He's here to help with the rape investigation. Please show him in.'

Hornsby handed Cory another of his cards

and settled in an armchair, crossing his legs. The sun bounced off the glossy shine of his wing-tipped shoes. He appeared to have a passion for his necktie, incessantly caressing it.

The private detective summarized his current work. He provided Rosalind with around the clock surveillance. His associates were investigating the rapes. All the targeted women were cooperative. Hornsby's firm had installed video surveillance systems in their homes.

Cory explained her concern for her personal safety and told him of Lewis' futile chase.

Hornsby's client had authorized him to provide any service that could lead to the man who raped their daughter, but he could not obtain anyone to guard Cory immediately. He assured her that in a few days someone would be available. Hornsby promised to have a video surveillance system installed at Cory's house at eight that evening. She scrawled her home address on a slip of paper and gave it to him.

Cory suggested that someone in his firm should tail Pope. Hornsby said they had done so from the time they entered the case until now, to no avail. Pope worked long hours and did not leave his apartment after work.

In a dull monotone, Hornsby spoke words of admiration and gratitude for Detective Lewis who had saved his life. The private detective suffered diabetes and was insulin dependent. While busy on a case, he had neglected to eat, producing low blood sugar and loss of consciousness. Lewis, recognizing Hornsby's condition got immediate help. Hornsby related the episode in a flat, detached manner.

The private investigator asked pertinent questions, took voluminous notes and told Cory to call if she had more information. Hornsby assured her of improved security and was out of her office in under twenty minutes.

Ann burst into Cory's office and related the strange phone call and the appointment she had made for her at three. She had checked every digit from one through nine to find the missing one the man had mumbled that supposedly constituted his phone number. There was no Robert Russell at any of the numbers. Ann had called Dr. Jolson who said he had not referred a Robert Russell.

A familiar name, where had Cory heard it? After a pregnant pause, it came to her — she had spoken to a Mr. Russell at Superior. She felt like a fresh fish thrown into a bucket of ice.

She looked up Superior's phone number. It was different from what the caller had given. Ann had made a three o'clock appointment with danger. *An appointment with Hamilton Pope!*

No longer plagued with the uncertainty of when or where he would strike, now she could concentrate on realizing a long held fantasy.

She told Ann of her suspicions and what she had learned from the police.

'Incredible! This is scary. No wonder you've not been yourself.'

'I'm sorry if I've snapped at you.'

'Lately when I talk to you, you grunt. That's why I didn't tell you the result of my interview.'

Cory had forgotten about Ann's clinical internship. 'I'm sorry. How did it go?'

'Not good. They spent more time with the younger applicants, and implied your recommendation was suspect.'

'I'm sorry. If they reject you, it will be their loss. Your maturity should count for, not against you, Ann.'

'I'll get another interview elsewhere where I'll be appreciated. Listen, Cory. I wish you'd told me before about your suspicions. Maybe I could have helped.'

'Thanks, but I don't want you in danger,

Ann. This has nothing to do with you. It's my lesson.'

'You can't cure all the ills . . . '

'All you need to do is cancel today's four and five o'clock sessions and go home.'

Ann pulled out the appointment book and started phoning.

Cory paged the detectives and requested police assistance.

Something told her to phone Frankie. There was no answer. Frankie was instructed not to leave the house except for office visits and a scheduled trip to the supermarket. Where the devil was she? Cory's concern deepened.

'Ann, please keep trying Frankie and put her through. If you don't reach her within the hour, call the sheriff for a security check.'

'Do you think something happened to her?'

'Very possible.'

Cory berated herself for not asking Hornsby to install special security in the office. Why didn't he think of it? It was his business. That man was just too bland. Ineffectual.

She phoned the company that handled her home alarm and requested immediate installation for the office.

Ten minutes later a technician arrived and attached a device on the floor under her desk that would activate a call to 9-1-1. The same equipment was affixed to the wall behind Ann's chair.

'You should go now, Ann.'

'No. I won't leave you alone.'

'Think of your own safety. You're exposed in the reception room to a vicious killer. The guy who attacked you. He thought you were me.'

Color drained from Ann's face. 'What?'

'You see why I want you to go. Don't worry about me, I won't be alone for long. The police should get here in time.'

'Aren't we protected by the new security system?'

'I installed it as a precaution, but by the time we'd get a response, it could be too late.'

'What about calling handsome Harry?'

'Who?'

'The private investigator.'

'Oh, the robot. Go for it. Tell him about my appointment with Pope.' She handed her his card.

This was Cory's big chance. Pope, off guard, unaware that she was ready for him, would be unprepared for what she would do to him. She had vowed not to let him get away with Grace's murder and who knows how many other crimes. She planned to terrify him as he did others.

Be sensible, she cautioned herself. The cops would not let her do their job and endanger herself, but if she insisted, and used Hornsby's agency for protection . . .

Ann poked her head into Cory's office. 'He'll be here as soon as he gets someone to guard Roz. It won't be long.'

'Go home, Ann. The cops are eager to close this case. To make an arrest, they must catch him in a criminal act. Like attempted murder. I don't want to subject you . . . '

'I know. You've made it plain, but I feel I'm more than just your Person Friday. You've saved my life.'

'I did what had to be done. I don't expect your obligation.'

'It's not what you expect; it's what I feel.' Ann's eyes watered.

'Thank you. You're a *mensch*, Ann. A real fine person.' Cory blew a kiss.

The picture of Pope, the predator becoming the prey, was better to Cory than runner's high. Better than winning a ten million dollar jackpot.

She recalled talks with Steve about a Judaic precept — a duty to defend all innocent human beings, to kill in defense was not wrong. It countered the commandment: Thou Shalt Not Murder and gave rise to numerous discussions. To take a life was an abhorrent act born of desperation, too horrible to imagine, but special circumstances would demand Cory to muster the courage. Those discussions had been theoretical. Now, she had a hard time imagining killing Pope. Deep in her Jewish psyche, she regarded stamping out a serial murderer's life — a *mitzvah*, a good deed. She wanted Pope to experience the profound terror he forced upon his victims. Cory had no knife with which to slash, nor a tool fierce enough to penetrate his anus, but she did have a smashing pair of high heel boots.

She had to get off that subject and focus on why she sat in her office. She was not an avenger, but a psychologist with two more patients to see today. Erin and Paige.

It pleased Cory to see a changed Erin. Her physical transformation symbolic of her growth. No longer the schoolgirl, she wore tailored clothes and her hair in a sophisticated french knot.

Midway through the session, Cory's anticipation of her date with danger intruded.

'Dr. Cohen, you seem distracted. Something wrong?'

'You're perceptive, Erin. I apologize. My thoughts were elsewhere. Thanks for bringing me back.'

'Oh, I have good news. That so-called

Patrick chap rang again. He promised to ring again Thursday. I heard canaries singing in the background. Isn't that a bit odd?'

'A prop to lure you. To make you feel he's gentle because he keeps birds . . . to make you feel so sorry for his loneliness that you'll invite him over. Quite a scam.'

'Well, let me tell you. He's quite an effective actor, really. So am I. You'd be proud of me, the way I play along.' Erin winked. 'That nice inspector, I mean detective, is so pleased with my cooperation. They traced the last call. It was made from the lobby of a hotel near where I live,' she gasped.

'Are you frightened, Erin?'

'No. If he shows up, they'll nab him. Mr. Hornsby had high tech surveillance equipment installed in my apartment and elsewhere in the complex. They set up a security office with monitors in the manager's office, so why would I be frightened? He won't set foot into my apartment.' Her words didn't match her expression. At that moment, if she was an animal, she'd have been a bunny rabbit. A soft, cuddly Irish bunny rabbit.

'This situation would make anyone nervous, Erin.' Cory wrapped her hands around a warm mug of coffee to stop herself from trembling.

'I guess I am, but only a wee bit. It's the

first time I've ever felt really important.' She gazed at the wall behind her therapist.

Erin said that having been raised in a large family, she was ignored. She wouldn't do that to her daughter Megan. She accepted her role as a parent and vowed to be a better mother than her mother was. In so doing, she would repair herself.

Erin had told Seldyn about the phone calls and they had agreed Megan would stay with him and his mother for a few weeks. Cory expected her patient to be jealous of the arrangement, but Seldyn's concern for their daughter's safety pleased Erin.

The ticking clock took away from Cory's pleasure in the young woman's progress.

An hour to go.

Cory shuddered. Coffee sloshed in her stomach. No panic attack. Not for me, she told herself as in a mantra. She closed her eyes and slowed her breathing pattern. She visualized her feet in high heel boots kicking Pope where it hurt the most. She heard him shriek over and over again — a harrowing scream, 'Stop — for God's sake. Stop!' His eyes widened in terror.

One more session to go.

Paige, too had cooperated with Hornsby who had provided surveillance equipment in her home. Her reward for calling the police was a relationship with Detective Sharpley, whom she called 'Bill.'

Her voice had become more audible and her language less pedantic. Cory noted a small gold heart had replaced the Phi Beta Kappa key on Paige's necklace.

'I think it intimidated people, Dr. C. I used it to bolster my ego, and to put people off. I wanted to avoid getting involved and hurt.'

'Good insight. It didn't put Bill off.'

'No. That is . . . I don't think so. I'm not sure he even knew what the trinket represented. He's no scholar, but he's very smart.'

Cory smiled. 'It goes with the territory.'

'Everything is much better, Dr. C. I've gotten things under control at work. I took your suggestion and have weekly staff meetings.' She sipped water from the designer bottle, she carried. 'My staff welcomes the chance to brainstorm. We're like one big happy family now.' She grinned. 'I've gone to lunch with a woman who supervises another group. That's helped, too. Would you believe it — we're thinking of double dating!' She blushed. 'I never did that in school.'

'It's never too late, Paige.'

'Dating a cop is hard. His hours are unpredictable.' She folded her hands on her lap. 'It's disappointing.'

'Disappointment comes from unmet expectations, Paige.'

She rubbed her chin. 'I wonder . . . maybe I do expect too much, Dr. C. Something to think about, huh?'

'With all your success in school and work, maybe you think it should be a natural outcome for all your goals.'

'Perhaps I'm not being realistic.'

The time drew near and the rest of the session blurred. Cory operated on automatic pilot. Paige smiled, laughed and appeared to be getting something out of it. Cory glanced at her Timex. Two-forty- five. *End of session.*

As soon as Paige left, Ann buzzed. 'The detectives are here,' she whispered . . . for the past couple of hours.

Time to put on the boots.

Her adrenalin pumped. Soon she would be face to face with Hamilton Pope and in a few minutes, he would be history. No more terrorizing defenseless women. Soon he would know what it meant to be at someone else's mercy and know terror — his own terror.

Cory began to wonder if the cops would allow Pope to enter her office and if she would have time for action before they apprehend him. Just a few seconds. That's all she needed.

Her plan came to a screeching halt when Ann rushed into the office.

'Mr. Russell's on the phone. He has to change his appointment because of an emergency at work. He'd like another appointment as soon as possible. What should I tell him?'

Cory sighed, feeling a combination of relief and disappointment. The theme of her life. 'Okay, give him Friday.'

Because his call could have been a tactic to get her off guard, they waited for him just in case he would show up.

At three-thirty, Ann and Cory met the three detectives in the reception room. Cory told them of Russell's recent phone call.

'Maybe he really had an emergency,' Detective Sharpley said.

'If he shows up Friday, I'll be prepared,' she whispered to Lewis. The dents she made in the carpet from her spike heels were apparent.

'Your boots could sure do a number on him, you know,' muttered Detective Lewis out of earshot of Sharpley. 'I'm familiar with your stunning karate kicks.'

'Please let me have a go at him,' she whispered.

'Don't worry, we'll be here to arrest him with pleasure.' Lewis grinned. 'If you don't make mincemeat of him first,' he said softly.

'Did you get my message about Frankie?' she asked.

He stared at her. 'No. What message?'

'Ann was supposed to call you, but with all this excitement, she must have slipped up.' Cory rolled her eyes. 'Wasn't Frankie instructed not to leave her house for two more weeks except to see me?'

Lewis nodded.

'Well, we've called her several times today and there's no answer.'

'You don't know she resigned?' Lewis asked.

'What? Impulsive, wasn't it?' Cory shook her head.

'She said she didn't like her assignment.'

'When did you find this out?'

'A day or so ago.'

'Why didn't anyone tell me?'

'She said she did.'

'Not exactly. She called it an option, not a fact.'

'It was probably wise,' Lewis said.

'She's bait. Shouldn't she have waited until you got that bastard?'

Lewis was probably glad to see Frankie leave the force, but Cory doubted he wished the former deputy harm.

'Who said she's smart? No one submits a

resignation effective at the end of the week. It's unheard of. She's a weird cookie.'

Cory figured Frankie could not tolerate being alone and having to listen to the voice in her head.

'Listen, we've put a pair of deputies nearby and their assignment didn't end with her resignation. We wouldn't endanger her. She planned to spend a few days hanging out at the beach. She asked to use the cottage with some friends, but wouldn't be taking any calls there. She said we owed it to her. Hernandez should still be right there, but I'll have someone check on her now,' Detective Lewis said, phone in his hand. 'We'll see you Friday, Doc.'

'This has been draining,' Ann said. 'Let's go to El Torito.'

Cory nodded. Her mouth watered at the prospect of tasty little fish tacos and raw veggies that would constitute dinner and welcomed the calm from strawberry Margaritas. Although disappointed with Ann for not calling the Sheriff about Frankie, Cory did not reprimand her.

They strolled the few blocks to the noisy, crowded café surrounded by small palm trees and red bougainvillea and managed to get a good table next to a window facing the ocean.

The sky changed from blue to lilac, like a

magician's silk scarves. The big orange sun dipped into the ocean leaving a lonely dark sky.

Mariachis wearing large sombreros strolled the restaurant playing traditional Mexican music. Red, green and yellow striped cloths covered the tables. Carved wood chairs with raffia seats and a coral colored tile floor offered a Mexican ambiance, enhanced by the aroma of fresh corn tortillas.

'You can bet I'm going to take self-defense classes,' Ann shouted above the din.

'Glad to hear it.' Cory sipped a frozen strawberry Margarita. The drink made her shiver.

They watched the choreographed graceful servers wearing white off-the-shoulder embroidered cotton muslin dresses and colorful sashes present trays of drinks, food and a festive spirit.

One of the Mariachis, a trumpet player with a tinny sounding horn stood next to their table, waving at Cory. She recognized him as the flower vendor she had met on her way to the hospital to see Jennifer.

Flashing on her ordeal, and the build up and disappointment of the day plus the icey drink made her shiver. On her mind were two questions: Did Hamilton fall for the bait? Was Frankie okay?

★ ★ ★

When Cory arrived home, she had three messages.

From Sergeant Lewis: 'Listen, Doc. I can't let you endanger yourself. You won't be alone with Pope. Understand?'

From Harry Hornsby: 'Coast TV will be there at eight.'

From Erin: 'Urgent. Please return call.'

Cory rang her and the young woman picked up right away.

'Thanks for ringing me back, Dr. Cohen. Sorry to bother you, but I've got a strange hunch. That so-called 'Patrick' rang tonight and asked if he could visit at seven-thirty Thursday evening. He said he'd bring pizza for Megan and me. He seemed over-eager for Megan to be there. When I told him she was with her father, he seemed angry, not disappointed, but out-of-control angry.' Erin sounded breathless.

'Erin, it is alarming. I'm glad you called. Phone the police too.'

'As soon as I ring off.'

Cory glanced at her Timex — close to eight. The doorbell rang. From her window she saw a white truck with the imprint COAST TV INSTALLATION & REPAIRS.

397

'Hold it a moment please, Erin, I have to answer the door.'

Two men in white jumpsuits stood at the entrance wearing identification badges. 'We're from Hornsby Security,' one said. She let them in and watched as they surveyed the house.

Cory returned to the phone. 'They'll probably assign a woman detective to take your place, but — wait. I have an idea. It's unorthodox, but I'm willing to do it, if you agree.'

'Unorthodox? You're so proper. What do you have in mind?'

After Cory revealed her plan, she phoned George Lewis and had a long chat. At his suggestion, she phoned Harry Hornsby and found him most agreeable.

55

Like a butcher on a mission to slaughter, Hamilton sharpened his knife. The target, easy like a lamb, was the psychologist. Today is the day!

At ten minutes before two, just as Hamilton was ready to leave, Mr. Russell's secretary summoned him to a meeting commencing at three, thwarting his carefully drawn plans. Expecting a day or so of advance notice, he smashed the receiver into the cradle. Clenching his fists into hard balls, he pierced his palms with his fingernails. Damn, damn, damn. The urge to go on a slashing rampage in his office nearly overtook him. Calm down, man, he told himself.

Hamilton locked his door, closed the blinds, disrobed except for underwear, and did push-ups until he was soaked in sweat.

In his private washroom, he sponged himself off and liberally sprinkled deodorant. Pleased that he had the good sense to keep a change of clothing at his office, he whistled a jingle and put on fresh shorts, shirt and tie. With an old towel, he shined his shoes. After brushing his hair until it glistened, his reflection in the mirror satisfied him.

His plot to kill that interfering bitch, Dr. Cory Cohen, quashed by the executive meeting only meant that he had to postpone it. He glanced at his Rolex. In a few moments he would have done away with her. Hamilton picked up his phone and punched in Dr. Cohen's number. 'This is Robert Russell. Sorry, I have an emergency and cannot keep today's appointment, but I shall pay for this cancellation. I still need an appointment. How soon can she see me?'

'Just a moment, sir.' After a few minutes the receptionist said, 'One o'clock Friday would be fine.'

Hamilton whistled the jingle again. Within a short time he would have his pleasure with Erin and dispose of the shrink. An especially productive week, he told himself. He smiled at his reflection in the mirror as he straightened his tie.

He checked his Rolex and focused himself for the conference. His earlier frustration had turned to excitement and pride about the deal Superior had consummated with Strauss. He was part of an organization fast becoming the largest in the industry. First Superior had taken over Behavioral Health and now they were joining a pharmaceutical conglomerate. Russell had assured him there would be no layoffs. Ecstatic at the prospect of a splendid opportunity, he strolled into his boss's office.

Robert Russell smiled, extending his hand. 'Hamilton, so nice of you to invite me to dinner. I hope my preoccupation with Strauss won't interfere. They're wining and dining me, fattening me up for the kill.' Russell laughed.

'Well, I'm looking forward to dining with you, Thursday.' Eye contact gave Hamilton the jitters, so he gazed at his boss' shoulder.

Soon the meeting started and went well.

When they adjourned, Hamilton felt proud of his composure and confident Strauss would enhance his career.

Later in the day, Russell called him to confirm their dinner appointment. Pleased, Hamilton left work and sped to Dr. Cohen's office garage.

He searched in vain for the old white BMW. He spied the receptionist's silver Camry parked in another part of the garage. Puzzled, he figured the shrink must have traded in her car. Exasperated, he searched for a new BMW. Spying a dark green twelve-year old 925, he figured she would not select a model older than her last. He noticed a new red 725 and considered it a good possibility. When he came across a new black

325, he became confused. Convinced that the red or black BMW was hers, he regretted that he had not brought more explosives. Thinking it a waste to plant a bomb in what could be the wrong car, he abandoned that plan for the day.

Arriving home, he pumped iron until exhausted. He had lifted heavier weights and did more reps than usual. In the mirrored gym he smiled at his image, admiring his well-defined muscles, slick with the moisture from his extra duty workout.

56

The next day, Lewis phoned Cory at seven in the morning and asked if she could meet him at her office within an hour before breakfast. Having ample time before her first patient, she agreed.

She figured her heart had enough of a workout yesterday to welcome a rest from heavy-duty exercise today. She hopped in the shower, dressed in navy wool slacks and red silk blouse and contemplated pulling her hair back with a white scarf, but it wasn't the 4th of July.

She headed to the office where she found Lewis dangling a Big Apple Bagel bag. 'Breakfast for the crime fighters.'

Ann and Cory smiled their gratitude. While Ann put up coffee, Lewis and Cory went into her consulting room.

'Doc, I thought it best if I came in person. Frankie's in Intensive Care in critical condition.'

'Damn!' Cory slapped the chair's arm rest. 'What happened?'

'While Hernandez was on stake-out at her place, a dumpster up the street caught on fire. These damn Santa Ana winds caused the flames to spread to the canyon, frightening the neighbors. Quite a commotion, Hernandez said people freaked out. Frankie was asleep in bed. Didn't hear a thing. Because she'd told him she hadn't slept the night before, he thought she'd taken a sleeping pill.'

Ann tapped on the door and entered carrying a platter of bagels and cream cheese. 'I'll get coffee now.'

'Anyway,' Lewis continued, 'Hernandez called in, explained the situation. He said Frankie was sleeping, and he'd be gone for a few minutes to help with crowd control. We had a team within range, so he figured it was safe, you know. After calling the fire department, he ran out to help. In the meantime, the perp came in through the bedroom window. Frankie probably didn't see or hear him. He was quick, Doc. He hit her on the head, raped, slashed and escaped. What a routine! Got to marvel at his efficiency. Probably added arson and did it all in record time. You know where I'd like to pin the medal?'

Cory squeezed her eyes shut. 'Where was the team on watch?'

'By the time they got there . . . who'd think . . . in the middle of the day. We need more resources, you know. But nobody wants to spend the money on our department.'

'No phone calls before his visit?'

'None. We'll get the sonofabitch, you'll see.'

'He could have killed her, but didn't. It's the same thing he did to Jennifer. I think Grace was murdered accidentally.'

'Me, too, Doc. Listen to this. We had to notify Frankie's family. Turns out she's from the same small town up north as Pope. Get this, her mother's name is . . . ready? Jane Adams. Here's a pisser — Frankie's brothers are Madison, Jefferson and . . . '

'Hamilton!' Cory shrieked. 'Holy cow! Franklynne A.? Of course — Adams-Franklin. With a mother called Jane Adams, she named her kids in Early American! Uh, wait — is their last name Pope?'

'Best we can figure, the mother dropped the last name. Either she gave it to her sons, or Hamilton adopted it.'

Cory gasped. 'Do you think he knew he raped and slashed his own sister?'

'About what he knew, I don't know, Doc. It could be that he suspected it and that's why this time, he did his stuff differently. He didn't call her — not even once. He moved fast because he got so excited about it, he couldn't wait. This kind of nut-case has a pattern that escalates, you know.'

'Maybe he changed his M.O. to fool you.'

'It's possible, but I think he's getting more

daring. Broad daylight. Doesn't speak well for his IQ. What do you say, Doc?'

'He didn't get caught.'

'Yeah, well . . . ' Lewis's face darkened.

'What about Frankie? Did she know the suspect was her brother?'

'I don't think so. As far as I know, she never said anything to anybody about that possibility. She attended briefings and got hot sheets. She never spoke about her family. Lou Kelly is still with the department. He's her ex-husband, you know. He said she was raised as an only child. She knew she had brothers, but had no contact with them. As far as he knew, Doc, the boys lived in foster homes.'

'That may explain Hamilton's rage at women,' Cory said.

The door slowly opened. Ann came in with two steaming mugs of aromatic roasted brew.

'Thanks, Ann. Have you tried these great bagels?'

'Yes. Food of the Jewish Gods.'

'Uh-uh, Ann. Jews have only one God. L'Chaim. To life.' Cory toasted her with a coffee mug. Ann smiled, closing the door behind her.

'Listen, Doc. It sure seems likely that he is her brother, but they had different family names and she may not have made any connection. Hamilton isn't an unusual name, nor is Pope, you know.'

'Yes, but they come from the same small town, and you said her brothers' first names were on her personnel file. Do we have anything on Pope's background to suggest a family relationship with her?'

'Only that his mother's name was Jane Adams. Isn't that enough?'

'Did she know that?'

'The information was available to her, Doc. She may not have read it,' he said, chomping on a bagel. 'Frankie was written up a lot. She reluctantly took this assignment to improve her standing with the department.' He sipped coffee. 'Fine brew. French roast?'

Cory nodded. Lewis had good taste. Well, it figures. He, too, was from New York. She had a flash of insight and realized she wasn't free of prejudice. She was a big city snob who placed undue value on sophistication and discrimination.

Lewis continued. 'Frankie couldn't tolerate the confinement, Doc. Things weren't happening fast enough. Hernandez said she was getting bitchy. Actually, more bitchy.'

'Didn't she realize what undercover work entails?'

'Well, she's got no patience, you know. She'd probably figured we'd wrap it up fast and she'd be promoted to detective. Fat chance! No one thinks she had what it takes,

Doc. No people skills, you know.'

'I sure do know. Since Pope didn't call first to set her up, he probably suspected she was his sister. Her name has an odd spelling. Wait.' Cory reached for a copy of her treatment request. 'I listed her name as Franklynne A. Kelly. He could have assumed or pretended she was his hated sister, and got off on that.'

'I figured that, too, Doc.' Lewis got up to leave.

'Will I see you later at karate?' she asked.

'I hope so, Doc.'

Cory thanked him for breakfast and realized she had missed the chance to ask him about Hornsby.

She sorted the mail stacked on her desk; announcements, a psychology journal, the phone bill and a handwritten envelope postmarked from Davis. With trembling hands, she ripped it open. A blue card fell out. On the cover was a pencil sketch of a little boy weeping. Unfolding it, she read:

Boo-hoo. I miss you. Guess who?

Davis Information supplied the only number for a doctor named Miller. Dr. Alan Miller. Cory called and the receptionist put Ron on.

'I was thinking about you, Cory. Glad you called.'

She figured she reached him in one of his rare good moods.

'I've taken time off and I'll be here for awhile. Can you meet me in San Francisco on Saturday?' he asked.

Hearing his smile, her doubts dissolved. She needed to share the news about Pope and blurted it out to Ron.

'I thought you'd knock it off, by now,' Ron groaned.

His words punched her in the gut. 'You don't understand. We're closing in on him. It won't be long and I'm . . . oh, what's the use.'

'You don't get it, do you, Cory? You know my father's ill. You haven't even asked about him or me. You don't even seem interested to know how long I'm going to be here. You've got only one thing on your tight mind. The only times you don't talk about that case is when we're jamming or having sex. There's more to a relationship than that.'

Unspoken words withered in her mouth like an untended garden. Ron held a mirror out to her and she didn't like what she saw. Unready to deal with it, she postponed the visit. He sounded relieved, but she was miserable.

57

Thursday, a big day. An important day. Hamilton sat at his office desk behind a locked door, whistling that familiar jingle that had become a habit. Unable to recognize it, he wondered if it was a commercial, designed with subliminal messages to motivate him to purchase a particular product. He reasoned that preferences for certain brands were the result of advertising. Hamilton shook his fist. Everyone cheated and tried to pull one over on him. Never knew who, where or when. Must be cautious. He forced himself to stop whistling, now ready to chart his course:

He'd have an hour and a half for dinner with Russell after work. Ample time would remain for him to drive to a rest stop, change his clothes, pick up a pizza, send a fax and arrive at Erin's before seven-thirty. Too bad her little girl wouldn't be there. Damn, damn, disappointing. Next time he'd select a single mother with a little girl and what a joy to kill them. First he'd do the kid, to strike horror on the mother's face. Imagining it, his penis stiffened. He stroked it to orgasm, stifling his moans of pleasure.

After conducting his personal hygiene ritual, he phoned a pizza place near Erin's house and ordered a large pepperoni pie. He requested it be ready at seven-twenty. He used Robert Russell's name and gave Superior's phone number. When the cops found the box they could trace it to Russell, as they would the pen.

His dinner engagement with Russell was for five o'clock at the elegant restaurant Russell recommended next to Superior's offices. At four forty-five he punched in Russell's phone number. 'Hamilton here. Are we still on at five?'

'Sure, Hamilton. I missed lunch and am hungry. I'll be there promptly.'

'I reserved under my name. They assured me a private, quiet table.'

'See you there,' Russell said.

At four forty-eight, Hamilton again rang Russell's office. No response. Everyone left for the day at four or four-thirty the latest. Stepping out of his office, he peered around the empty corridor. It was quiet except for the hum of the air conditioner as he jogged towards Russell's office. With his handkerchief, he opened the door, snatched the pen and closed the door behind him. He flew down the two flights of stairs without breaking a sweat. Striding to the restaurant, he noticed the sky darkened. Good. Soon it would be winter, his favorite season, but too short in southern California. He pushed the huge, heavy wood door and entered Bookers.

The maitre d' ushered Hamilton to a large table in a windowed corner. Fica trees in large clay pots separated tables. Thick plush carpets and upholstered chairs absorbed sounds.

At first Hamilton was awed to be a patron in this elegant restaurant, designed to resemble an English gentlemen's club with dark wood panels and brass fixtures.

He began to feel ill-at-ease, out of his element, especially with that uppity host who walked as if he had a broomstick rammed up his ass, and the way he clasped those huge green velvet covered menus as if they were passports to paradise. How pretentious!

Russell rose to greet him. Hamilton's stomach pitched at the prospect of a handshake, but he shook his boss's hand firmly, quickly releasing it. He sat down, discreetly wiping his sweaty palm on the bottom of the tablecloth.

When the server arrived, Hamilton ordered very rare prime rib, a baked potato with sour cream and chives, Yorkshire pudding and a Caesar salad. Russell told the server he would have the usual and requested the wine steward. 'I hope you don't mind, but I do like wine with dinner. Put it on my tab,' he told the wine steward.

Hamilton could feel his face reddening with humiliation, but vengeance would soon be his. He ignored Russell's order and declined the wine when offered by the steward. Hamilton had an urge to take the metal bucket containing the bottle of wine and ice and dump it on his boss's head. Instead he breathed deeply and regained his focus. The waiter filled his water glass. Hamilton asked him to leave a full pitcher on the table.

'Strauss chose us over Preferred,' Hamilton said.

'Yes, indeed.' Russell swirled the ruby red liquid in the crystal wine glass.

'Why don't they buy both Preferred and Superior?'

'There are anti-trust laws.' He sniffed the wine.

Buttering the warm sourdough bread, Hamilton asked, 'If they took over both companies they'd have most of the mental health care contracts in the country?'

Russell nodded and sipped the wine.

'Superior doesn't yet have the majority of the contracts, so anti-trust isn't an issue. I get it. Later, we'll market and gradually gain a stronghold.' Hamilton gazed at the full moon and stars in the dark velvet sky from the window behind his boss.

'Hamilton, I admire your intellect and ability. You've done a great job.'

'It sounds like past tense. What do you mean?' Hamilton narrowed his eyes.

'When we merge with Strauss, my intention is to place you in a position in which you can do the most good for the company.'

Hamilton was elated. In succession, he drank two glasses of water.

'What would that be?'

'Vice-President of Provider Relations. You wouldn't let those wimps get away with anything. You'd work them like slaves for a pittance.' Russell smiled.

A sudden wave of nausea hit Hamilton. He would hate that job. He could not tolerate the barrage of complaints by providers. His access to treatment requests, though possible, would be difficult. 'What kind of raise are we talking about?'

'Substantial. I won't know exactly until this is *a fait accompli.*'

'How soon will that be?'

Russell shrugged his shoulders.

Hamilton felt his bladder and bowels about to explode. He excused himself and rushed into the men's room. After he attended to the matter, he washed his hands and face, combed his hair and returned to the table.

He sat gazing out the window to distract himself from images of blood splats everywhere, like strobe lights whirling around the room. To prevent a panic, he focused on his dinner, but the red juicy meat added to his confusion. Hamilton wondered what marvelous drugs Dr. Higushi would prescribe for this problem. He took several deep breaths and focused on the conversation.

'The managed health care business is changing rapidly. I enjoy my work and want to continue. With rapid changes in the industry, I'm concerned for my future. One day, sooner than we imagine, the government may adapt new statutes which would abolish this industry,' Hamilton said, waving the server away.

'True. Although it will be a long time coming, we should take every advantage while we can. Make the most of it before it's too late. Make your big bucks now, Hamilton. Invest wisely. Retire early. That's my plan.'

Hamilton, jealous of Russell's financial acumen, also admired it. Pity he would not have time to exploit it. He would grab what he could tonight.

The discussion progressed. The realization that Russell was more capable than he, ruptured Hamilton's self-esteem. Ruled by lust for the power of Russell's job, Hamilton hadn't thought about his own readiness for the challenge. Sudden awareness that he could miss elusive subtleties, chilled him, but his plans were as good as etched in concrete.

After leaving Russell, he sped to a gas station. He entered the restroom and quickly changed his clothes. Nausea and vertigo overtook him. Leaning on the wash basin, he heaved several times, rinsed his mouth and hurried to his next stop.

The pizza restaurant reeked of garlic. Nauseated again, he demanded a container of ice water and gulped it down.

In the convenience store, as he started to send the fax to Superior, he noticed his hands tremble. Why bother with the fax? Wasn't the evidence he'd plant at Erin's sufficient? Would it do more harm than good? Hamilton had always thought things through carefully, logically, but now he worried that small details may have escaped him. His self-confidence began to unravel.

58

'Are you sitting down, Doc?' Detective Lewis asked.

'Yes. What's up?'

'I'm calling with an update. Jane Adams Pope was murdered last year. The murderer was never apprehended. Guess how she was killed, Doc?'

'No!' Cory shrieked. 'Was she slashed?'

'Yes. We came up empty in our search for Madison and Jefferson Pope or Adams. Maybe they were adopted. On the good side, Frankie's condition is stable.'

'Thanks for letting me know. Are you going to pick up Hamilton?'

'We still don't have sufficient evidence for a court order. There's no alternative.'

Cory had one, but for the moment she would keep it to herself. Between sessions, she paced. Ann brewed a lot of chamomile tea and Cory took many potty breaks.

After three back to back cancellations, Cory told Ann to close up shop.

'I'm afraid for you. You're welcome to stay at my place. Tomorrow is the big day. If you need anything, or want to talk, please call.'

'No thanks. As I always, say, Ann: You're a real mensch.'

On the way home, Cory wondered about the madness she had planned. If it did not go well, what would it do to her family?

There's a ten hour time difference between Israel and California, and her folks stayed up late for her call.

Rachel spoke first and announced that she was not ready to go home. She was catching on to Hebrew and made friends with her tutor, Moshe. Israeli dancing was her latest passion. Cory hoped her tutor was, too.

Noah picked up the phone. 'Love you, Mom.'

Cory's dad probably yanked the phone away because the next thing she heard was his rattling in Hebrew.

'Shalom, Dad. This is Cory in California. My Hebrew is confined to a few words of prayer.'

'Don't be such a wise-tush. So, I forgot for a moment. So do me something.'

'I guess you're steeped in the language. Are you having fun?'

'More than I ever imagined.'

'I'm glad for you, Dad. Maybe you'd like to settle there.'

'Trying to get rid of me, are you? Besides there are already too many violinists here.'

The conversation was predictable; the banter she and her father engaged in through the years. When she hung up, she was happy that her family was safely away from her. Danger from an Arab terrorist was less imminent than what she figured awaited her — and Pope.

59

No sooner had Cory arrived home, when the phone rang. It was Harvey asking her to jam. Her first impulse was to refuse because she didn't want to be reminded of Ron. Pleasurable memories of him saddened her, but she wanted Harvey to see Pope's photo. She accepted Harvey's invitation.

When Cory arrived, she met musicians, new to her, of her father's generation. Music bridged the abyss of age and their poise, energy and experience inspired her. She drifted away from the danger lurking outside, into the music's charms. She expected to miss Ron's tenor sax, but the impeccable timing of a mellow trumpet was like a bright jewel decorating the electric guitar tones. A slight caress on the bongos was all the percussion needed to back Harvey's bass. Even without keyboards, they sounded pretty good.

After the session, they went into the kitchen for the platter of sandwiches Harvey had prepared. Cory took him aside and pulled out the photo. He donned his glasses and scrutinized the photo under the light of a table lamp.

'Same deep cleft in the chin. Yeah, I'm sure it's him. Where did you get it?'

After she told him, he shook his head. 'Look, Cory, you're getting a reputation as a high-risk chick.'

'What does that mean, Harvey?'

'You turn off Ron with your heroics. It's none of my business, Cory, but is that what you want? You seem good for each other. He rarely smiled until you came around.'

'Thanks, Harvey. When things settle, I'll try patching it up. I know I'm obsessed with helping to catch the bad guy . . . it's too hard to talk about now.' She gave him a goodbye peck on his cheek and thanked the musicians for the privilege of playing with them. Cory drove home with a reservoir of unshed tears.

She was in danger. It was said that before you die your whole existence spreads out before you — as if watching the landscape of your life from a train trudging along the coast passing various vintages and styles of houses. Cory imagined the occupants and the lives they lived. And so it was with the events of her past. She wondered if the fleeting segments really happened or were fantasies. From her readings in neuroscience, she knew the stories we tell ourselves elicit the same brain chemistry as the reality we live.

Cory, an infant is rocked in the arms of her

mother. A moon-shaped, tear-stained face stares down at her. The sunken, dark eyes, moist. The mother's tears start again. She often cries. This time Cory tastes the salt of her tears and she cries, too.

There are no other images of the woman who bore her, who gave her life, but failed to teach her how to live. Try as she could, she could not resurrect any other memories of her. It was as though the mother wanted to vanish from her child's life to make it seem she had never been part of it. She could have been a simple wet nurse. In forty-five-years of her child's life, she had not sent a letter, a gift, or made an inquiring phone call. She must have wanted to erase her American interlude. Her pitiful mistake.

When Cory had first met the man who was to be her husband, he seemed surprised to learn of her mixed race. The evening they had met flashed before her.

They are at a crowded party, sitting across from each other. Snatches of laughter sprinkle the buzz of conversation in the background. When their eyes meet, she marvels at the attraction. His smile dazzles. He walks over to sit beside her, speaks, but his words are muted as the image fades.

The birth of each of Cory's children appears like film clips. Events fan out.

Rachel's first ballet performance. Noah's first photography exhibit. The move to the west coast. And now. Her life had become precarious because she knew too much.

Did she think of her birth mother now because her life could be over soon? Was the woman trying to send her a message? Maybe she did care and sensed her daughter's danger because they are linked in some inexplicable way. It was time to forgive, but Cory had not learned how. She knew it must start with her mother.

She is now eight years old. Aunt Tess pours a 'glassela tea mit lemon.' Gingerly, Cory grasps the ring of the delicate shiny silver filigree container encasing the goblet. She feels grown up, sipping tea at the lace covered dining table. She eyes the lemon poppy seed cookies. Aunt Tess pushes the platter toward Cory and says, 'Ess mamala.' Eat, little mother.

'No matter how well the family treated your mother, she wouldn't allow herself to warm to us,' Aunt Tess says, filling the glass with warm, sweet tea.

Cory tries to feel for the mother she did not know, and at eight she cannot. She can only feel her own selfish sorrow, bound up in an unforgiving nature.

When her friend, Steve became forty-years

old — the age when Jews were considered mature enough to understand the Kabbalah, an aspect of Judaism, they had many talks about it. One concept similar to karma, speaks of reincarnation in much the same way as Buddhism. It teaches that we are here on a mission to learn a lesson not learned in a former life.

Forgiveness was Cory's lesson. Her mother was the instrument. She had to forgive her before she could forgive others. She wondered if her study of psychology was designed to teach her to understand people in order to pardon them. Cory accepted her refusal to condone reprehensible acts, but as Betty had noted, she was judgmental and critical and that she could change. She would forgive her mother for her character flaw. The birth mother had not abandoned her on the steps of an orphanage, but presented her to those who would cherish her. What lessons this woman could have taught Cory were better not learned. Unless the sudden awareness that Cory's anger clouded her reason and propelled her toward danger was a message from the unknown mother. Did her long-ago-mother urge caution? Would Cory listen?

60

Patrick was due at Erin's at seven thirty. Cory had time to stretch, warm-up and practice karate before dinner. Exercise energized her. The scent of basil and garlic signaled the lasagna was ready. After eating a small portion, she pushed the plate away and headed out to fulfill her mission.

Erin rang Cory through the lobby entrance at six forty-five and surprised her with a tight hug. Their relationship had rapidly changed.

Cory's eyes searched the plain, uncluttered room. The sole item of interest in Erin's apartment, an antique oak-framed mirror hung opposite a closet in the foyer. The small hallway led into a large living room in which one corner served as a dining area. A dark wooden dining table stood in front of a large sliding window overlooking a garden and waterfall below. From eight stories above, she heard the sound of the rushing water. On the table, farthest away from the window, lay a green plastic place mat in a clover leaf shape with 'Megan's Place' printed on it. A large puffy cushion was tied on the chair to enable the child to reach the top of the table.

Cory scanned the sparsely furnished living room, gazing at the blue faux leather couch, an upholstered red plaid chair, a coffee table and a TV. She wondered if Erin was embarrassed by the paucity of her household belongings. She hoped the young woman didn't think Cory judged her unkindly by them.

Cory's eyes drifted to a box of crayons and a sheet of crumpled paper that lay on the floor next to a stuffed pink bunny rabbit.

An acrylic framed photograph of a little girl stood on the coffee table. She bore a striking resemblance to Erin. Same fine red hair, green eyes and freckles. A front tooth was missing from her broad grin.

'This must be Megan. She's adorable,' Cory said.

Erin blushed. 'She is rather cute. Would you like something to drink or munch. I think there's time.'

'No thanks.'

'I've got good news. I'm now a volunteer at the Old Globe Theater. A lovely setting . . . reminds me of home, just a wee bit. And guess what? A giant coincidence. I ran into an Irish woman who went to university with one of my brothers. I've made a chum.'

'How nice.'

'There's more. I've saved the best for last. Seldyn wants to reconcile! Mainly because of Megan, but I can make it work. I've learned from my therapy. I've expected too much and given too little. Sel's a fine dad and I'm afraid I'd taken him for granted.'

'I'm happy for you, Erin. The love the two of you have for your child can bring you closer to each other.'

'He wants us to take a cottage with a safe play yard for Megan. He doesn't want us living in a high rise condo. I am so pleased about that. This place is so different from where I grew up. Maybe that's why I've been irritable.'

'You're not the only one who has found it hard to adjust here, Erin. It's culture shock.'

'I thought Seldyn would solve all my problems. I must do that myself.'

Distracted by the upcoming event, Cory acknowledged, but couldn't fully appreciate the new Erin.

'You've taught me so much. When you made this suggestion for tonight, I was shocked. Of course flattered, too. It made me feel so fine that you respected me and took me into your confidence. I guess unusual circumstances bring out unusual reactions in people you'd least expect.'

'That's for sure,' Cory said.

'How strange, we've become co-conspirators.'

'After this unconventional experience with you, Erin, our relationship has changed. I can't be your therapist any longer, but I don't think you'll need much therapy anyway. You've grown a lot.'

'Thanks, Dr. Cohen — Cory.' She laughed. 'Seldyn thinks so, too. You know, I didn't quite care for you at first. I thought you cruel and abrasive. I couldn't relate to someone from a way-out culture — not even an American. But you aren't way out, I mean. Whoops!' Erin covered her mouth with her hand.

It was clear the young woman had realized she had said too much about her therapist's heritage. She watched Erin wring her hands.

'And now I must really care because I'm truly worried about you tonight. Are you sure you can carry this off?' Erin asked.

'Want to watch?' Cory grinned.

'Brr.' Erin shrugged her shoulders. 'Only if I could see it on the telly. By the way, the cameras are so well hidden, you didn't notice them, did you?'

Cory glanced at the corners of the room. 'No. Where are they?'

Erin pointed to the air ducts, and motioned Cory toward the closet. Inside it, several TV monitors reflected the entire apartment.

'They've put up mini cameras so small you can't see them. They're all over.'

'I'm impressed, Erin. They've gone to great expense for this operation.'

She escorted Cory into her small bedroom that contained a queen size bed, a desk with a cordless phone, and a dresser. On the bed was a sweatshirt. She handed it to her therapist. 'Here, don this. My four leaf clover shirt will be a fine talisman.'

Cory slipped on the large gray sweatshirt, Erin's name printed green in the form of four leaf clovers. Cory wore black tights and the treasured boots. She tied her long dark hair in a tight bun and wrapped a green and blue print scarf around her head. Tinted glasses concealed her eyes. An ample addition of rouge on her cheeks, forehead and chin helped the illusion. She studied her reflection in the hall mirror, Erin standing next to her. They were the same height. At first glance Cory could pass for a young woman for which she thanked good genes and attention to health. Besides, Erin had followed instructions and installed low wattage light bulbs.

Her patient's eyes widened as though stunned by the metamorphosis. 'What a charade! You look positively great! I hope he's never seen me.' She grimaced. 'You should do quite nicely.'

'This disguise is meant to avoid suspicion and get him into the room. In a matter of minutes, the deed will be done.'

Erin sat on the bed, her fingers smoothing the satin quilt. 'The one good from this flaming thing was a wake up call to me. I shudder to think what could have happened if I'd gotten involved with that madman.'

'Erin, you showed good sense. You matured in a short time. It's rare and wonderful. I'm pleased that Seldyn and you are ready to reconcile.'

'I should expect it to be bit precarious, but I'm optimistic. That's a change already. Sel said I used to be a pessimist. Now, I do hope you'll be safe. What exactly is the plan?'

Cory wanted to tell her, but it wasn't right. A therapist in her patient's house, wearing her clothes, pretending to be her, was unorthodox enough.

'After I open the door and he tries to attack me, the private investigator will make a citizen's arrest. You will alert Sergeant Lewis in time for him to take over. Later, the victims will make a positive identification, and his fingerprints and DNA should assure a conviction. Hopefully, he'll be locked up forever.'

'But this is California, Dr. Cohen! The land of misguided juries.'

Cory banked on her own brand of justice to insure Pope would be incapable of repeating his cruelty. She glanced at her wristwatch. 'It's time for you to let in Hornsby. Please call Sergeant Lewis right away. Don't stick around. This place will be a media circus.'

Erin flinched. 'I'll be across the street shooting pool. Good luck.' She grabbed Cory's hand. 'Here. Take this to remember me. It's a wee token for good luck.'

Cory uncurled her palm and found a small gold four leaf clover charm.

She pictured Grandma shaking her head, glasses perched on the tip of her nose. *What kind of psychologist would do such a thing? Your patients will think you're too sick to treat them.* Despite Grandma's admonition, Cory thought she would have felt proud of her. A knock on the door stilled Grandma's voice.

Through the peep hole, she glimpsed Harry Hornsby. When she opened the door, he gaped at her and laughed loudly, drowning out the roar of the waterfall. 'What a hoot! You are Dr. Cory Cohen, aren't you?'

Nodding, she smiled.

'I must grab some food,' he said, dashing into the kitchen.

'Damn, there's nothing here for me,' he

said a few minutes later, slamming a cupboard.

Earlier than expected, the phone rang twice; a signal from another detective from Hornsby's agency observing the entrance. When it rang again, Cory picked up after the third ring and punched the tape recorder to the 'Play' position. In Erin's voice it announced: 'Hello . . . can't hear you very well. I'm letting you in.'

Hornsby ran into the hall closet a few feet away, keeping it open a crack. They had made a plan. After one kiai — a horrifying animal-like shout, used in karate — designed to frighten an opponent, the detective, an experienced marksman would come out with his revolver and make a citizen's arrest.

Cory flexed and stretched her muscles while she waited for Pope to come up to the eighth floor. The room felt too warm. Stifling. She slid open the window and inhaled the moist night air. A navy blue sky with a full moon sparkled with stars like sequins. She heard a light tap at the door.

Her finger hit the 'play' button of the tape recorder, 'Door's open, come in.' Stashing the device under the cushion on the chair, she drew slow, deep breaths.

The door creaked and slowly opened. With one hand placed under his sweat shirt, he swiveled the knob, then shoved the door with his knee — a clever way to avoid fingerprints, Cory figured. His arms created a shelf for the pizza box. Muscular, dark bearded, he wore a knit cap and black sweats. Instantly, Cory recognized him as the menace who had tried to kill Ann in the garage. He plopped the pizza box on the dining room table that stood between them. A noxious odor akin to rotten onions pervaded the room.

Cory's heart thumped against her chest like a kettle drum. Her stomach pitched. She told herself not to be afraid. She peered into the cruel, unfocused eyes of Hamilton Pope and smiled.

He leered at her right shoulder with the look of a hunter about to kill his prey, his cold dark eyes flickering like little black marbles. His face, damp and pale, as though drained of blood. A repulsive smell of vomit and sweat emanated from him. He lurched toward Cory. Like an animal in front of a moving car, she froze.

He yanked the scarf from her head, loosening her hair. Sprinting behind her, he pulled the scarf around her neck tightening it. She couldn't scream — couldn't breathe, afraid she would pass out. With all her force, she jabbed her elbows into his chest. She struck steel.

Where the hell was Hornsby? Couldn't he see the monitor in the closet? She had depended on him. Now, she would have to rely on herself, but could she foil this strong monster?

She jerked her body backward until Pope crashed against the wall, releasing his grip on the scarf. She thought she heard his skull crack. She pivoted to face him. He seemed dazed. His eyes rolled back. Suddenly, he sprang at her. Cory jumped out of his way, but he caught her leg and flung her to the floor.

They struggled, tumbling over each other. His stinking body, hard as a giant oak.

'KIAI!' she yelled in his ear, hoping to break his hold and his ear drum. He clutched his head. Damn it, Hornsby! Get out here — now!

Pope looked stunned — his eyes glazed. He rose from the floor, shot a deadly glance, his breath foul. 'What the hell . . . you're not that mother-bitch, Erin. You're the shrink bitch.' He belched a foul stench and rubbed the back of his head.

For a moment, apart from the roar of the waterfall and the drumming in her chest, all was quiet. And then she heard Pope's labored breathing — a primitive hiss — reptilian. He looked sick, but he would get no pity from

434

her. Cory prayed Erin's good luck token would work, and he would just collapse without her effort.

The pattern of his ragged breathing changed, becoming like the snort of an animal on a hunt. Cory's adrenalin rushed. Expecting to see a blade in his hands, her fists clenched and her body flexed, ready to pounce.

Pope thrust his hand into the pocket of the black sweat suit jacket and whipped out his shiny knife much like the knife Cory had given the police. She calculated a distance of two yards between the table and herself. She riveted her eyes on him.

He staggered toward her, spittle dripping from his mouth.

The food she had eaten earlier, came back to haunt her. She swallowed hard, tasting bile. Nauseated, her knees grew wobbly. She felt hot, dizzy . . . faint. No! Don't let go, she cautioned herself. She had come so far. Don't! No! Don't give in. Stay alert. She filled her lungs with air, Okay, big shot. Here goes!

'KIAI,' she bellowed, her throat sore.

Pope grunted, twisting toward Cory. She stepped to the side, evading the knife, but he grabbed her hair, tugging so hard, her scalp burned. In pain and fury, she yelled, 'KIAI!'

What the hell is wrong with Hornsby? She hadn't expected to get into a scuffle, but now ... Pope wrenched her head back. The cold blade touched her cheek, as in her flashbacks. This time, she felt the nick. Blood trickled down her neck, moistening her chest. She wanted to wrest her head free, to bite him, but it was too risky. In a split second, he could kill her. Lifting her hands, she pressed hard on his wrist, but couldn't release his grip on the knife. Her fingernails pierced his skin and she pushed harder — heard a snap — hoped she had broken his bones. Moaning, he let go of her head. Cory swerved away. He lurched at her, clinging to the knife.

'KIAI!' Cory thundered.

Tottering, he darted his eyes toward the hall mirror. He must have seen the reflection of the door opening.

In a micro second Lewis raced in, poised — gun drawn. 'Freeze!' he shouted.

Pope gasped. Sweat streamed down his face and into his eyes.

Whirling around, Cory kicked his wounded hand. Wheezing, he dropped the knife. She plunged her fingers into his gooey eyes.

Pope let out an ear piercing wail as his hands gripped his face.

'How does it feel, you sonofabitch? *This* is

what you deserve,' Cory spat, swinging her leg high. Her heel plunged into the soft tissue of his testicles, before she pivoted aside. Behind him was the large open window. Blinded, he howled in pain, then swaying, fell backward, plummeting down-down-yelling-yelling. An unforgettable grotesque sound masked the roar of the waterfall.

★   ★   ★

'This wasn't how it was supposed to turn out,' Cory told Lewis. 'I intended to disable, not kill him.'

'I saw the whole thing, Doc. You did *not* kill him. You protected yourself. He fell out the window. He wasn't pushed, you know,' Sergeant Lewis said.

'But I had opened the window and faced it. Unconsciously I must have known how it'd play. I'll have to live with that.' Cory sat on the floor, cradling her knees in her arms and rocked while Lewis held a compress to her bloody cheek.

Cory had sought justice knowing it was only a concept and rarely a reality. Retribution did not bring relief.

'Where's Hornsby?' Lewis asked.

'Oh, my God, he hid in the closet. I

wondered why he didn't come out when I screamed. Something must have happened to him.'

Lewis flung open the closet door. There was Hornsby slumped on the floor, unconscious.

'Hypoglycemia — low blood sugar.' Lewis called in for help.

Within minutes, ambulance sirens screamed louder and louder and abruptly halted. Paramedics raced into the apartment. They checked Hornsby's medical tag bracelet and injected him with an I.V. of glucose. 'He'll come around in a few minutes,' one of them said. 'That's some gash, let's take care of it. Do you want us to take you to the emergency room, or do you want to see your own doctor?'

'No, I can go myself.'

'No, you won't, Doc. I'll drive you,' Lewis said.

Cory heard the commotion of another ambulance and police cars, then a loud rumble. 'Probably TV vans filled with media vampires filming the body for the evening entertainment,' she said.

Lewis nodded and left to attend them.

Cory sat on the floor and tugged off her boots — shivering, dazed, afraid to look out the window. The blood from her wound had stopped gushing. Gingerly, she patted her throbbing head — grateful to find her hair intact.

Lewis returned and draped a khaki wool blanket over Cory's shaking shoulders.

Forgiveness, the lesson she had to learn in this life must include forgiving herself. She had a long way to go.

Cory stared at the floor and blinked at the boots she had shed, wanting no part of them anymore.

'They should be your trophy. I'd have them guilded. You saved taxpayers' money and prevented countless crimes, you know.'

She trembled, tightening the blanket wrapped around her.

'With money for a defense team and no prior convictions, in this state he might have gotten off on an insanity plea, you know. And . . . if he was convicted, he was clever enough to escape. Dr. Cory Cohen, you're a heroine.'

'Heroin is the name of a drug. I guess I'm a hero.'

Sergeant Lewis laughed as he raised his hand holding Cory's boots.

★   ★   ★

The next day, Sergeant Lewis accepted Cory's invitation to breakfast. Over coffee

439

and pecan pancakes, they discussed the morning's headlines:

SERIAL RAPIST FELLED

The alleged beach rapist, Hamilton Pope, jumped to his death, last night while fleeing from authorities. Pope, 40 years old, Vice President of Superior Health Care, is believed to have committed seven rapes and killed two women in the San Diego area.

'Our secret, Doc?' He winked.
'Of course.'
Later that day Betty arrived at Cory's house with flowers and champagne. 'Rejoice.'
'Do you want me to counsel you on the merits of celibacy?' Cory asked.
'It can wait,' Betty said, popping the bottle cork.

Epilogue

Upon learning the news of Pope's demise, the survivors he had raped reported an immediate reduction of symptoms.

For three years, profits soared after Strauss took over Superior. Strauss became the largest and most powerful managed mental health care corporation in the country.

After a prolonged legal battle, victims and their families won an unprecedented settlement, causing Strauss to file bankruptcy.

Public outcry against managed care brought significant changes to the health care system. A law providing consumer freedom of choice through government health plans, stipulated that patient care can only be monitored by professional peers. Confidential psychotherapy was restored.

★　★　★

Sergeant George Lewis was promoted to lieutenant.

Frankie Kelly recovered and became an insurance investigator.

The Caldwells reconciled and moved to a rural area.

Mallory Nelson passed a dental hygienist course. She continues to play volleyball.

Paige Warren received a promotion to Vice President of the Seattle office.

Jennifer D'Amico and Oliver Baxter formed a partnership in a karate studio.

Steve Glass became an ordained rabbi.

Ann Abrams continues as Cory's Person-Friday.

Grace Myles lives on in Cory Cohen's thoughts.

Ron Miller remains in Davis. He visits San Diego to surf and sit in on jam sessions, but maintains distance from Cory. In a brief discussion with her, he said his interest waned during her obsession with the villain. Cory understood. She said she found his moodiness intolerable. They were right about each other, but not for each other.

The knife wound Pope had inflicted on Cory's cheek required sutures. It left a scar. Faintly visible, it would heal with time.

We do hope that you have enjoyed reading this large print book.

Did you know that all of our titles are available for purchase?

We publish a wide range of high quality large print books including:
Romances, Mysteries, Classics General Fiction Non Fiction and Westerns

Special interest titles available in large print are:
The Little Oxford Dictionary Music Book Song Book Hymn Book Service Book

Also available from us courtesy of Oxford University Press:
Young Readers' Dictionary (large print edition) Young Readers' Thesaurus (large print edition)

For further information or a free brochure, please contact us at:
Ulverscroft Large Print Books Ltd., The Green, Bradgate Road, Anstey, Leicester, LE7 7FU, England. Tel: (00 44) **0116 236 4325 Fax:** (00 44) **0116 234 0205**

Other titles in the
Ulverscroft Large Print Series:

SLAUGHTER HORSE

Michael Maguire

The Turf Security Division is surprised and suspicious when playboy Wesley Falloway's second-rate horses develop overnight into winners. Simon Drake investigates, but suddenly there is a new twist — someone is out to steal General O'Hara, the star of British bloodstock, owned by Wesley Falloway's mother. With a few million pounds at stake, lives are cheap; Drake finds himself both hunter and quarry in a murderous chase where even his closest associates may be playing a double game.

MERMAID'S GROUND

Alice Marlow

It's been five years since Kate Williams' beloved husband died, leaving her with two young children to raise. Now she's built a good life in one of Wiltshire's prettiest villages, and she has her dream job, as gardener at Moxham Court. For the last year, Kate has had a lover, roguishly attractive Justin Spencer, but he won't commit to more than a night here and there. When she takes in a male lodger, Jem, Kate's secretly hoping his presence will provoke a jealous reaction in Justin. What she hasn't reckoned on is exactly how attractive Jem will turn out to be.

HOT POPPIES

Reggie Nadelson

A murder in New York's diamond district. A dead Chinese girl with a photograph in her pocket. A plastic bag of irradiated heroin in an empty apartment. A fire in a Chinatown sweatshop. The worst blizzard in New York's history. These events conspire to bring ex-cop Artie Cohen out of retirement and back into the obsessive world of murder and politics that nearly killed him. The terrifying plot uncoils first in New York — in Artie's own back yard — then in Hong Kong, where everything — and everyone — is for sale.

A FANCY TO KILL FOR

Hilary Bonner

Richard Corrington is rich, handsome and a household name. But is he sane . . . ? When journalist Joyce Carter is murdered only a few miles from Richard's west country home, his wife suspects he has been having an affair with her, and forensics implicate him in the killing. But Detective Chief Inspector Todd Mallett believes that Joyce's murder is part of something much more sinister and complex. There have been other deaths; the senseless killing of a young woman on a Cornish beach, another in a grim London subway . . . And somewhere on the Exmoor hills a killer waits. Stalking his prey. Ready to strike again . . .

RUN WILD MY HEART

Maureen Child

For beautiful Margaret Allen, travelling alone across the western plains was her only escape from a loveless marriage — a marriage secretly arranged by her father as part of a heartless business scheme. In a fury, she left her quiet, unassuming life behind and ventured out on her own . . . Cheyenne Boder set out to claim a cash reward for finding Margaret and bringing her home. But the handsome frontiersman found a promise of love in her sweet smile and vowed to unearth the hidden passions that made her a bold, proud woman of the west!